Blessings
Vicki Irwin
Numbers 6:24-26

A Journey for

Rebecca

Vicki McBee Irwin

WestBow
PRESS®
A DIVISION OF THOMAS NELSON
& ZONDERVAN

Copyright © 2022 Vicki McBee Irwin.

All rights reserved. No part of this book may be used or reproduced by
any means, graphic, electronic, or mechanical, including photocopying,
recording, taping or by any information storage retrieval system
without the written permission of the author except in the case of
brief quotations embodied in critical articles and reviews.

This is a work of fiction. All of the characters, names, incidents,
organizations, and dialogue in this novel are either the products
of the author's imagination or are used fictitiously.

WestBow Press books may be ordered through booksellers or by contacting:

WestBow Press
A Division of Thomas Nelson & Zondervan
1663 Liberty Drive
Bloomington, IN 47403
www.westbowpress.com
844-714-3454

Because of the dynamic nature of the Internet, any web addresses or
links contained in this book may have changed since publication and
may no longer be valid. The views expressed in this work are solely those
of the author and do not necessarily reflect the views of the publisher,
and the publisher hereby disclaims any responsibility for them.

Any people depicted in stock imagery provided by Getty Images are
models, and such images are being used for illustrative purposes only.
Certain stock imagery © Getty Images.

Scriptures taken from the Holy Bible, New International Version®, NIV®.
Copyright © 1973, 1978, 1984, 2011 by Biblica, Inc.™ Used by permission
of Zondervan. All rights reserved worldwide. www.zondervan.com The
"NIV" and "New International Version" are trademarks registered in
the United States Patent and Trademark Office by Biblica, Inc.®

ISBN: 978-1-6642-5801-3 (sc)
ISBN: 978-1-6642-5800-6 (e)

Library of Congress Control Number: 2022903010

Print information available on the last page.

WestBow Press rev. date: 04/22/2022

Dedication

I dedicate this book in memory of my parents
Cyrus and Burniece McBee, who went to heaven in 2020.

Trust in the Lord with all your heart and lean not on your
own understanding; in all your ways acknowledge him
and he will make your paths straight. (Proverbs 3:5–6)

Love is patient, love is kind. It does not envy, it does not boast, it is not proud. It is not rude, it is not self-seeking, it is not easily angered, it keeps no records of wrongs. Love does not delight in evil but rejoices with the truth. It always protects, always trusts, always hopes, always perseveres. Love never fails. (1 Corinthians 13:4–8)

Acknowledgments

I would like to thank Kathy Hunt and Nathaniel McBee, who patiently helped when called upon.

Jack and Joyce Worrill, who are great prayer warriors, and I greatly appreciate their prayers and guidance on my first book.

Most importantly, I thank our heavenly Father, who allowed me the ability to write this story.

One

As the sun was peeking through the blinds, Rebecca lay in bed wondering how the day would go. She had a job interview at eleven and was praying it would bring good results. Her last job had been such a disappointment. The hours, pay, benefits, and even the drive to work had been great; her boss, on the other hand, had not. When Rebecca refused the demands he made of her, she'd been given a choice: do as he asked, or she would be fired. So she quit.

Ever since her husband had died, life had been incredibly challenging. Why did things have to happen this way? She was trying so hard to do what was right but felt she was always met with another obstacle.

After getting out of bed, she headed for her favorite chair to do her morning devotions. She opened her Bible and started reading in Philippians 4. As she was reading, verse 13 caught her eye. She read it again: "I can do all things through Christ my Lord who strengths me." So true, and how she needed that verse today. Closing her eyes, she took a moment to give thanks.

Rebecca headed to her closet, unsure of what to wear for the interview. She finally decided on a navy-blue pantsuit. At the last interview she had gone on, some of the women had on jeans, baggy shirts, and sandals. Rebecca had felt so out of place, but when they called her to say she had the job, they informed her that she would be working for one of the managers and would need to dress professionally. The ad in the paper for this job had specified an upper-management position, so she assumed she would need to dress more on the professional side.

Wondering how many others had applied and what her chances were, she thought of the scripture from that morning. She repeated Philippians 4:13 to herself again as she pulled up in front of the company, a feeling of calmness came over her, and she knew God was certainly with her; otherwise, she would have been a bundle of nerves.

She looked at her watch; she had eight minutes to get parked and find where she needed to go. Another lady walked up and went inside just ahead of Rebecca. She looked so sad, as if she had the weight of the world on her shoulders. Not saying a word or even looking toward Rebecca, she disappeared behind the door.

As Rebecca entered through the main entrance, she was greeted by a very attractive lady. "May I help you?"

"Yes, I am Rebecca Clark. I have an interview with Mrs. McKay at eleven o'clock."

Looking through some papers, the lady said, "Yes, Mrs. McKay is expecting you. Take the elevator to the fourth floor, and a lady at the desk will take you to Mrs. McKay."

Rebecca thanked her and took the elevator to the fourth floor, saying a prayer as she went up. When the doors opened, a lady was standing and waiting for her.

"You must be Rebecca," she said. "My name is Lynn Jones. If you will follow me, I'll take you to Mrs. McKay."

Lynn knocked on the door and waited till she heard Mrs. McKay say, "Come in." As they entered, Mrs. McKay was already coming out from behind her desk to greet her. She was an older lady—Rebecca guessed she was in her early seventies—but very beautiful. She moved with such grace and was so sure of who she was. Lynn quietly left the room and closed the door behind her.

"Rebecca, I'm Irene McKay. It's a pleasure to meet you," Irene said to Rebecca.

"Thank you," Rebecca said, shaking her hand. "It's a pleasure to meet you too." For some reason, Rebecca felt as if they had met somewhere before, but she couldn't remember where.

Mrs. McKay led Rebecca over to a small table where they took a seat. "I was very impressed with your résumé, Rebecca. Tell me about your previous job. You stated you were only with the company for three months. With your capabilities, why did the company let you go?"

Rebecca, not wanting to go into what kind of person her boss was, replied, "I felt it better to pursue a position somewhere else."

Mrs. McKay knew well the company that Rebecca had worked at and had heard of the demands her boss made on the women he had eyes for. She respected Rebecca for her decision to leave and for the fact she didn't cast stones toward her former employer. "Rebecca, with your qualifications, what do you feel you can do for this company, and why do you want to become a part of it?"

After Rebecca took a deep breath, answering Mrs. McKay's questions came with great ease. She felt God was beside her guiding her answers, and she had never been on an interview where she was so comfortable. Again, she felt as if she had met Mrs. McKay before and that there was a connection between them somehow.

Nearly two hours had passed when Mrs. McKay asked, "Rebecca, would you mind coming over to my house this evening, say around five o'clock? I would like to go over some things with you."

Realizing she had the job, Rebecca said five would be fine.

Mrs. McKay gave her the address, walked Rebecca to the door, patted her on the back, and said, "See you at five."

Giving thanks all the way to her car, Rebecca looked at the address in her hand. She thought she should drive by to see exactly where she would be going this evening, for she did not want to arrive late.

From the company office, it took only about fifteen minutes to get to the street that was listed. Rebecca read the house number on the paper, but she couldn't figure out where the house was. Then she saw the house number at the entrance of a gate. *Oh my,* she thought. *It's beautiful. At five o'clock today, I will be going inside that home. Oh wow.*

Five o'clock came quickly, and Rebecca was so thankful she had gone by earlier to locate Mrs. McKay's house. Turning onto the driveway, she thought, *Lord, are you sure you have me at the right place? I know I said I would go wherever you led me, but this is beyond anything I have ever imagined. I'm sure you know what you're doing. I need some guidance and reassurance.*

As she walked up the steps, Rebecca couldn't help but take in all the beauty of the landscape, knowing inside would be just as beautiful.

She rang the doorbell, and a lady with a loving smile and warm, kind eyes opened the door.

Before Rebecca could say a word, the lady said, "You must be Ms. Clark. My name is Mary. It's so good to meet you. Ms. Irene has told me all about you. Please, just follow me."

Rebecca stepped into the house and saw that it was as beautiful as she had imagined, plus warm and relaxing. The smell of something delicious filled the air.

A door opened, and Irene McKay came out looking just as she had that morning. She was a take-charge person, but Rebecca felt so at ease with her.

Reaching out to shake Rebecca's hand, Irene asked, "Did you have any trouble finding the house?"

Rebecca, trying not to look around at the beauty of the house, replied, "No. It was a very pleasant drive, and I noticed it is not that far from your office."

"It is very convenient for me. By the way, would you like a cup of coffee or a glass of tea?"

"Thank you, Mrs. McKay, but I'm fine for now."

As Mary turned to leave, Irene asked, "Mary, what time will dinner be?"

Looking at her watch, Mary said, "Dinner will be ready at six fifteen." Then she turned to Rebecca and said, "It is a pleasure to meet you, Ms. Clark." She left Mrs. McKay and Rebecca to get down to business.

Irene looked at Rebecca and said, "Let me explain why I have invited you over tonight. I have a few health issues and need someone to help with the company. I'm not stepping away completely, but I need someone whom I can trust to handle the biggest portion of decisions in running things. I have everything I need to work here at home, but the company needs someone there that they can go to physically. Do you know anything about McKay's Company?"

Thankfully, Rebecca had done some research about the company before she went on her interview. "I know that the company has been passed down for four generations. It started with only family members working, and as it grew, they began to hire others to help. The property that this house sits on has been in the McKay family for four generations also. The company is well known, and they stand behind their work. Turnover in the factory is very low."

Irene sat back and took a deep breath. "My dear Rebecca, you have certainly done your homework. I was very impressed today at the office and felt right away you were the one for the job; that's why I wanted to meet with you tonight. Let me show you what all the job entails and what is expected of you."

A tap came at the door, and Mary said dinner was ready. Looking at her watch, Rebecca couldn't believe how quickly the time had gone by. They went to the dinner table and enjoyed a wonderful meal while they talked about the details of the job.

After dinner, Irene said, "Rebecca, I would like for you to start tomorrow. Be here at nine. Of course, you will be paid for today since we covered a lot this evening, but tomorrow we will set up pass codes and show you the different accounts. You do have a lot to learn, so for the next few weeks, you will be working from here. I'll give you a key to the house so you will be able to come right on in every morning to work. It will be better to start you here away from the office where you won't be interrupted by phone calls and people."

As Rebecca left to go home, she thought about how different this had been from any job interview she had ever had—yet it all felt so right. Lifting up a prayer of thanks, she said, "Lord, you said to trust and believe in you, and today has been so unusual yet such a blessing. Thank you, Father, for this job and for being here for me. I couldn't have made it without you."

Rebecca got up early the next morning, making sure she had time for her morning devotions. She knew she had about a forty-five-minute drive ahead of her, provided traffic was not bad. She headed for the McKays' home, this time feeling like she was not really going to work but going to a friend's house for the day.

As Rebecca walked up to the door, Mary opened it with that same smile and loving eyes, but this time she greeted Rebecca with a hug. "It is so good to see you this morning, Rebecca. Ms. Irene is already in the office. Would you care for some coffee this morning?"

"Yes, I would, Mary. Thank you."

She walked inside and found Mrs. McKay sitting behind her desk, already busy with the computer. Rebecca said, "Good morning, Mrs. McKay."

"Oh, good morning, Rebecca," she replied. "Are you ready for today? We have so much to cover."

As Rebecca took a seat beside Mrs. McKay, Mary came in with a pot of coffee and two cups. "You ladies let me know if you need anything at all," she said, and with that she disappeared.

"Oh, by the way," Irene said, "if you see a young man around here, that would be Sammy. He works here and can do most anything. Sammy is a very special person—very loving and with a big heart. Some people are taken back by his loving nature, but he means no harm. When you meet him, you will know what I mean. He never meets a stranger and never forgets a face."

The two women worked through the day, taking only a few minutes for a quick snack at lunchtime, and before Rebecca knew it, it was six o'clock. Mary knocked at the door to tell them dinner was ready. After dinner, Irene gave Rebecca a key to the house and told her she would see her the next morning at nine o'clock.

Until Rebecca got home that night, she hadn't realized how exhausted she was. She wondered if she would ever be able to handle all that Mrs. McKay was expecting of her. But she determined that she was up for the challenge—and a challenge it was going to be.

Two

ONE DAY, WHILE SITTING AT THE DESK WORKING, AS USUAL, Rebecca didn't hear Mrs. McKay come in. "Good morning, Rebecca."

Nearly jumping out of her skin, Rebecca replied, "Oh! Good morning."

"I'm sorry. I didn't mean to startle you. I thought you heard me come in."

"That's okay," Rebecca assured her. "I was just deep in thought on what I was reading on the computer."

"I understand, I have been there myself. I would like to talk to you for a few minutes, if you are at a good stopping place with what you are doing."

"Absolutely" said Rebecca. "My eyes could use a break anyway."

"Good." Irene sat down across from Rebecca. "Are you aware you have been with me for a little over two months? I'm very impressed with how well you have caught on to all that I have put before you. Now I would like to make some changes," Mrs. McKay began.

"First, I would like for you to call me Irene. Working as closely as we have, I believe we can be on a first-name basis from now on." Rebecca nodded with a smile.

"Next, I think it would be very beneficial if you would move in here. We have the room, and you will not have so far to drive to work. From here to the office, you will have a fifteen-minute drive.

From where you live now, you have a forty-five-minute drive just to the house. Mary and I would love to have you here." Irene paused a moment to let all of this sink in.

Then she continued, "Last, I think you are ready to work downtown at the office. Tomorrow we will go in, look at your office, and see if any changes need to be made. Working at the company will be a lot different than working here. You will need to go out on the floor and let the workers know who you are and that you are there for them.

"Lynn Jones will be your personnel secretary," Irene added. "Charlotte Bailey, as you know, handles payroll and is the chief financial officer. Gloria Rogers basically handles all orders, incoming calls, and so on. Michael Allen is over security. Each department has its own supervisor, who reports to Lynn with any problems. In time you will learn who is who. Working here, you have gotten familiar with the names of all the employees, and soon you will have faces to go with the names. Remember that I mentioned Brad Brewer, the company attorney? He pops in at the office from time to time, so you will eventually have the privilege of meeting him." She paused and looked at Rebecca's face. "Well, what do you think?"

Looking back at Irene, Rebecca replied, "You want me to move in here? In this house? I have a house. It's small, but it's my home."

"I'm don't mean to make you feel like you don't have a home, Rebecca," Irene explained. "I would like you here so we can talk in the evenings, go over things about your day, and discuss whatever you may need help with. And most of all, this house would become your home. We feel very close to you. You can bring anything you want here. I hate the thought of you going to a house at night with no one there. Here you will have Mary and me, and of course Sammy. He thinks the world of you. I'm sure he would be more than happy to help you move."

"Oh, I would hate to bother Sammy," Rebecca said. "He has so much to do around here—taking care of the lawn, the horses, the pool. I don't know how he does it." She took a moment to decide what to say. "Let me think about this. I wasn't expecting you to want me to move in here."

"Of course. I totally understand," Irene said with a smile. "Why don't you take the rest of the day off? Think on all we have talked about. Pray about it, then meet me here in the morning at eight o'clock and we will start your first day at the company."

As Rebecca drove home, she couldn't imagine living with Irene. The woman was wonderful. She never seemed to get upset over anything, always so easygoing. As she pulled into her driveway, the house seemed so small—nothing fancy at all. The lawn could use some love, that's for sure, but the house was all that Rebecca had in memory of her late husband and mother-in-law.

Opening the door, she looked around and saw that everything was pretty much the way Mamie Clark had left it. When Rebecca's husband Ray had died in the car accident, she was beside herself. She remembered sitting outside the hospital in shock, crying, not knowing what to do. A kind lady had stopped by and was such a blessing to her. The lady held her hand, prayed with her, and was such a comfort to her. Rebecca had wished so many times that she had asked the lady for her name.

A picture of Ray sat on the nightstand. Rebecca held the picture in her hand, remembering how they had first met. Her mind traveled back to that point in her life. She had been going through a very hard time. Her parents had been missionaries for years, and instead of going with them to a third-world country, she had wanted to stay in the States to go to college. She had been with them on many trips, which were very rewarding, but now she wanted to go to college and get a degree in management. She had sent word to them about her graduation date, and they had promised to be there.

Two days before graduation, Mr. and Mrs. Holland from the Ministry of Foreign Affairs came to see her. Inviting them into her tiny apartment, Rebecca was hoping they had news of her parents' arrival time. But Mr. Holland handed her a letter, which she immediately opened. As she read, tears started streaming down her cheeks. She looked at them both and said, "This can't be true. Someone has made a mistake."

The letter informed her that both of her parents, Mr. and Mrs. Stanley James, had died in an explosion at the camp they had been in. They had been trying to get to a plane that would take them back to the States when a missile hit the camp, killing all inside.

Unable to read anymore, Rebecca thanked Mr. and Mrs. Holland for coming by and said that she needed to be alone. Nothing they could say would ease her pain.

She wasn't sure what she was feeling. Both her parents were gone. She would never see them again. There wasn't even a body to bring back to the States for burial. She had saved up so much to tell them, and now she would never be able to share anything with them.

On the day of graduation, as she was doing her morning devotions, she remembered a scripture she had heard her father say many times. In 2 Timothy 1:8–9, the Bible says, "So do not be ashamed of the testimony about our Lord, nor of me his prisoner. Rather join with me in suffering for the gospel by the power of God. He has saved us and called us to a holy calling, not because of our works but because of his own purpose and grace."

Knowing her parents gave their lives doing what they truly enjoyed and loved, she had to find peace. She needed to be happy for them because they had always been together in all they did, and they were together when God called them home.

I'm going to walk across that stage today and hold my head up high for I know that's what they would have wanted. Besides, they are with me, here in my heart. And that's what she did.

After the ceremony, a lady approached Rebecca and said, "Hello, I'm Mrs. Simpson. I'm looking for someone to help me in my office, and I was told you would be the perfect one. It's not here in Colorado; my office is in Texas. Would you like to have lunch so we could discuss a few things—that is, if you don't mind moving?"

Looking around, Rebecca thought, what do I have here that

would keep me from moving. "Yes," she answered, "I am very much interested in what you have to say."

Rebecca took the job, and by the end of the week, she was on her way to San Antonio, Texas. Mrs. Simpson met Rebecca at the airport in San Antonio and took her to an apartment she had found close to the office. "I came across this apartment yesterday and took the liberty of going ahead and leasing it for you. I hope you don't mind. You stated you were selling your car, so until you decide what kind of car you want, this apartment is close enough for you to walk to work."

The apartment was sufficient till she could learn her way around town and decide where she might want to move and what kind of vehicle she would need. She was to start work Monday morning at seven thirty.

It didn't take Rebecca long to unpack and get settled in her new home. As she walked around and familiarized herself with the area, she came across a little section of the town that had a river running through the center. Shops, restaurants, galleries—you name it, it was there. The day was sunny with a gentle breeze, so she stopped for lunch and chose to eat outside near the water. Her mind was rehashing all that had happened in the last few days when she was startled by a man asking if he could use the extra chair at her table. He was dressed in a military uniform, as were many others around her. He took the chair and apologized if he had bothered her in any way.

Going back to her thoughts, she got out a small notepad from her purse and began to make a list of things she needed to do and people she needed to contact. She hadn't really noticed the guys near her table, but soon they were getting ready to leave and the one who had borrowed the spare chair came over and introduced himself. He was Ray Clark, and he wanted to know if he could have her name and phone number. He said that he would like to call her the next time he got a pass to town.

Thinking he was probably a long way from home and, like her, could use a friend, she wrote down her number on a napkin. His grin broke into a wide smile. Napkin in hand, he said, "Hope to call you soon," and then he was off with the other GIs.

Two weeks passed when one morning, he called. "Hey, this is Ray Clark. Remember me from the Riverwalk?"

"Yes, I remember," she said. "How are you doing?"

"I'm doing great. I called to let you know that I have a weekend pass and wondered if you could meet me around eleven at the Riverwalk. Then we could go for lunch."

Still thinking he needed a friend to talk to, Rebecca said she would be there.

On Saturday morning, Rebecca thought she would go a little early to look around some more. As she walked up, she saw that Ray was already there, and she noticed how truly handsome he looked in his military uniform.

Ray was so easy to talk to. They talked about his life and what made him go into the service, then they talked about her life. He had lost his father about two years earlier, and his mom lived in Kentucky. Talking about her parents was very hard for her, but Ray seemed to know exactly what to say to comfort her. Soon it was time for him to go back to the base for the evening, and he wanted to know if they could get together the next day.

As she held his picture there in her house, she thought, *who would have ever thought I would meet my future husband in San Antonio, Texas?* He had completed basic training and was assigned a position there for additional training. They married about six months later.

Mamie Clark was the best mother-in-law anyone could want. Rebecca just loved her, for she reminded her so much of her own mother. They talked on the phone at least three times a week. Ray and his mother were so much alike, always looking for the positive in everything and never raising their voices; they insisted on being very prompt when they had to be somewhere and always kept their word when they said they were going to do something. She had needed them both in her life and every day thanked God for them.

On May 22, 2016, Rebecca was to meet Ray for dinner at a new restaurant that had just opened downtown. Just in case traffic was heavy, and to make sure she got a table, Rebecca had left an extra thirty minutes early. After securing a table at a window that looked out on a lawn of flowers in bloom, she decided to look over the menu. An hour had passed with no sign of him, even though she had called his cell phone four times and sent several texts. No reply.

The waiter kept coming over to her table to see if she was ready to order. She thought maybe he had to stay late for work, yet no one had answered his work number when she had called. It was now nearly two hours since she had sat down at the restaurant. Watching the door, she saw Ben, one of Ray's buddies, come in. She waved at him, hoping he and Ray were together, and he came over to her and sat down.

"Rebecca, I've got some bad news," he began. "Ray has been in an accident and was taken to the hospital." "Her heart nearly jumped out of her chest, and she was unable to move. *Lord, please don't let this be serious,* she thought. *Don't take Ray away from me too.* Ben told her he would drive her to the hospital.

They went into the emergency room, and Ben went to the desk and said something to the clerk. In a few minutes, a nurse came out and took them both back to the room where Ray was. He looked terrible. All she could do was cry and say, "Ray, I'm here. I need you."

A doctor asked Rebecca if he could speak to her in the hall. As he talked, Rebecca was only hearing bits and pieces of what he was saying. Her thoughts were, *Lord, we need you. Help Ray. Please don't take him from me.* Ben was still at her side when a nurse asked the doctor to come back into the room. Rebecca was not sure how long she had been standing there when the doctor came back out and said, "I'm sorry. We did all we could do. His injuries were just too severe."

She went back into Ray's room, held his hand, and took a long look at him. She realized just how bad his external injuries were and could only imagine the extent of those injuries on the inside. It was so much more than the doctors could repair in the short time they had to work. *Lord, I don't understand why this had to happen,* she thought. *We were so happy and had so many plans. Right now, I feel so lost and alone. Please, Lord, help me.* She knelt over to kiss Ray on his cheek and whispered, "I love you. Thank you for the joy and happiness you have given me." Turning away, she told Ben she needed some time to herself. She thanked him for his help and told him she would talk with him tomorrow about arrangements for Ray.

Outside, the sun was beginning to set and a slight breeze blowing, Rebecca walked over to a bench near a tree. Her tears were flowing, and in her mind she kept saying, *Why? Why did this have to happen.* A lady came over, sat down beside her, took her hand, and started talking to her. She started praying and put her arm around Rebecca, telling her God was with her. This stranger was an angel from God, which Rebecca so desperately needed. The lady's touch was so soft, her words so gentle and kind. She even followed Rebecca home just to make sure she made it home safely.

Rebecca had called Ray's mother, Mamie, and together they made the funeral arrangements. It seemed like only yesterday, yet it had been three years. Four months after Ray's death, Mamie had called Rebecca to tell her she had been diagnosed with cancer. It had already spread, and treatment was not an option.

Rebecca quit her job and then packed up and moved to Kentucky to be with her mother-in-law. She loved Mamie dearly and knew Ray would have wanted her to be there for his mom. Mamie had been so touched by Rebecca's kindness. She was also a blessing to Rebecca for she was such a godly woman who taught Rebecca so much. She also told Rebecca about everything in her house. Ray's dad had made so many things in their home, and some things had been handed down from Ray's grandparents.

A year later, Mamie passed, leaving everything to Rebecca. With Mamie gone, she knew she needed to find a job and try to get on with her life. Looking around at the house now, she didn't know if she wanted to leave or stay there. Irene had made her a good offer, but was she ready to move out? When she had graduated from college, she never dreamed her life would have taken her down the path she had been on, but as she looked back, she saw that when one door closed, another one opened. That's the way God works. He never closes a door and keeps it shut; he always has another door for you to open.

Is this a door in my life that needs to close? she wondered. *Living at the McKays' home would be a new journey in my life. God has never let me down, but still, I feel a little uncertainty—just not sure what it is.* Everything Irene McKay had said to her made perfect sense, but she couldn't part with this cozy little house just now. *Do I want to rent it?* No, she didn't think so. *Maybe I'll just let it sit for a while and see how things work out at the McKays'. If they don't go well, I'll have my little home to come back to.*

Now, what do I take with me and what do I leave behind?

Three

SATURDAY MORNING, SAMMY AND ONE OF HIS FRIENDS ARRIVED AT nine o'clock sharp. Rebecca had decided to take only what was necessary, knowing she could come back at any time to pick up anything else. In no time, the truck was loaded, and they were pulling into the driveway at her new home. *I'm actually going to live here*, she thought. *Rebecca Clark living in this beautiful home.* When she traveled with her parents, she had lived in some rough places. College dorms at least had beds and running water; Ray and she had a decent home in San Antonio; and Mamie's little house was nice, just small. *Now look at what I'm moving into*, she thought. *Girl, you have definitely come a long way.*"

Mary came to the door to let them in, smiling from ear to ear. "Ms. Irene had to go into town, but she will be back soon. What can I do to help you, Rebecca? Your room is all ready for you. Come and I'll show you which room is yours."

They had given Rebecca the master bedroom. When she walked in, she stood in amazement at its size. The closet would make a room all on its own, and the bathroom was something from a magazine. Looking around, Rebecca still couldn't believe this was for her. What had she done to deserve such a fine place to live? Closing her eyes for a minute, she just had to say, "Thank You, Lord, for your blessings on me."

As they were unpacking, Rebecca turned to Mary and asked,

"Why is Mrs. McKay giving me the master bedroom? Is this not her room?"

"This was Ms. Irene's room for years," Mary answered, "but now she is content to be in a room not quite as large. The room she chose and has fixed up is cozy and very comfortable. She is quite happy and pleased with her move."

In no time, Mary and Rebecca had everything in place. Rebecca was grateful she had brought only what was necessary for the furniture in Mamie's house certainly would not go with the décor in this one.

"By the way, if you should want to change any of the furniture or add to it, we have an attic full of furniture," Mary said. "Ms. Irene changes things around from time to time, but you are welcome to look, and if you see anything you like, we can have it brought down. Just let us know." Mary left the room, and Rebecca wondered if she had read her mind about Mamie's furniture.

After working in her room a bit longer, Rebecca decided to go to the kitchen and look around. For as many times as she had been in this house working, she had never really taken the time to see what was where. Mary was working at the stove, and as soon as she saw Rebecca, ask, "Can I help you with anything?"

"No, I just thought I would look around," Rebecca replied. "I have never really been in the kitchen. I don't know where anything is. Mary, I don't know what you're cooking, but it smells delicious. What can I do to help you? I enjoy cooking, I just haven't been cooking much lately; it's hard to cook for just one person."

"Honey, I know what you mean. Sometimes I get carried away with the cooking, and Ms. Irene and I have leftovers for several days."

Rebecca laughed. "There is nothing wrong with leftovers. In fact, that's what I eat most of the time. You cook one night and eat on it for five."

Irene walked in and said, "Mary, surely since it is Rebecca's first night here, we are not having leftovers." They all laughed.

Rebecca remembered when her parents had friends over, the laugher and fun they had. And when Ray had his buddies from the base over, they always seemed to gather in the kitchen to eat and cut up. For some reason, remembering this did not make her sad. She was able to smile about those good times.

Four

WALKING INTO THE COMPANY ON MONDAY MORNING, REBECCA was excited to finally meet the employees. She had seen their names in the computer so often. She knew who had been with the company the longest, insurance information on each one, which departments they worked in, who was married, who was single, and if they had missed any days of work—she felt like she already knew every employee. Now to put faces with those names.

An announcement had been made on Friday that Rebecca would be touring the company on Monday and that all employees would get a chance to meet the new CEO. Irene took Rebecca around the plant, and all the employees seemed so happy to see both of them. Rebecca could tell that the employees had great respect for Irene, and Rebecca knew why. She treated everyone like family, not just the workers at her company. How would she ever fill the shoes of this wonderful lady?

As they made their way through the plant, they came upon the lady Rebecca had seen the day she had come for her interview. Still wearing a sad look on her face, she managed a smile toward Rebecca. Her name was Rachel Mills. After the tour, Rebecca addressed the company over the intercom, saying that her door was always open to each one of them. She was there to help them in any way she could and wanted to hear about anything that they felt needed attention. If they didn't talk to her, she couldn't help.

Then they made their way upstairs to the main offices. They meet Tina Guffey, who was over Human Resources. Lynn Jones, whom Rebecca had already met on the day of her interview, would be her personal secretary, and Charlotte Bailey was the chief financial officer. Gloria Rogers handled all incoming calls and did some ordering. As they were all talking, Brad Brewer came in, not realizing Irene would be there.

"Brad, what a surprise!" Irene said. "I wasn't expecting to see you here today, but I'm so glad you are here. Come meet the new CEO of McKay's." Irene turned to Rebecca. "This is Brad Brewer, the company's attorney. He comes around occasionally. This is just perfect—you get to meet everyone you will have contact with."

Brad shook Rebecca's hand and then turned to Irene. "How are you feeling? I understand you have been a little under the weather, but I must say, you look as marvelous as always."

"Thank you, Brad. I'm feeling wonderful, and with Rebecca here I feel even better. Now if you all will excuse us, Rebecca and I need to go over some things. If you need anything, we will be in her office."

As they turned to go into the office, Rebecca noticed the name on the door. Irene's name had been removed and her name added. Feeling tears sting her eyes, she looked at Irene. Without saying a word, Irene patted her on the back and said, "Let's go in, shall we."

"Mrs. McKay, the office is just perfect," Rebecca gushed. "I can't imagine changing anything."

Looking at Rebecca, Irene said, "I really wish you would call me Irene or Ms. Irene. I would feel so much better."

"I'm so sorry. I have called you Mrs. McKay for so long, it's just hard to say Irene. But I will try."

Rebecca went behind the desk and saw that everything was in place. She already had the keys to everything in the company, knew all the passwords, and met all the employees, so she was all set to get to work. Before Irene left for the day, they went down to the nearest cafe and had lunch, and then Rebecca went back to her office to really start her new job.

While they were gone to lunch, Brad went into Charlotte's office and closed the door behind him. "What do you think of this new lady?" he asked.

"Don't worry, Brad. I'll keep a close eye on her," Charlotte assured him. "She won't give us any problems. I'll make sure to keep things the way they are."

"I hope so. It was easy when the old lady was here because she relied on you for everything. Now with this new blood in here, she might get to snooping into things she shouldn't."

"Don't worry," Charlotte repeated. "I have everything covered. You take care of your end, and I'll take care of this end."

As Rebecca sat at her desk, she remembered some of the things she had been working on while at the house. Now that she was at the office, she could take a better look into them.

Five

REBECCA REALLY DID ENJOY HER JOB, AND THE PEOPLE WERE ALL wonderful, except for Charlotte. It was as if Charlotte was always looking over her shoulder, asking if she needed help with anything. Rebecca tried to be nice, but she was uneasy with her, and as she did some digging around in the files, she began to understand why. She made some phone calls and asked people to call her on her personal phone instead of the office line, and if she needed an email, she didn't use the company's email address. She didn't want Charlotte to catch on to what she was doing.

Charlotte was always well dressed and wore only the latest styles. Her accessories complemented whatever she had on. Rebecca took notice of what car Charlotte drove and even went by where she lived. Slowly, pieces of this puzzle were coming together. But Rebecca knew she had to have everything she needed before going to Irene.

That night, when everyone went to bed, Rebecca quietly slipped into the study to check her email. Sure enough, in front of her was the information she needed. Just as she was ready to hit the print button, she heard a noise from the back door. She turned down the lights and slowly made her way toward the sound. She saw a shadow of someone in the kitchen. It was a man, and she knew it wasn't Sammy. Looking for something to use as a weapon, she picked up a brass candlestick, ready to use it on whomever was coming through the door. Just then she heard Irene say, "Mark, you made it home. It's so good to see you." And she gave the man a big hug.

With the brass candlestick in hand, Rebecca walked around to the kitchen to see who this man was. When he saw Rebecca with the candlestick raised and ready to hit someone, he stepped in front of Irene to protect her.

Irene realized that Rebecca didn't know who Mark was. "Oh, Rebecca, it's okay. This is my son, Mark. Mark, this is Rebecca Clark, the lady I told you about."

"You have a son?" Rebecca asked.

"I'm so sorry. I should have told you about Mark. You can put the candlestick down now."

Feeling a little foolish standing there holding a candlestick, she put it down and managed to say, "Hi."

Mary came running out just as Rebecca was putting the candlestick down, not knowing what was going on, then saw Mark. "Oh, Mark, you are home!" she cried. She gave him a big bear hug. "Are you hungry? Would you like me to fix you something to eat? Sit down and tell us all about your travels!"

"No, Mary, I'm not hungry. Thanks anyway. I'm fine, just tired. Would you mind if we talked in the morning? It's been a long, tiring month. Usually, I get a chance to rest up, but here lately that's not happened."

"Sure, honey," Irene replied. "You get some rest, and Mary can fix you a big breakfast in the morning. We can all talk then. It's so good to see you and have you home. Do you get to stay very long this time?"

"For a little while, Mama. It's good to be home and good to see you and Mary. Sorry, Ms. Clark, if I scared you. I truly apologize."

"No harm done," Rebecca replied. "If you will excuse me, I'll go put the candlestick back where it belongs." With that, she made a quick exit, put the candlestick back, and wanted desperately to go back to the study. But with Mark there, she figured she had better wait till she knew she could be alone before printing everything up.

She headed for her room and, once inside, locked the door behind her. She was still shocked that Irene had never mentioned Mark to her, and she wondered why. Even Mary had never said anything about Irene having a son or any children. Maybe Rebecca would find out why the next day, but for the time being she needed to concentrate on other matters.

Looking at the clock on the nightstand, Rebecca saw that it was three o'clock in the morning and thought for sure everyone should be asleep. Quietly she made her way to the study, closing the door behind her. As soon as she touched the mouse, all the information she was wanting to print was still there. She was so thankful no one had been in there, for with the noise earlier, she had forgotten to shut the computer down. She printed up all the information, which was several pages, and slowly separated the papers, attaching receipts she had been able to find, as well as some photos. With all this laying before her, Rebecca wondered how Irene would take all this. What would Mark think? No matter what, she had to let Irene know what was going on.

When she headed back to her room, she saw that it was six o'clock. It had taken longer than she thought to sort through and arrange the papers in the correct order. She had the oldest information on top, with what followed in consecutive order down to the present. Hearing someone in the kitchen, she knew Mary was up, getting ready to prepare a big breakfast for Mark. She wondered if he was an early riser and Mary was wanting to have everything ready for him. Part of her wanted to go to bed, but she knew she didn't want to be late for breakfast, not that day anyway. A shower would wake her up, and she needed a clear mind when she presented Irene with so much information.

"Good morning, Mary," she said when she entered the kitchen after getting ready.

"Good morning, Rebecca. Hope you were able to sleep well, after all the excitement last night," Mary said.

"My blood was pumping for sure. I thought someone was breaking in to kill us or rob us, possibly both. My mind was going in so many directions, and all I could find to defend us was that brass candlestick. I had no idea Irene had a son or that he was coming in."

"Mark would never hurt anyone, but then you didn't know that," Mary said. "I can see why you were so worked up. Your face was so pale, yet you were prepared for a fight. You will like Mark. He is such a sweetheart. Ms. Irene thinks there is no one like her Mark"

"Anything I can help you with, Mary?" Rebecca asked. "You know how much I enjoy cooking."

"Oh, Rebecca, that would be so helpful. Would you like to make biscuits? I mean homemade biscuits, not the kind that comes out of a can."

"I would love to! I'm sure they won't be as delicious as yours, but I'll do my best."

"Who did you used to cook for?" Mary asked. "You mention from time to time how much you used to enjoy cooking. Did you have a family to cook for, or did you work in a restaurant?"

Not wanting to talk about her past and bring on so many questions that she did not want to answer right now, Rebecca ask, "What pan would you like for me to use, and about how many should I make?"

Irene walked into the kitchen. "Rebecca, my dear, good morning. Hope you slept well last night."

"Good morning, Irene. Yes, I slept very well. And you?"

"Well, I have slept better. I was so excited about seeing Mark, and then I thought of you and how you must have felt. After tossing and turning, I got up at about four o'clock, and when I came through the house, I saw the light on under the study door. Went to your room and it was empty. Apparently, you couldn't sleep either. I started once to knock on the office door, but then thought I would wait till morning and after breakfast we could talk. Is everything all right at the company? I don't want you to work all day and then come home and work through the night. You need your rest."

"It's nothing that can't wait till after breakfast," Rebecca answered. "Besides, I need to get these biscuits made or Mary won't let me back in the kitchen." She looked at Mary for some backup.

Mary said, "If you have some juicy gossip, we can talk, but if it's something boring about your work, it can wait till after the biscuits are made." All three of them laughed, for Mary was not one to gossip, nor was Irene. Whatever someone told them, they shared with no one.

As they were getting the table set, Mark came in. "I'm not sure what all has been cooked, but it smells delicious." Looking at the table, he asked, "Mary, did you cook everything in the kitchen?"

"No, didn't have that much time," she replied as she gave him a wink. On the table was bacon, ham, hash browns, eggs, gravy, biscuits, muffins, a bowl of fresh fruit, orange juice, and coffee.

"I'm glad you didn't. Just look at the table. Don't know where you would have put anything else."

Just as they were ready to sit down, Mark asked about Sammy. About that time, Sammy popped around the corner. "You guys wasn't going to eat without me, was you?" Going straight to Mark, he gave him a big hug. "Man, I've missed you, Mark. So glad you're home."

"No, Sammy, we would not start without you," Mark answered. "Besides, I need someone to help eat all this. Mary cooked enough for an army."

Looking over the table Sammy said, "That's okay. It will give us something to snack on later in the morning. Do you think you might want to go for a ride? I'll make sure your horse is all ready if you want."

"Maybe later," Mark replied. "I'm sure you have taken good care of Tilley. I'll come out to the barn and see how he's doing."

To Rebecca, it seemed like breakfast would never end, and she hoped Mark would go out to the barn to check on his horse. That way she could talk to Irene alone. Finally, she got up and took her dishes to the kitchen. Mary told her she would clean up and didn't need any help, so Irene said it would be a good time to talk.

Irene intended to talk about Mark, while Rebecca intended to talk about the company. When they entered the study, Rebecca looked at Irene. "I know you want to talk about Mark, but can I go over some things first with you?" Rebecca asked. "I feel this is much more important. Please sit here behind the desk. I need to explain and show you what I have come across."

She continued. "Remember that, when I first came to work here, you showed me how the billing worked; how everything was posted and listed; and how the employees, hire dates, insurance, and everything is here in the computer? You gave me a password that allowed me to go into any file that the company had. One day, I clicked on a screen that showed what bills were paid, to whom they were paid, and who ordered certain items. If you will notice here, back in 2010, checks were mailed out to a mortgage company. And here checks were sent to a travel agency and here to a jewelry company in New York.

"I researched the mortgage company checks and found that McKay's does not have a mortgage on the business or your home," Rebecca explained. "The checks were paying for a home on 1654 Lavender Drive, where Charlotte Bailey lives. Also, I requested a list of any jewelry purchased on your account from the store in New York called Alexander's Jewelry, telling the owner that we needed it for insurance purposes. Since you are one of his best customers, he was more than happy to help. He sent me pictures of all the jewelry that had been purchased since 2010 and charged to you. Now, one day you showed me a piece of jewelry that was your mother's. As you were talking, I made a mental note of the other jewelry in your box. None of it matched the pictures. Then, one day, Charlotte wore a bracelet I recognized, so when the time was right, I took a picture of it on her arm. And here she is wearing the necklace and earrings from this picture that Alexander's sent."

"And last, I spoke to the travel agency Charlotte uses and

28

found that the credit card bills were signed by Charlotte Bailey or Brad Brewer. It seems they take trips together and charge them to the company credit card—trips like Hawaii, Aruba, St. Thomas, Jamaica, and others. Not anywhere could I find that the company held any meetings in any of these places. When the bills come to the office, Brad signs off on them, no questions asked."

Irene sat in shock, not saying a word. As she looked first at one paper and then another, tears ran down her cheeks. "I trusted Charlotte and Brad with the company," she stammered. "They always said, 'You have no worries. McKay's is doing great.'"

"Oh, Ms. Irene, the company is doing great, but it could be doing so much better if Charlotte and Brad weren't taking from you. They are living it up on your money! Plus, when they take trips, they are not taking their families with them. It's just the two of them. I overheard Charlotte and Brad talking about Hawaii, how beautiful it was, and how everyone should go at least once. I looked up Brad's home address and drove by to see what kind of home he had because Charlotte's house is beautiful. As I was driving by, a lady was getting the mail, so I stopped to see if she was Mrs. Brewer. She was, and I pretended to be looking for a home in her area. I told her who I was and how I knew Brad. She was very nice and invited me in for tea. While we were talking, I mentioned that someday I would like to start traveling and my first trip would be to Hawaii. She said, 'Oh, I have always wanted to go to Hawaii. Maybe when Brad retires and has more time, we can go.' Right then I knew that Brad and Charlotte had taken the trip together."

Just then Mark knocked on the door and popped his head in, and when he saw Irene, he stepped inside. "Mom, what's wrong? Why are you crying?"

"Oh, Mark, you are not going to believe this," she said. "It' just awful."

He knelt beside her and asked, "What's awful, Mom?"

Irene began explaining everything to Mark. When she finished, he looked at Rebecca. "How long have you known about this?"

"This is what I was working on last night when you scared me," Rebecca answered. "I was just about to print more proof when I heard a noise. I didn't know who it was that was breaking in—or so I thought—and then I had to wait till after things settled down. I came back in to finish up so that after breakfast everything would be ready for your mother to look at."

"*That's* what you were doing when I saw the light on in here this morning," Irene said. "I should have come on in. Oh, Mark, what are we going to do?"

"I have my own personal attorney," Mark replied. "Let me have him go over all this and get his advice on what steps we need to take from here. This is very serious, and we want to go about this in the proper way." Mark left the room to make the call.

"Rebecca, what would I ever do without you?" Irene said gratefully. "You are truly a blessing from God. Do you realize you could become a private detective as good as you are?" She wiped her eyes. Her heart was so heavy because of all that she had learned about two people she trusted and what they had done behind her back.

"I have been praying hard about this because I wasn't sure how you would take it. It was not my intention to be a snitch, but we are not talking about a few hundred dollars. It's much more than that."

"No, child, you did the right thing," Irene assured her. "You hear about things like this happening in companies, but I just never thought it would happen to mine. Charlotte and Brad have been with the company for a long time. I never went back over anything they did—just took their word for it. Especially since Brad was to look over what Charlotte did and sign off on things."

Mark came back into the room. "Okay, Joe Lewis, my attorney, will be by after lunch to look over all this. He wants you both here to answer questions he will probably have." He looked at Rebecca. "Thank you for what you have done. You don't know how much I appreciate this."

Then he looked at Irene. "Mom, are you okay? You still look a bit pale."

"I don't know how to look or feel," she answered. "This has been such a shock. But at least it is out, and we can start dealing with it."

Rebecca thought a breath of fresh air might do her good and give Irene and Mark some time to talk alone, so she asked to be excused. When she walked outside, she came upon Sammy.

"Hi, Ms. Rebecca," he said. "That breakfast was great this morning. Didn't you enjoy it?"

"Yes, it was good. Say, which horse is Mark's? I think he called him Tilley."

"Come with me," Sammy replied "I'll show you Tilley. I take really good care of all the horses. I like to talk to them, they don't fuss at me, and we get along so well."

"Sammy, why would anyone ever want to fuss with you?" Rebecca asked. "You are always so kind and good to everyone."

"Well, not everyone thinks so. Ms. Susan used to always fuss at me. I could never do anything right. She wasn't like you, Ms. Rebecca. You are always good to me. That day you gave me a hug for helping you move, I was on cloud nine. Ms. Susan wouldn't ever think of doing something like that. I know I have some disabilities, but she always reminded me that I wasn't normal. It made me feel bad, so I tried to stay away from her."

"Sammy, there is nothing wrong with you," Rebecca said. "You are a very special person. God made all of us, and he made us just the way he wanted us to be. You have a way with the horses—not everyone can do that. And look at the lawn and landscaping. Do you think I could do that? That's one of the first things I noticed when I came here. As I came down the drive, it was all so beautiful. This is a masterpiece, and you did it. Ms. Irene told me she just lets you do what you want, and this is the result. I don't know who this Susan person is, but she is so wrong."

"Ms. Susan was Mark's wife," Sammy explained. "She is gone now. Don't tell anyone, but I was glad when she left. No one was happy when she was around. If you said one thing wrong, she let you know about it."

"Oh, I didn't know Mark had been married. In fact, I didn't know Ms. Irene had a son until he showed up. But don't worry, Sammy. I promise not to say a word about what we have talked about this morning. Now, where is this horse named Tilley?"

At a quarter after twelve, Joe Lewis arrived at the McKay home. Mark met him at the door, and Rebecca could tell that the two knew each other well. Irene was in the study still going over papers and checking things in the computer when Mark and Joe walked in. Not sure if she was needed at this time, Rebecca decided to stay in the den until they requested her presence.

Thirty minutes had passed when Mark came to the door. "Rebecca, would you mind joining us in the study? Joe is here, and he has some questions for you."

As Rebecca entered, Irene said, "This is Rebecca Clark, the one who found all this. She has simply been a blessing to us."

"Hello, Ms. Clark. I'm Joe Lewis. In looking over all the information, everything seems to be in order. You certainly have uncovered a lot. Have you spoken to anyone at the company about what you were doing or what you thought was going on? Would anyone suspect you were up to something?"

"No, Mr. Lewis, I have been very careful. Much of my research was done here at night, but some I had to do through the day," Rebecca explained. "When I needed someone to return my call, I used my private cell phone number, and when I sent emails, again I used my personal email account instead of the company one. I didn't want to raise any flags by looking into the business accounts that Charlotte might notice. One thing I didn't talk about earlier with Irene was the employees' pay. All employees received raises every year, but one employee received not only raises but also bonuses. Charlotte makes over $150,000 a year, and this year she has received two good bonuses. Also, if you look, Brad's paycheck has increased considerably in the last five years."

Looking at Rebecca, Irene said, "Charlotte makes *how* much a year? And who authorized those bonuses? McKay's has never given anyone a bonus, Rebecca. We always give decent raises to all our employees. I can't believe I have been so blind to all this. I just never thought about anyone taking from the company. Is there anything else you have discovered that I don't know about?"

"I hope there is nothing else," Rebecca replied. "When I first discovered that something didn't seem right, I had no idea it would lead to all this. It blew my mind, and that's why I kept on searching the files and digging deeper. The password you installed gave me access to so much information. You said that you wanted me, as CEO, to know this company inside out. But some things I still have not investigated."

"You know, Ms. Clark," Joe began, "as Mrs. McKay's attorney now, I will need access to your emails and will need to look at your personal phone log. When this is all over, you might want to consider changing them, but for now everything must be gone over."

"That's fine," Rebecca said. "I totally understand." She gave Mr. Lewis all the information he needed, and then he gathered up the papers and said he would be getting back in touch with them in a few days. But until they heard from him, he advised, they were to just continue as usual.

"With this information," he explained, "we have enough proof to arrest them, but I want to have some warrants and other things in hand before any moves are made."

Mark said to Joe, "Let me walk you out. I really do appreciate your coming over and helping my mother out."

"Yes, Joe," Irene agreed. "I'm so glad Mark was able to recommend someone to help us out. I was in such a state of shock when Rebecca informed me of all this that I wasn't sure what to do."

Joe and Mark went outside, leaving Irene and Rebecca alone. "Are you going to be okay, Irene? I'm so sorry to have to be the one to tell you all this, but you needed to know."

"Yes, I will be fine," Irene said with a sigh. "This was such a shock and disappointment. Wonder what they will do to Charlotte and Brad? What will this do to their families? How will this affect the other employees? So many questions with no answers."

Rebecca went over to Irene and took her hand. "Mr. Lewis will take care of all this. He will let you know what you need to do and when." Irene nodded.

"You know, Irene," Rebecca began, "in the beginning, I'm sure Charlotte was a very trustworthy employee. She may have been going through some hard financial times at home and made a bad choice on how to handle it. At the time, taking a little money may have seemed like a harmless thing to do, but it turned into greed or lust to have more. I'm not sure how Brad got wrapped up in this, but the two became partners in crime. Like you said, this just doesn't affect them; it affects so many others."

She continued. "When Charlotte is gone, you will need to find someone to replace her. This needs to be your decision because I am too new to the company. The employees know you and know you will do right by the company and what's best for them."

"That hadn't even crossed my mind," Irene admitted. "Who could we get? Lynn was hired a few years after Charlotte. Do you think she could do the job? I know she is your personal secretary and you like her very much, but she has a better knowledge of the company than any of the others."

"This isn't a decision you have to make today," Rebecca said. "Take your time and look around. You will know when you have found the right person—that I am confident in."

She paused for a moment and then asked, "Ms. Irene, would it be all right if I went for a drive to try to clear my mind and sort some things out? That will also give you and Mark some time to talk things over and discuss what all has happened and what you may want to do."

"Yes, I'm certainly going to need plenty of advice," Irene conceded. "I know what I'd *like* to do, but it's best not act too hastily.

Yes, go enjoy yourself, dear, and Rebecca, thank you again. I'm sure this hasn't been easy on you."

About five minutes later, Mark came back into the study. "Where's Rebecca?" he asked.

"Oh, honey, she went for a drive," Irene answered. "She thought the two of us might want some time alone. She is very thoughtful."

"Well, Mother, we do need to talk about so many things."

Six

MONDAY MORNING CAME MUCH TOO SOON FOR REBECCA. HOW WAS she going to walk in and pretend nothing was going on? She hoped Brad would not be there; she didn't want to see the two of them together.

When she arrived and saw Lynn at her desk, Rebecca asked if she had any messages. "Yes, Charlotte called and said she wasn't feeling well today," Lynn replied. "She had been under the weather all weekend and was trying to get in to see a doctor today."

"That's good. I mean, I hope she gets to see a doctor," Rebecca stammered. She closed her office door behind her, thankful that Charlotte was not coming in. She buzzed Lynn and asked that any mail that would normally go to Charlotte be brought to her so they could stay caught up. She wondered if she would find any more surprises.

Three more weeks had gone by when, one morning before lunch, Lynn buzzed Rebecca and said that Irene, Mark, and a Mr. Lewis were there to see her. "Yes, Lynn, show them in," Rebecca replied. Suddenly, she had knots in her stomach. This was the day that the bomb was going to hit the company. She thought she had prepared herself for it, but now she wasn't sure.

Irene, Mark, and Joe came in looking very calm. Irene said, "Rebecca, let's all sit over at the conference table, and Joe will go over what is about to take place. I thought it best for him to talk to all of us at one time. I'm sure that people started talking when we walked in. I could feel them watching us as we went by."

Mark said, "You haven't been in the office for a while, I haven't been here in years, and they have no idea who Joe is, so I'm sure we raised some eyebrows. But we have more serious business to worry about right now. Okay, Joe, you have the floor."

"Well, after going over all that Ms. Clark provided, I had some of my people who deal with cases like this do a little more research. It seems Mr. Brewer may have been the one to bring Charlotte on board with him. He has been skimming money from the company since way before she was hired. When he found out about her financial problems, he was able to convince her that, if she did certain things, he would cover for her, and from there things just escalated. Charlotte went from living in a small two-bedroom home to a home with over four thousand square feet, a pool, and a tennis court. On her old salary and her husband's, there was no way they could afford a home like that. The furnishings in her home more than likely were paid for by the McKay company. Her children are involved in several activities that are quite expensive, and she did take some trips with her family that were very nice, but she took more trips with Brad Brewer. By the way, Ms. Clark, how did you find Charlotte's home address? In all the records, it gives her old address."

"She had some personal mail on her desk," Rebecca answered, "and I knew that wasn't the address in the computer. I drove by both homes, and that's how I found out which was her actual address."

Joe was very impressed with what Rebecca was able to find out. "Very good. Like I said, she never changed it here at the company, so if anyone looked up her address they would not have known. In fact, her niece lives at the address listed in the computer, so she was able to still get mail at that address."

Joe continued. "As for Brad Brewer, he already had a nice home, but he too moved up. Being an attorney, he knew how to get around certain things, and with Charlotte in the picture, he had better access to the company's money without raising any suspicion. Unfortunately for them, their lifestyle is getting ready to change, but it's fortunate for you, Mrs. McKay, that your company stayed in good standing financially." Irene nodded.

"As we speak, Brad Brewer is being read his rights," Joe told the group. "One of my partners along with the police are at his office now. Ms. Clark, if you would be so kind as to ask Charlotte Bailey to step into your office, I will let the police know to come on up."

Knowing what Charlotte was about to face, Rebecca felt sorry for her, but she also wanted to see justice done. Irene did not deserve what Charlotte and Brad had done to her. As Rebecca entered Charlotte's office, Charlotte was just getting ready to leave.

"Charlotte, I see you are getting ready to go somewhere, but I would like to see you in my office first."

"Oh, Ms. Clark, can it wait?" Charlotte pleaded. "I have a lunch date in about ten minutes, and I don't won't to be late or keep them waiting."

"I'm sorry, but your lunch date will have to wait. If you will come with me."

"Ms. Clark, are you sure this can't wait till I come back?" Charlotte persisted. "I have made reservations at the Landing."

"Lunch will wait," Rebecca said firmly. She had turned and headed toward her office when Charlotte said, "I don't mean to be disrespectful, Ms. Clark, but this is a very important luncheon. Your meeting will just have to wait till I get back. I'm sorry to be like this, but this is very, very important."

Just then two police officers walked up. Charlotte looked at them and then at Rebecca.

"What's going on? Why are they here?"

"Please, Charlotte, come with me to my office," Rebecca said.

As they walked in, Charlotte saw Irene, Mark, and some other guy she didn't know.

Irene asked Charlotte to take a seat and introduced Joe Lewis to her, saying, "Mr. Lewis is the new attorney for the company." Charlotte went white. She looked from one person to the next, not saying a word.

Mr. Lewis handed Charlotte some papers to look at. After a few minutes, he said, "Ms. Bailey, please keep in mind that anything you say can be used against you in a court of law. You have the right to an attorney. If you can't afford an attorney, the court will appoint you one. Do you understand what I have just said?"

With tears in her eyes, Charlotte just nodded her head.

Joe asked her if anything in those papers looked familiar to her. At that point, Charlotte lay her head down on the table and began sobbing uncontrollably. He motioned for one of the officers to handcuff her.

"Oh, please don't do this to me," she protested. "Please. I'm so sorry for what I've done. I don't want to go to jail. And please don't let my family find out. It will kill them. Surely there is something I can do to make this up to you!"

As the officer was putting the handcuffs on her, she continued pleading with them. "You can't let them take me out of here in these cuffs! What will the people who work here think? They will start talking and think only the worst. Please have some sympathy for me. Mrs. McKay, I have worked a long time for you. Please understand and help me!"

Irene turned to Charlotte and asked," What understanding did you have as you stole from this company?"

As Joe gathered up the papers, the officers led Charlotte out. "We have a search warrant for her home, as well as for Mr. Brewer's. Both families will be asked to leave with only the clothes on their backs till we inventory everything. Both will likely serve jail time, but there's no telling how much. Mrs. McKay, we will do all we can to see that restitution is made."

Patting Irene on the back, Joe turned and walked out.

"Mark, can you take me home?" Irene said. "I don't feel well. To be honest, I'm not sure how I feel. Are you coming home, Rebecca, or are you going to stay here?"

"Think I will stay here for a while. Like you, I'm not sure how I feel. It's like I just watched a movie play out before my eyes. Part of me feels sorry for Charlotte, and part of me knows she must pay for what she did. I'll be home later."

Mark helped Irene up. Her legs were so wobbly that she wasn't sure she could walk. "It is so hard to believe this happened in our company." With tears running down her cheeks, she took Marks's arm and left.

Rebecca had no idea how long she had been sitting behind her desk just staring out across the office. She wasn't even sure if she had been thinking. What happened there that day was so awful that she couldn't even begin to think what Charlotte's husband and children were going through. Then she thought of Brad Brewer and what his wife must be experiencing and thinking. She would soon find out about the affair Brad and Charlotte were having. Would she lose her home too? Would she divorce Brad? This mess was getting so enormous and so many lives were affected by it.

Rebecca decided she might as well leave. With a headache and knots in her stomach, she was not able to get any work done anyway. As she headed out the door, she saw Lynn sitting at her desk and wiping her eyes. It was obvious she had been crying.

"Everything is going to be all right, Lynn," Rebecca assured her. "We had some problems that needed to be attended to."

"Ms. Clark, I'm not sure what all happened today," Lynn began, "but may I ask if Brad was involved also?"

"Why do you ask that?"

"Well, since I have become your secretary, I have noticed Brad and Charlotte together a lot. In fact, I walked in one day and they were kissing. She told me if I wanted to keep my job, I had better keep my mouth shut. Do you remember when, about two weeks ago, I received some red roses? They were from Brad. When he came in that day, he asked me how I liked the roses. I told him they were nice, and he said they were for keeping my mouth shut. As I left for home that night, I threw them in the trash as I went downstairs. I have been trying to figure out how to tell you but didn't want to cause any problems."

"Yes, Brad and Charlotte are in some serious trouble. I would appreciate it if you didn't discuss this with the other employees, though. You will know more later. I'm going home now. If you need me, call; otherwise, I will see you tomorrow."

Seven

AROUND FOUR O'CLOCK THE NEXT MORNING, REBECCA DECIDED TO get up. She had worn herself and the bed out. Turning on the lamp by her bed, she picked up her Bible. "Heavenly Father, help us as we try to get through another trying day. Help me to stay focused and to give the employees just what information is needed without revealing too much for they are going to want to know what is going on in the company. Help Irene as she faces all that is before her. Dear Father, be with the families of Charlotte and Brad. Their lives went from normal to destroyed. Thank you again for helping us get through yesterday. I don't know what we would do if we didn't have you. I love you and thank you for loving us. Amen."

When she opened her Bible, it fell open to Isaiah 41. As she started reading, verse 10 seemed to speak to her: "Fear not, for I am with you; be not dismayed, for I am your God; I will strengthen you, I will help you, I will uphold you with my righteous right hand." As she pulled the Bible close to her chest, she knew God was with her.

Rebecca decided to go into work early. She wanted to be there before the employees started coming in. Michael Allen, the security guard at the gate, waved as she pulled in. As she got out of the car, he walked over to her. "Ms. Clark, you are here really early. Is everything all right?"

"Yes, Michael. Thought I would try to catch up on some work."

"I saw what happened yesterday," he added. "I hate to sound

A Journey for Rebecca

nosy, but is everything all right with the company? It's not going to shut down, is it?"

"No, everything is good. We just had some issues that needed to be addressed. If any of the employees ask, let them know their jobs are secure."

One employee down, many more to go, she thought. As she worked, she kept looking at the clock on her desk. At nine o'clock, she figured she might as well make her rounds through the plant.

As she walked around, she made sure she gave each employee time to ask questions. Some she just chatted with, but she made sure she spoke to everyone. For the ones who did inquire about what had taken place the day before, her reply was, "The company had some issues that needed to be addressed. To our knowledge, all is well."

It took three and a half hours to make the rounds, but she felt so much better. McKay's had some good people working for them. Heading back to her office, Rebecca cut through the break room. She heard someone talking over in the corner so she stopped to listen. This was not break time—who else was in the break room?

She went over to see whose voice she had heard and found Rachel Mills. She was on the phone asking the caller to give someone a Tylenol and asking if that person could possibly lie down in the sick room. She needed to work and would not be able to pick this person up until she got off of work. When Rachel saw Rebecca, she told the caller that she had to go and hung up.

"Rachel, I'm sorry," Rebecca said. "I didn't mean to interrupt your phone call. You didn't have to hang up if it was important."

"No, it's okay. I really need to get back to work. I know we are not to be on our phones till break or lunch." The phone rang again and Rachel looked at it, not sure if she should answer it.

"Do you need to answer that call?" Rebecca asked.

"Yes, I really do," she replied. She answered and told the caller that the soonest she could pick the person up would be around five o'clock.

"If you need to leave work, you can," Rebecca whispered. "Is it important?"

Putting her hand over the phone, Rachel said, "My little girl is at school, and they said she is running a fever. If I pick her up, I have no one to leave her with so I can come back."

"You can tell the school you will be right there to pick her up. Your daughter is more important than your work right now."

With a look of relief, Rachel said to the caller, "Ms. Ward, my boss just gave me permission to leave work, so I will be there in a few minutes to pick her up. Thank you." She hung up the phone.

"Why did you think we wouldn't let you leave work?" Rebecca asked.

Dropping her head, Rachel simply said, "I need to work. Thank you for letting me off." With that, Rachel went to her locker to get her things and left.

Rebecca went back inside the factory to find Emma Bowman. "Emma, are you at a stopping place? I would like to talk to you for a minute."

"Yes, ma'am, I am," Emma answered.

"Good. Follow me, please." Rebecca decided to go outside where a picnic table was, hoping to keep down employee gossip if possible.

After they sat down, Rebecca began, "Emma, I would like to ask you a few questions. This has nothing to do with your job or work. How well do you know Rachel Mills?"

"Rachel is very quiet," Emma replied. "I've worked beside her for almost a year, and she says very little. If we are alone, sometimes she will talk more, but if anyone is around, she won't hardly say a word."

"I don't normally ask question about the employees, but I'm concerned about Rachel," Rebecca explained. "What we say here today needs to go no further. If you would tell me what little you know, I would appreciate it. She always seems so sad, like she has the weight of the world on her shoulders. And she just received a call from the school saying that her little girl is sick. I would like to help her, but I don't know what to do because I know nothing about her. Usually when I'm talking to the employees here, they mention a spouse or their children, but Rachel says nothing."

"Ms. Clark, please don't say anything to Rachel about what I tell you," Emma said. "She has told me a little, and it's like I'm the only friend she has. She has only shared with me in the last three or four months. It's taken me this long to earn her trust."

"I understand, and I promise not to say a word. I just need some insight on how to help her if I possibly can."

Emma sighed. "Rachel has had a very tough life. I don't know what happened to her parents, but she was raised first by one family member and then another. When she graduated from high school, she wanted to go to college, and the only way she could do that was to work and pay her own way." Taking a deep breath, Emma looked at Rebecca with tears in her eyes before continuing. "One night after class, some guys jumped her, and they raped her. From what she said, they roughed her up and left her for dead. I don't know any other details other than that she became pregnant from that ordeal and had Sarah."

Rebecca shook her head sadly.

"Rachel has also mentioned working in a day care," Emma went on. "The owner let Rachel and Sarah live at the day care at night while Rachel worked there during the day. That way she could work and look after Sarah. But the owner became sick and had to close the day care. From what I have gathered, Rachel worked there for several years—I'm not sure how many." Emma paused to think of anything else.

"Ms. Clark," she said when she remembered something. "Do you remember back about two months ago when those apartments over on Finley Street caught fire and burned completely down? Everything was a total loss. Well, Rachel and Sarah were living there. Rachel was here at work, and Sarah had not made it home from school when the fire broke out."

Not sure of some things, Rebecca asked, "Who watches Sarah while Rachel is at work?"

"No one," Emma answered. "Sarah is about six or seven. When she gets off the bus, she lets herself in and stays inside till Rachel gets home."

"Oh, Emma, this is so sad," Rebecca said. "I can't imagine going home to an empty house at that age. Who watches her in the summer while Rachel is at work?"

"I really don't know," Emma answered. "I take it she is there all day by herself till Rachel gets home."

Placing her hands over her chest, Rebecca said, "This just breaks my heart. Does she not have neighbors or someone who could watch her while she is gone?"

"There was an elderly lady who lived next door to them, and I think she always made sure Sarah made it safely in the house when she came home after school," Emma explained. "But again, this is something Rachel doesn't talk about often."

"Where are they living now?"

"Well, a few days after the fire, I asked her where they were living, and she said out of her car. She didn't have a checking account, and what money she had saved got burned up in the fire, so she was waiting till payday to try to find a place. Her car has been giving her trouble, and she was saving up to have the car fixed. They stayed about four days with my husband and me, and then my neighbor told us about a small house for rent. Rachel went and looked at it. It's not much but it was furnished. We took her to the Red Cross, and they gave her some items for the house and some clothes, plus my neighbor and I gave her some things. It's really not much of a house, but the rent was what Rachel could afford at the time."

"Why haven't you said something about this before now?" Rebecca asked. "We could have been helping her."

"Ms. Clark, Rachel is a very private person. She doesn't want anyone feeling sorry for her or asking questions."

"I can understand, but she needs help. She needs friends—people to help her in a time like this. What do you know about her little girl?"

"She talks about Sarah's drawings. Apparently, she is pretty good. She goes to Meadows Elementary, and she loves school. That's about it. I didn't know Sarah was sick till you just told me."

"Emma, I really appreciate what you have told me, and again, this conversation is between the two of us. Would it offend you if I gave you a hug? Hugs seem to help at times like this."

"Oh, a hug would be perfect," Emma replied.

After they hugged, they walked back inside the plant. Rebecca went straight to her office to pray about this, for her heart was so heavy for Rachel and Sarah. After praying, Rebecca called Meadows Elementary. She told the lady who answered the phone who she was and why she was calling, hoping to get to talk to Sarah's teacher. The lady put her on hold, and while waiting, Rebecca whispered a prayer asking for God to please intervene because she was only wanting to help. The lady came back on the line and asked if Rebecca could be at the school at 3:00. Ms. Reagan, the teacher, could speak to her then.

"Yes, that will work, and thank you so much." When Rebecca hung up the phone, she whispered another prayer. "Thank you, Father. I know it was you who made this possible."

Meadows Elementary looked to be new. Rebecca parked her car and headed for the building, but a police officer stopped her. He asked Rebecca if he could help her. She explained that she had an appointment with Ms. Reagan, and he called the school office to verify her appointment. Then he escorted her to the door that led to the office. The lady behind the desk asked for her name and who she was to see. Rebecca couldn't remember school being like this when she was in school; things had really changed. She was told to have a seat and Ms. Reagan would be in to see her shortly.

In a few minutes, a young lady came in and asked if she was Ms. Clark. The two shook hands and then went to Ms. Reagan's classroom. The room was so neat and orderly. Taking a seat, Ms. Reagan asked how she could help her.

"Sarah's mom, Rachel Mills, works for me at McKay's. I

overheard her talking to someone here at the school about Sarah this morning. Rachel didn't want to leave work, yet was concerned about her daughter. I'm aware that they have gone through a tough time and was hoping you could enlighten me on how I could possibly help them. Rachel is very quiet and says little. I didn't know if maybe Sarah may have said something that could be of help to me."

"Oh, Sarah is a very sweet and lovely child," Ms. Reagan began. She always does her work and helps the other children if they need help with their work. She is very well behaved, well mannered—you couldn't ask for a better child. Sarah loves to draw and make things. Here on the board, Sarah drew all these leaves by hand, and we put each child's picture in the middle of the leaves. As you notice, all the leaves are different colors, and each child picked which color they liked best. This one is Sarah's." She pointed to an orange leaf.

"She is a beautiful child," Rebecca agreed. "Just look at that smile. "It was as if Sarah had reached out and touched Rebecca's heart. She wondered how she would feel seeing Sarah in person if a picture could move her so deeply!

Trying to look away from the picture, Rebecca asked how Sarah's attendance was.

"She is here every day and always early," Ms. Reagan said. "Her mother drops her off on her way to work. I always put a little something in her backpack to eat when she gets home. I'm sure you know about the fire."

"Yes, that's one of the reasons I'm here. Again, Rachel doesn't say much at work, and I didn't know if Sarah had said anything?"

"I know they lost everything. Sarah wore the same clothes for several days, and she said they had to live in her mother's car till they could find a new home. I kept Sarah after school with me till her mother could come by and pick her up because she had nowhere to go. You know, that poor child never complained. She kept the best attitude about it all."

"Ms. Reagan, do you know what was wrong with Sarah this morning?"

"She was running a very high fever and throwing up, had diarrhea, and could barely get around. When I took her to the school nurse, she said Sarah needed to see a doctor or be taken to the emergency room. When her mother came to pick her up, the nurse insisted that she take Sarah to the hospital. Her mother had to carry her out to the car she was so weak. I called Rachel about an hour ago, and she said they had admitted Sarah to the hospital. I'm not sure if I should go by today or wait till tomorrow to see her. They were running tests on her and may not want her to have visitors."

"Oh, I did not know she had been admitted," Rebecca said, "but then I have been away from the office. Can you tell me what Sarah likes? I would like to get her something."

"She talks about unicorns and angels a lot. She hopes to someday have her own room and put angels and unicorns in it."

"Thank you, Ms. Reagan, for taking the time to talk to me. You have been most helpful. If at any time you think of anything I can do for them, please call me. Here is my card. Call anytime."

While sitting in her car, Rebecca wondered what it was about the picture of Sarah that had gotten to her. For some reason, she couldn't get it out of her mind. Was God trying to tell her something? If so, what?

On her way to the hospital, she decided to stop at a toy store. Rebecca was so shocked at all the different toys. Without children of her own and being an only child to parents who were out in the mission field so much, she never really had a lot of toys. She felt lost and out of place as she walked up one aisle and down another. Finally, a clerk asked her if she could help her find something.

"Yes, by any chance do you sell angels or unicorns?" she asked. The clerk took her to where she needed to go, but there were still so many choices. She wondered how children today ever decided what they wanted—there was too much to choose from. Then Rebecca spotted an angel, and she knew she had to have it for Sarah. She took it to the checkout counter, and the clerk gift wrapped it in unicorn paper. This was perfect.

The Pink Lady at the information desk of the hospital gave Rebecca the room number for Sarah. As she neared the open door, she saw Rachel sitting in a chair by Sarah's bed, holding the child's little hand. Rebecca knocked softly at the door, and Rachel turned to see her boss standing there.

"Oh, Ms. Clark!" she exclaimed. "We weren't expecting you. Thank you again for letting me off today. I'll be at work in the morning."

"No, you won't, Rachel," Rebecca replied. "Your daughter is sick, and you are going to stay here with her. You have some sick days saved up, and you can use them. I brought this for Sarah. Whenever she feels better, you can give this to her." Rebecca handed her the gift.

"Thank you, Ms. Clark, but you didn't have to get her anything. I'm sure she will like it. I had forgotten about the sick days. Do you know how many I have?"

"You have as many as you need. Remember, I have the final say-so in this. Now, how is your little girl?" They both looked at Sarah, who appeared to be sleeping.

To Rebecca, the child looked so pale. She had an IV in her little hand, and she just lay there. "Have the doctors said what is wrong with her?"

"They ran a lot of tests today, but they haven't said what the results are," Rachel answered. "She has been like this ever since I brought her in."

"Have you had anything to eat today?" Rebecca asked.

"No, I'll find something later," Rachel said. "I don't want to leave Sarah."

Just then, a nurse came in to check Sarah's vitals. She said there was no change.

Rebecca turned to the nurse and said, "Excuse me. Is it possible that you could stay in here with Sarah while I take her mother to get something to eat? We don't need them both as patients."

"Certainly, go get some food, and I'll stay till you get back," the nurse replied. "You need to eat, and taking a break from this room will do you good. Trust me—as a nurse, I know what a break can do for you."

Rachel looked at the nurse and said, "I really appreciate this, but I don't want to leave her. She may wake up, and I won't be here for her."

"Ms. Mills, I'll call you if she wakes up," the nurse assured her. "Don't worry. Now go with your friend and get something to eat. You need to take care of yourself as well."

Rebecca put her arm around Rachel, and the two went down to the cafeteria. When they arrived, Rebecca said, "If you will find us a seat, I'll get a tray."

As they went through the line, Rebecca said, "Rachel, this is for you. I grabbed something before I came. You need to eat and stay strong for your little girl."

At first, Rachel just picked at her food, but then she began eating. Rebecca wondered when the last time Rachel had really been able to have a decent meal.

As soon as Rachel finished her meal, she was eager to get back to Sarah. As they were walking down the hall to the elevators, they came upon a chapel.

"Rachel, do you mind if we stop in here?" Rebecca asked. "I'd like to say a prayer for Sarah."

"You go ahead, Ms. Clark. I'm going back to her room in case she's awake."

"Rachel, Sarah could use our prayers," Rebecca said.

"Sorry, but I don't have time for that," Rachel said. "Excuse me, but I need to get back to Sarah." She turned and rushed down the hall toward the elevator.

Opening the door, Rebecca wondered what it was about the chapel that made Rachel not even want to step inside. She took a seat and started praying. Both Rachel and Sarah were in much need of prayer.

After praying, Rebecca went back to Sarah's room to check on her and Rachel.

Rebecca looked at Sarah and noted that she didn't seem to have moved at all. Rachel had tears streaming down her cheeks. "Have you heard any news?" Rebecca asked.

"The doctor came by and said Sarah has a bacterial infection," Rachel said. "They are putting her on some strong antibiotics, and she will need to stay in the hospital for a few days. I need to be here with Sarah, but I also need to work."

"Rachel, don't worry about work. Your job will be waiting on you when you are able to come back. Just concentrate on taking care of Sarah and yourself. Remember, you have sick days you can use."

"Ms. Clark, I do appreciate this," Rachel replied. "This is the best job I have ever had, and I don't want to do anything to lose it."

"You're not going to lose your job, especially when you have a reason as justifiable as this for missing. Besides, Mr. Callahan speaks very highly of you. Good, loyal workers are hard to find."

"Oh, Ms. Clark, I can't thank you enough for your kindness. You have such a caring heart."

"I care about all my employees," Rebecca responded. "We are family as far as I'm concerned, and we all need to help one another. The Bible says in Matthew 22:39 that we are to love our neighbors as ourselves."

"Do you really believe all that religious stuff, Ms. Clark?" Rachel asked. "I noticed you have a lot of scripture things on the walls, you have a moment of silence every morning at work, and I've seen you pray with some of the workers. Why?"

"My parents were missionaries. I have seen what God can do, and through my own life, he has done so much. I can't imagine not having him in my life. Don't get me wrong—I have had my own share of heartaches, but by faith, God has brought me through it all. Do you have a Bible?"

"No, I lost all faith in God years ago," Rachel said. "When I really needed him, he turned his back on me. Sarah and I are making it on our own just fine."

Reaching over, Rebecca put her hand over Rachel's. "I would like to talk to you about some things later that may help you. We all have our troubles and trials; no one is spared. At times it's as if it's more than we can handle, but it's God that gets us through it. We can't get through anything on our own."

Sarah moaned a little, and Rachel jumped up to go to her. The child moved just a little but never said a word.

"I appreciate your coming by, Ms. Clark. Maybe we can talk again some time."

"Yes, let's talk soon." Looking at Sarah, Rebecca said, "I hope she is much better by morning."

As she left the room and went to her car, Rebecca hoped she would be able to break through the wall Rachel had up. She wondered what had happened that would cause her to lose faith. Maybe it was having Sarah.

As soon as Rebecca got home, Irene asked her if everything was all right. Rebecca had turned her phone on silent and had missed several calls. "I'm so sorry, Irene," she answered. "I forgot to turn my ringer back on. I went to the hospital to check on one of our employees whose daughter had to be admitted to the hospital today. Is anything wrong here?"

"My dear, things are fine," Irene said. "I knew you said you would be a little late getting home, but that was several hours ago. I was wanting to let you know to clear your calendar for Thursday and Friday. We are flying to New York."

"Oh! Have I forgotten a meeting, or are we going to New York for another reason?"

"No, dear, we have not had a chance to talk, and we really should have a long time ago. Mr. Bruce Stafford is hosting a dinner in honor of Mark. Mark is announcing his candidacy for state senator, and the dinner will be held at the Winchester Opera House in two weeks. Time has really gotten away from me with all that has happened, but anyway, we need to go buy the perfect dresses for us to wear, and I know the perfect New York designer for the job. Besides, it will help to get away for a few days."

"Am I supposed to go to this dinner?" Rebecca asked. "I don't know Mark that well, and I don't think I would fit in someplace like that."

"Oh, you will fit in fine," Irene assured her. "Besides, this will give you an opportunity to meet more people around here, and they will meet the new CEO of McKay's. We will leave Thursday morning around seven o'clock for we have an appointment with Phillip at noon. He designs the most absolutely beautiful gowns, and I trust his judgment completely. Can't wait for you to meet him."

"I don't know. I'm not used to dressing up in fancy evening gowns. I will feel so out of place. Are you up for a trip to New York? With all that you have gone through lately, going to New York might not be a good idea."

"Honey, the time is perfect. We really need to get away, and the dinner will be a perfect chance for you to meet other people. Who knows how many bachelors might be mingling there?"

"Oh, no, I'm not interested in looking for a man," Rebecca replied, shaking her head. "Please don't try to play matchmaker for me. I have my work, and that's all I need. Oh, by the way, do you remember Rachel Mills?"

"Rachel Mills—that name does sound familiar. In fact, I believe I interviewed her. If she is the lady I'm thinking of, she is shy, but I've heard she is a very good worker."

"She is *very* shy," Rebecca replied, "I was nearby when the school called her today to tell her that her little girl was sick. In fact, her daughter had to be admitted to the hospital and will probably be there for a few days. I went by to see them, and that child broke my heart when I saw her. She just lays in the bed, so lifeless. She has a bacterial infection and is on some strong antibiotics. I told Rachel not to worry about work, that her daughter was more important, and her needs came first. She has some sick days she can use—I'm not sure how many. When you interviewed Rachel, did she say anything about her previous jobs?"

"I would have to go back and pull her resume. I make notes on the resumes so that, if I ever need to, I can refresh my memory about the candidates. Is there a problem other than her child being in the hospital?"

"She needs help in a lot of ways, and I'm just trying to figure out what to do," Rebecca answered. "For now, would you be sure to keep her and her little girl in your prayers? The little girl's name is Sarah."

"Sarah!" Irene exclaimed. "That was my mother's name. I always said that, if I ever had a little girl, I would name her Sarah, but I had a boy. Don't think Mark would like to be called Sarah, although Johnny Cash wrote a song about a boy named Sue."

They both laughed, and then Irene continued, "With that being said, I think I shall turn in. Sleep well, Rebecca, and don't forget we will be going to New York on Thursday."

Rebecca did not want to go to New York, especially this week; she wanted to be here to help Rachel if she could. And she certainly did not want to go to some formal dinner in two weeks with highly affluent people. Rachel's situation was more important to her, and the dinner was important to Irene. Caring for both, Rebecca wasn't sure what to do. Pray—that's what she would do. She needed guidance.

Eight

EARLY THE NEXT MORNING, REBECCA WENT TO THE HOSPITAL before going to work. She walked in and found Sarah propped up in bed, still looking very pale. When she saw Rebecca, a big smile came across her face.

"Hello," Sarah said. "Do you work here? My name is Sarah."

"No, I don't work here. My name is Rebecca Clark. Your mom and I work together. I came by to see how you are feeling. Is your mom here?"

"Yes, she had to go sign some papers," Sarah replied. "She will be right back."

"How are you feeling today, Sarah?"

"I'm okay. Can I lie back down?"

"I'm not sure," Rebecca answered. "Let me press the call button for the nurse and see if we can lay your bed back down. Have you been raised up long?"

The speaker crackled and a nurse asked, "Can I help you?"

"Yes, I'm a friend of the Mills family," Rebecca said, "and Sarah wants to know if she can lie down. They have her propped up in the bed."

The nurse replied, "Someone will be right with you."

In a few minutes, a nurse came and helped Sarah lie down. She took Sarah's vitals and asked her some questions. The nurse then turned to Rebecca and said, "Her fever is down some, but we can't get her to drink anything. We will be back in again to her turn and move her around. We don't want pneumonia to set in." Rebecca thanked her, and the nurse left the room.

Just then, Rachel came in, looking surprised to see Rebecca.

"Hello, Rachel," Rebecca began. "I thought I would stop in and see how you two are doing before I went to work. The nurse just left and said Sarah's fever was down some and that they would be back in later to turn her. They want to make sure she doesn't get pneumonia."

"Ms. Clark, I wasn't expecting to see you here this morning," Rachel said. "Sarah feels so bad that she doesn't want to move. When she finds a comfortable position, she lays very still. And when they come to turn her, she doesn't say a word, just moans a little." She looked at her daughter and said, "Oh, Sarah, this is Ms. Clark, my boss from work. She came by last night and brought you a present."

Rachel handed the package to Sarah, who asked her mother if she would open it. When Rachel took out the angel, a smile broke out across Sarah's face. "Oh, she is beautiful. Can she lay with me?" Taking the angel, Sarah held it close to her.

"Thank you, Ms. Clark," Sarah said quietly. "I like her." Then she turned and closed her eyes for she was so tired.

Rebecca looked at Rachel and asked, "How are you doing this morning? Did you sleep any last night?"

"I slept a little. You can't get much rest with the nurses coming in and out all night to check on patients."

"Maybe you will be able to get some rest today," Rebecca said. "Can I get you anything? If you want to go eat, I would be happy to sit here with Sarah."

"Thank you, Ms. Clark. I'm good. I do appreciate your stopping by. You really don't have to. Sarah and I will be just fine."

"Rachel, I came by because I care. Remember what I said last night: the employees at McKay's are all family. We help one another out, no matter what the situation is.

Let us help you."

Tensing up, Rachel looked down at her sick daughter, so pale and frail looking. "Ms. Clark, Sarah and I have made it on our own for years. We will be fine. Thanks again for all you've done."

Rebecca reached over to pat Rachel on the shoulder. Rebecca wanted so desperately to help her but just said, "If you need anything, Rachel, please call."

Rebecca left the room and walked down the hall, where she passed one of the cafeteria workers. She asked her if it was possible to have a tray of food sent to room 453. Rebecca explained why, and the worker told her where to go to order the meals. So Rebecca went and purchased three meals a day for Rachel for as long as Sarah was in the hospital, and she asked that Rachel never know who paid for her meals. This way, hopefully, she would eat and not go hungry.

Lynn was busy at her desk when Rebecca walked in. "Morning, Lynn, Rebecca said, "Could you bring your calendar and come into my office?"

"Good morning, Ms. Clark. I just made a fresh pot of coffee. Would you care for a cup?" Lynn asked.

"You know, Lynn, that would be nice. Yes, thank you. Could you tell me what the calendar looks like for this Thursday and Friday? I need to be off those two days."

"You have a few things scheduled but nothing that can't be changed," Lynn answered. "Will you be in the office next week?"

"I think so. Irene informed me last night that we would be going to New York this Thursday. If it had been anyone else, I would have said no, but who can say no to her?"

"Oh, you're going to New York? That is awesome. Are you going to see a play?"

"No, we are going shopping," Rebecca answered. "I'm not at liberty to say anything else right now, but this is not something I want to do. Trust me."

"I'm sure you will enjoy your trip. Going to New York sounds so exciting, and going shopping can't be all that bad. I'll clear your schedule for both days. Anything I can do for you while you're gone?"

"No I can't think of anything. Should something come up, shoot me a text and we will go from there. Has Mr. Lewis called by any chance?" Rebecca asked.

"No, but if he does, I will certainly let you know," Lynn replied. "If it's all right, Ms. Clark, could I possibly leave after lunch today? I have a doctor's appointment that I had forgotten about. It was on my calendar, but for some reason, I overlooked it. I'm not sick, just my yearly checkup."

"Not a problem, Lynn. Just glad it's for you and not me," Rebecca joked.

Smiling, Lynn turned back to her work.

Later that day, a knock came at Rebecca's door. It was Emma.

"Ms. Clark, do you have a minute?" she asked. "I know it's time to go home, but have you heard from Rachel and her little girl?"

"Emma, come in. Yes, the little girl was admitted to the hospital and is very sick. I went by yesterday to see her, and then this morning I went by before coming to work. Last night the child just laid in the bed and didn't move. This morning they had her propped up a little in the bed and her fever had come down some. She has a bacterial infection and is taking some strong antibiotics."

"Do you think it would be all right if I went by the hospital and saw them?" Emma asked. "I want Rachel to know I care and have been worried about them."

"That's a very good idea," Rebecca answered. "It might help Rachel to see you and know how much you care. Since you're going to go by, I'll wait and go another time. If you don't mind, let me know how they are doing. Here is my cell phone number." She handed Emma a business card.

"I certainly will, Ms. Clark," Emma replied. "Thanks. I'll call you later."

Rebecca had wanted to go by and see them for herself, but she thought it best not to. Besides, she needed to pack for New York. She wasn't sure what to take, and worse, she wasn't sure what she needed to buy, but with Irene McKay by her side, she knew it would be only the best.

It was seven thirty that evening when Emma finally called. "Sorry for the delay," she began. "After leaving the hospital, I had an errand to run. Rachel looks so tired. I'm not sure if it's stress or staying at the hospital. Both can bring you down. Sarah was a little better. Her fever was coming on down, but she doesn't want to eat."

"Do you know if Rachel is eating?" Rebecca asked.

"Yes, she is. They are bringing her a tray from the cafeteria. She said since Sarah was not able to eat, they brought a tray in for her. That is thoughtful of them to do that. That way Rachel doesn't have to leave Sarah. She said Sarah wouldn't be able to leave the hospital until she was able to eat and walk up and down the hall."

Emma continued. "Ms. Clark, some of us were talking today at work, and we wondered if we could donate some of our sick days to Rachel. That way she would still have money coming in, and she could stay home with Sarah for a few days after she's discharged so they could both rest up."

"Emma, that is a wonderful idea," Rebecca replied. "Let me know who wants to donate a day, and we will find out how many days are needed. This is what Rachel needs—her work family to help her out when she needs it the most. Emma, you are such a blessing."

As she hung up the phone, Rebecca thought, *God is working in so many ways. That wall that Rachel has built up will soon come down. Just like the walls of Jericho did.*

Since she had so much to do before leaving for New York, Rebecca decided to go visit Rachel and Sarah around lunchtime the next day. When she walked in, she noticed that Sarah looked so much better.

"Look, Mama," Sarah said. "Ms. Clark is here." Rachel was standing by the window, looking out. She still looked very tired.

"Hello, Ms. Clark," she said. "How are you today?"

"I'm fine, Rachel. And how is our little girl doing?"

"Sarah is doing better," Rachel answered. "Her fever finally broke."

Sarah spoke up. "The angel you gave me took my fever away. She is a special angel, and I love her so much."

Rebecca's heart almost leaped out of her chest. She didn't know what it was about Sarah, but something was pulling on her heartstrings.

"That's wonderful, Sarah!" Rebecca said. "It's so good to see you sitting up in bed. Is there anything you would like to eat? I would be happy to get it for you."

"No, I'm good. Thank you."

Looking back at Rachel, Rebecca asked, "Can I get you anything?"

"No, thank you," Rachel replied. "Sarah and I are taking one day at a time. With luck we might be able to go home Saturday or Sunday. The doctor said it would take a while for her to get over the infection. It will leave her weak."

"Why don't you take all next week off from work? That way you and Sarah can rest up from all you have been through."

"Thank you, Ms. Clark, but I need to go back to work. I don't have enough sick days for another week off."

"Actually, you *do* have enough sick days. You see, some of your coworkers have donated sick days on your behalf so you can take care of your daughter and rest up yourself before coming back to work."

"They did that for me?" Rachel asked in disbelief. "They don't really know me. Why would they do that?"

"Rachel, that's what friends do—they help one another out in a time of need. Your coworkers are your friends, like I said the other day. We are like family, and you are a part of that family. We all go through hard times and never know when we will need help."

Putting her hands over her face, Rachel broke down and cried. She couldn't believe what she was hearing. The people she worked with really cared about her and Sarah. "I don't know what to say. Can you thank them for me?"

"No, that you need to do yourself," Rebecca answered. "It will be better coming from you than from me. It will also help your relationship with your coworkers."

Nodding her head, Rachel indicated that she understood. She went to Sarah, took her in her arms, and said, "Oh, Sarah, we are going to be all right."

"Mama, will we be home on my birthday?" Sarah asked.

"Yes, honey, we will."

"Will I be able to go and pick out a cupcake for my birthday?"

"We will have to wait and see how you are doing," Rachel began, "but yes, we will go and get you a cupcake one day next week."

"Is Sarah's birthday next week?" Rebecca asked.

"Yes, Sarah will be seven next Tuesday," Rachel answered.

"Every year, Mama lets me pick out any cupcake I want for my birthday," Sarah explained. "They are all so pretty, it's hard to decide." The smile on Sarah's face and the excitement in her voice over getting a cupcake touched Rebecca's heart again, especially as she realized that because of how little they had, even receiving a cupcake brought such joy. It reminded her of the children she had seen in the orphanages when she was with her parents in foreign countries. They were so excited to receive the least little thing.

"Sarah, I hope you continue to get better and go home soon, especially for your birthday," Rebecca said. "And Rachel, call the office should you or Sarah need anything. I will be out of town for the next few days, but Lynn, my secretary, will be taking all calls and will help you."

"Ms. Clark, thank you for stopping by and for the good news," Rachel said. "I feel so fortunate to be working for you. Smiling, Rebecca turned to leave the room and said, "We are always here for you. You two take care"

As soon as Rebecca got to work, she told Lynn to grab a notepad and a pen. "We have some work to do before I leave for New York," she said.

Lynn and Rebecca spent the next two hours making plans for the next week. When they had finished, they looked at what they had accomplished and felt good about what was to take place. Then they set out to take what was on paper and turn it into a reality.

Nine

SAMMY AND IRENE CHATTED ALL THE WAY TO THE AIRPORT. So many other things were on Rebecca's mind that she had no idea what the two were talking about. When they arrived at the airport, Sammy said he would be waiting for them on Friday evening and hoped they had a great time. Irene was so excited about the trip, while Rebecca found it hard to stay focused on what she was saying.

After they found their seats on the plane, Irene turned to Rebecca. "Now that we have some time together without any interruption, I want to tell you about Mark. When he went off to college, his goal was to become a family doctor, which he did. After several years, he went back to college to study law. He was a doctor during the day and a law student at night. So many things about medicine and the law that he felt he needed to be educated on both. Mark is very smart and has no trouble remembering anything. He receives high honors in all that he does, and I am very proud of him. Anyway, Bruce Stafford approached Mark about running for state senate. This is a new challenge for Mark and something that had never crossed his mind, but he finally agreed to be a candidate. Men from everywhere seem to take such an interest in his running for state senate. I saw part of the speech Mark will be giving next Friday, and I was very impressed. He doesn't know I saw it, so I can't say anything to him, but it was good, not to brag."

Trying to take in all that Irene had just told her, Rebecca said,

"So that's why we are on our way to New York to get a dress. Do you buy many evening gowns from this Phillip guy?"

"Yes, I have bought a few. You will like Phillip. I don't know how he does it, but he can design a dress that is perfect for any woman in just a matter of minutes. Sometimes he has a gown already in his shop that you would think he made just for you. It's amazing to watch him. We can also shop around in other shops if you like or go sightseeing. Our top priority is seeing Phillip and getting his help."

Getting to New York was one thing; getting a taxi was another. Irene was calm as always, indicating that she had done this on several occasions. She knew exactly where Phillip's store was, so Rebecca just followed along. Their first stop was at the Beekman Hotel to drop off their luggage. It was just beautiful, and Rebecca told herself she should have realized that Irene would want only the best. Next, they went to Phillip's Fashions. Rebecca was amazed at all the beautiful gowns.

"Hello, ladies," a woman greeted them. "May I help you?"

"Yes, we are here to see Phillip," Irene said. "We have an appointment. My name is Irene McKay."

"Yes, Mrs. McKay, Phillip is expecting you. Please have a seat while I get him for you."

Soon, Phillip came in, walking straight toward Irene.

"Mrs. McKay, how are you?" he asked. "It's been a while since you have been in. As always, it's a pleasure to see you."

"It's a pleasure to see you as well, Phillip. You look as handsome as always," Irene replied. "Oh, this is Rebecca Clark, the lady I spoke to you about. We are here in need of gowns, and like I said on the phone, we need them rather soon."

"Yes, don't worry," Phillip said. "Since you sent me the pictures, I am already ahead. But Ms. Clark, the picture she sent doesn't do you justice. You are much more beautiful in person, and the gown I have for you is perfect. I chose a blue that will go with your eyes perfectly. Come, let me show you."

Rebecca looked at Irene and asked quietly, "You sent him a picture of me?"

Irene smiled at Rebecca. "Yes, dear. Time is of the essence."

They followed Phillip to the back of the shop, and he soon emerged with a gorgeous dress. It was an off-the-shoulder gown with a split up one side that extended to a little above the knee. The color was the most beautiful blue Rebecca could have imagined. "Ms. Clark, what do you think?" he asked. "Shall we try it on?"

"Yes, Rebecca, you must try it on. While you do that, I'll see what Phillip has picked out for me. I'm sure it will be perfect."

"Yes, Mrs. McKay, yours is just as beautiful," Phillip assured her as he reached into a garment bag. "Here, what do you think?"

"Oh, yes, Phillip! I knew you would come through for us," Irene said excitedly. "I must try it on. The champagne color is perfect, and the lace bodice with a matching jacket is exactly what I need."

Rebecca stepped out to see what they thought of her gown. She felt like a million dollars in it.

"Oh, the shoes!" Phillip exclaimed. "I forgot to bring them out." He dashed to the back of the shop again.

He returned with a beautiful pair of shoes. "Here, try these on," he said, handing them to Rebecca. "They will do wonders for the dress. Mrs. McKay, I have picked out shoes for you also."

Rebecca looked at Phillip and asked, "How did you know what size dress I would need and what size shoe I wore?"

Irene spoke up. "Rebecca, my dear, while you were at work, I looked at your clothes so I could tell Phillip what size you wore, and of course I sent him a picture of you. I told you he was good. Look at you! the dress was made just for you, and the shoes are a perfect match. Yes, Phillip, we will take that gown. Now, I'll try mine on."

When Irene stepped from behind the dressing room door, she looked totally different. Rebecca couldn't believe how a dress could transform someone. "Oh, Irene, that gown is perfect for you!" "I can't believe how the gown fits you so."

"My dear, Phillip here is the guy you want when you need a

gown. I can't imagine using anyone else. Yes, Phillip, you have come through for me again. What would I ever do without you?"

"Mrs. McKay, it's always a pleasure serving you, and seeing the glow on your face brings me so much satisfaction, as well as yours, Ms. Clark," Phillip replied. "I will have the gowns packaged up and sent to your hotel. Are you staying at the Beekman Hotel again?"

"Yes, we are. Thank you so much. Rebecca and I may be seeing you again very soon."

"I'm here anytime you need me, Mrs. McKay. Ms. Clark, I hope you enjoy your gown as well."

"I'm sure I will," Rebecca said, "and thank you for all you have done. This has been a wonderful experience"

As they left the shop, Irene asked Rebecca, "Well, what do you think?"

"Irene, that man is amazing. Just by knowing my size and looking at a picture, he made that gown. He didn't even have to alter it any! It was a perfect fit."

"If Mark does as well as I think he will, we may be coming back for more gowns," Irene smiled. "What is it they call that? Frequent flyers? (laughing at the comment)"

Laughing, Rebecca said, "I was thinking more of *repeat customers.*"

As soon as they got back to the hotel and Rebecca had some time alone, she called Lynn to check on Rachel and Sarah. There had been some improvement in Sarah's condition, but it still looked like it would be Sunday before she would be released from the hospital. Lynn was still working on all that they had discussed before Rebecca left, but all was going well.

After dinner, Irene asked Rebecca, "What would you like to do this evening?"

"To be honest, Irene, I would like to go back to the room so we can talk," Rebecca answered. "I have been working on a few things and need your input."

"Is it something urgent?" Irene asked, surprised. "We are in New

York! Wouldn't you rather go see the sights or something besides staying so focused on work?"

"I realize this is a good opportunity to get out and have fun, but my mind is on other things. If I could choose, I would rather go back to the hotel."

"That's fine, my dear. You have seemed distracted all day—really, all week. I could tell something was heavy on your mind. Come, let's see what we can do to help you with whatever you're working on."

They left the restaurant and took a cab back to the hotel. Once in the room, Irene said, "Okay, now tell me what has you so preoccupied? Where is your mind taking you?"

"Irene, I know everything is not settled with Charlotte and Brad yet. This could go on for many more months, maybe a year or more. But I have been wondering, what are your plans for the money that is coming back to you?"

"Well, we have already received a good amount and will get more in time," Irene answered. "Why do you ask?"

Taking a deep breath, Rebecca asked, "Have you ever thought about building on to McKay's? We own several acres around us, and we have enough room to add a day care for the employees' children and a gym."

"A day care and a gym? Why would we want to do that?" Irene scoffed.

"Okay. In talking to the employees, I found that so many must get up early to take their children to a day care. If the child should get sick, they must leave work, pick up the child, go to the doctor, and get an excuse from the doctor for them and the child, possibly missing a day or two of work. If we built a day care, we could build it big enough to have different areas for the children: one area for babies, one for toddlers, and so forth. We could have a physician's assistant or a registered nurse to work in a clinic there. Not only would they see the children, but employees who got sick could go to the clinic as well. The employees who used the day care would have the cost taken from their paychecks, and if they took a week off, they would not be charged. They would only pay for the days they use."

Irene thought for a moment. "Rebecca, I had never thought of that," she replied. "Let me think on this, but I do like the idea. You know, I have a friend who recently decided to retire. She had been a medical doctor for years, and now she wishes she hadn't retired. She just told me last week she was thinking of going to the health department to see if she could get on there, even if for a few days a week. She would be perfect for the job. Yes, I do like this idea."

"Well, I have another idea to share, I mentioned a day care *and* a gym. One side of the building would be for the children, and the other side would be a gym for those employees who like to work out. We could have instructors to help them. The gym could be divided into a men's area and a women's area. I think it would be best to keep it separate. Also, we could have a female instructor for the women and a male for the men. We will have showers for them to use after they work out. This would be a big plus for those who use the day care because they could work out and not have to hurry after work to pick up their children. Everything would be right there."

"Do you ever let your mind rest?" Irene asked. "I must say I'm impressed with your ideas. This could really be a big plus for the company. I don't know anyone around who offers anything like this for their employees. I'm sure you have checked on the cost and time frame we are looking at. I want to talk to Mark about this. With him being a doctor and a lawyer, he might be able to guide us to the right people to talk to. Did you come up with this idea just by talking to the employees?"

"Sort of," Rebecca answered. "Really, it's one employee I have taken a great interest in. Do you remember me telling you about Rachel Mills and her daughter Sarah?"

"Yes, I do. How is the child getting along?"

"Hopefully she will be released from the hospital on Sunday. Some of the employees gave up their sick days to donate to Rachel so she can be home with Sarah next week."

"That is wonderful!" Irene exclaimed. "I would never have thought to do all that you're doing. I know the employees are grateful to have you. I must have the names of the employees who gave up days for Rachel. I want to send them each a card."

"Well, it's not just the ones who gave up sick days for her," Rebecca explained. "Irene, everyone at the company has contributed in some way. Rachel is going to be so surprised when she finds out all that has been done for her."

"So when are you going to surprise her with all you have planned? If possible, I would like to come along with you."

"If all goes well, our plans are for Sunday, when Sarah is released. Tuesday is Sarah's birthday, so we plan to also have a little party for her."

"Oh, this sounds like so much fun," Irene said. "Do you mind if I come along? I want to contribute to what you are doing for them. What kind of birthday gift can I get? How old did you say the little girl is?"

"She will be seven on Tuesday," Rebecca said. "I have a few things in mind. When we get home, I'll show you what my plans are. Lynn Jones has been handling things while I have been gone, and she is doing a remarkable job. Everyone has been such a blessing and so eager to help."

Ten

On Sunday after church, everyone knew what they were to do. Emma went to the hospital to help Rachel.

Rachel protested, "Emma, Sarah and I are fine. I'm sure you have many things to do on your day off."

"Well, you know, sometimes your car doesn't want to start, so I thought I would come by to take you both home."

"But I need my car" Rachel replied. "Hopefully it will start."

A nurse came in with a wheelchair to get Sarah. "Are you all ready to go?" she asked.

"Oh, yes!" said Sarah, holding tightly to her angel doll.

The nurse pushed Sarah out in the wheelchair while Rachel and Emma followed along. Once outside, they saw Emma's husband Frank standing by their car to help them load up.

Rachel looked at Frank and said, "I really do appreciate this, but I have my car here and will need it next week."

"I'm going to drive your car home, just in case it decides to break down," Frank explained. "I'll know what to do. You go ahead and ride with Emma. I'll follow behind."

Rachel showed Frank where she had parked and gave him the keys. "It may give you a little trouble. I haven't driven it in a few days."

Once they were all loaded up, Emma made small talk to distract Rachel, hoping she would not pay attention to where they were going. Finally, Rachel said, "Oh, Emma, you missed the turn to my house. We were talking, and I didn't realize we had passed it."

"That's okay," Emma replied. "We can take the scenic route. It might help to ride around before going home. You two have been in the hospital for several days, and I'm sure a change of scenery will do you both good."

After a few minutes, Emma pulled into the driveway of a cute little house.

"Is this where you live?" Sarah asked.

"No, I don't live here, but I *do* have something to show you both," Emma said. "Come on. Let's get out!"

"Emma, I think it would be better if Sarah and I stayed in the car. I don't know who lives here, and I don't feel like being social with strangers today."

Nodding, Emma looked in the back seat. "Come on, Sarah. You can come with me, and maybe your mom will decide to join us."

"Emma," Rachel protested, "she just got released from the hospital! I don't think it's a good idea to expose her to strangers." But Sarah was already out of the car, not waiting to see if her mother was coming. Rachel scrambled out of the car to follow them.

As they were walking to the house, Rachel caught up and said, "Okay, I'll come with you, but I don't want whoever lives here to get too close to Sarah. Her immune system is really weak right now."

Emma took Sarah by the hand and said, "She will be fine. Let's go around back and go in that way. I think that would be much better."

As they turned the corner to go into the backyard, a large group of people yelled, "Surprise!" and then started singing happy birthday to Sarah. Both Sarah and Rachel had tears in their eyes. The backyard was packed with Rachel's coworkers, including Rebecca. They stepped back to clear the middle of the yard, where a huge birthday cake with Sarah's name on it sat on a table. As Sarah walked up to the cake, she couldn't stop crying. This was the biggest cake she had ever seen, and it was for her. Someone was taking pictures, and presents were everywhere. They knew about the fire and that Rachel and Sarah had lost everything.

Rachel was at a loss for words. She had never had anyone treat her with so much love and kindness. Saying thank you just didn't seem like enough for all they had done.

After all the gifts were opened, Rebecca said, "We have two more surprises for you two. Let's walk around front to the garage." Rachel and Sarah followed her around, and when they opened the garage door, they saw a nice car inside. "This isn't a new car, but it is in excellent condition and reliable," Rebecca said. "With the help of a very nice car dealer and your coworkers, you now own a car to take yourself and Sarah wherever you need to go."

Rachel could not stop crying. "I haven't done anything to deserve this," she sobbed. "I truly don't know what to say."

Everyone started approaching Rachel to hug her and tell her they would be available for her and Sarah anytime.

Rebecca spoke up, "Now, remember I said there were *two* more surprises? This is one of them, and now for the other." She took Rachel's and Sarah's hands, and together they walked into the house. "This is your new home for as long as you need it," Rebecca said with a smile. It was completely furnished.

Rachel thought she was going to pass out. She had to sit down, shaking all over.

"Are you all right, Mama?" Sarah asked, afraid something was wrong with her mother.

"I'm fine," Rachel answered. "I just can't believe all this. It's like a miracle."

"Mama, it *is* a miracle. It's the angel doll! Angels do miracles. My teacher Ms. Reagan told me that God sends angels to look after us, and that's what the angel doll is doing. She is looking after us."

With that, Rebecca could not stop her own tears. She thought, *Who would have ever known what that angel doll could mean? This may be what Rachel needs to open up and let God back into her life.*

Everyone seemed to be having a great time. God had showered

blessings on all who had come to help, and the smiles, tears, hugs, and laughter proved it.

After everything was cleaned up and everyone gone, Rebecca stayed to talk to Rachel. "Rachel, this is my house," she explained. "I lived here till I moved in with Mrs. McKay. I started to sell it but then thought I would keep it for a while. I'm glad I kept it. What it needs is someone to give it a little love. It's just lonesome sitting here by itself."

"Ms. Clark, I am so overwhelmed by all this," Rachel replied. "I'm so afraid it's a dream and that I will wake up and it will all be gone."

"It's no dream," Rebecca said with a smile. "This house means a lot to me. It's full of memories and love. Now you and Sarah can make your own memories and fill it with your love."

Sarah called from another room, "Mama, come look at the bedroom! I have my very own room and bed!"

When Rachel walked into the bedroom, she saw that it was decorated with angels and had a unicorn bedspread and pillows and a large area rug. "I even have my own closet, Mama, so we won't have to share one!" Rachel and Rebecca laughed. Sarah's eyes sparkled as she danced around her room.

"I need to bring my presents in here and put them away," Sarah continued. "Did you see all the new clothes I have, Mama? I can't wait to go back to school and tell my teacher and friends. This is the best birthday ever!" Holding tight to her angel doll, Sarah said, "I love you, my angel," and she gave her doll a big hug.

Rachel couldn't believe that even the cabinets and refrigerator were completely stocked. She could not remember ever having anything this nice. Emma had even gone to the other house and brought back what little Rachel and Sarah had. Rachel began to realize that she really did have friends. She had always felt everyone was against her and that she had only Sarah, but now she had so many friends who really cared, not only for her but for Sarah. She was truly blessed.

Sarah lay down across her bed. The day's events had worn her out, but as she lay there, she held tightly to her angel doll with a heart-melting smile.

That night at Irene's house, Irene told Mary all about the surprise party.

"Mary, it was a party to remember. That child and her mother cried so many times over what they had received. I wouldn't have missed it for the world. Rebecca and the people at the company outdid themselves. We have so much and take it for granted. Rebecca took me by the place where Rachel and the little girl had been living. It was horrible, but that's all she could afford, and that little girl is just precious. So appreciative of all she got today. It was so uplifting."

"Sounds like everyone got a blessing at that party," Mary commented. "When did you say the little girl's actual birthday is?"

"It's Tuesday. Why?"

"I'll make a special batch of cookies that we can take to her," Mary said.

"Speaking of sweet treats, do you know that, every year, that child got one cupcake for her birthday and never complained? In fact, she looked forward to her birthday. If Rachel had any extra money, Sarah got a small, inexpensive toy. To Sarah, this was a lot."

"That's it!" Mary exclaimed. "We'll fix some cupcakes and a batch of cookies for her birthday."

"That's a great idea!" Irene agreed. "I'll help you decorate them. I haven't had this much fun in years. Ever since Rebecca told me what she had planned, I have been so excited. Mary, we need to do more fun things like this."

"Yes, ma'am. You know, Ms. Irene, things are finally perking up around here. With Rebecca here and now Mark running for state senate, I wonder what is possibly coming next."

On Tuesday, right after lunch, Mary and Irene went over to visit Rachel and Sarah. When they handed Sarah the box, she was so surprised.

"I thought I had gotten all my gifts on Sunday!" she cried. When she opened the box and found all kinds of decorated cookies, she said, "Oh, Mama! Look how pretty!" Then she offered everyone a cookie.

Mary said, "Oh, by the way, we have something else for you." She handed Sarah a long, wide, white box. Mary helped her place it on the table, where Sarah took a deep breath and smelled the box.

"It smells so good. Is it more cookies?" When she took the lid off the box, she found that it was filled with all kinds of cupcakes. Some had flowers, some had cute smiley faces, and some had icing of different colors. "Oh, my! Are all these cupcakes mine?" she asked.

"I heard you like cupcakes, and I couldn't decide what kind to make, so I made a little of everything," Mary said. "Hope you like them!"

"Ms. Mary, they are beautiful!" Sarah exclaimed. "I'm not sure I want to eat them!"

Irene suggested, "Let's take a picture of you and all your goodies so you can always look back at them. Do you know which is your favorite?"

"I think they all are," Sarah answered. "I have never seen so many pretty cupcakes."

Rachel and Sarah were so happy that Mary and Irene had come by for a visit. They were still excited about the party from Sunday and talked about how much they were enjoying their new home. Sarah had to give them a grand tour of her room, and she told them how the angel doll had come to take care of them.

Eleven

FRIDAY NIGHT CAME MUCH TOO SOON FOR REBECCA. SHE WAS really dreading going to the Winchester Opera House that night. She wondered if Mark was a good speaker and if he planned to give up medicine as a career. She thought about him being a doctor, then a lawyer. He did seem very knowledgeable no matter what he talked about or to whom. As she put on her dress, she wondered what the other ladies would be wearing, whether she would fit in, and what she would have in common with them that would enable her to carry on any kind of conversation. The people she worked with were all down to earth. She felt very relaxed around them, they were her family, and she loved them all. These people, though—would they be like Brad and Charlotte? A knock at her door startled her. It was Mary checking on her.

"Rebecca, do you need any help with anything?" she asked.

"I'm doing okay," Rebecca answered. "You can come in, though. I can always use a second opinion."

Mary stepped inside the room. "Rebecca, my dear, your dress is gorgeous! It looks stunning on you."

"Thanks, Mary. Should I wear any jewelry? And if so, what kind?"

"Okay, honey," Mary said flatly. "What gives?"

"What do you mean?"

"You don't look happy. What happened to that wonderful smile and the sparkle in your eyes? Has something happened?"

"No, everything is fine," Rebecca replied. "I'm just not sure what jewelry to wear. What do you think? I don't really have anything fancy."

"We can take care of your jewelry problem in a minute," Mary persisted. "What's wrong? Talk to me, Rebecca. Is everything all right with Rachel and her little girl?"

"To my knowledge, they are very happy," Rebecca said, smiling. "I went by last night, and Rachel talked almost nonstop. She has changed so much, and Sarah is looking better. She doesn't look so pale, and she is beginning to eat better. I think by Monday Sarah should be able to go to school and Rachel will be able to come back to work. Oh, Mary, with where they live now, Sarah's teacher lives three houses down and said she would keep Sarah with her after school till Rachel gets home. Sarah doesn't have to go home to an empty house anymore. Isn't that wonderful?"

"Now *that's* the Rebecca I know," Mary said. "Smiling and eyes lit up like a Christmas tree. That is good news. I can't imagine being that young and left alone so much. That Sarah is one special little girl. She loves her mama and tries so hard to do what Rachel tells her. Now that you're back to your old self, what had you so down when I first came in? And don't tell me 'nothing.' I know better."

"Really, Mary, I'm fine. Having never been to a function so formal, I'm concerned about what to wear and what not to wear," Rebecca admitted. "So what do I need to do about jewelry?"

"So it's tonight that has you down. Why?"

"I won't know anyone but Irene and Mark. They will be visiting with the people; I'm sure they will know everyone there, and I will be standing around like a knot on a log. I can't go walking around behind Irene like a little child holding onto her mama's dress. I would rather stay here and try to get caught up on some work from the office."

"Rebecca, you need to leave work alone for a while," Mary

replied. "You are constantly working or trying to figure out a way to help the company out. Who knows? You might meet a nice, handsome, single man tonight, and if you stay home, you will miss out on him."

"First, Mary, I'm not looking for a man. I'm content with my life just the way it is. Second, I enjoy trying to do things for the employees. They are a great bunch of people and so appreciative of anything I can do for them."

Rebecca paused for a moment. "In fact, remember us talking about George Clure, who works at McKay's? Well, he has a brother who owns a car lot, and do you know that when we were trying to figure out how to get Rachel a car, George went to him and told him about the situation. His brother picked out a car and gave George a price, which George gave us. We made an announcement that anyone who would like to donate any money for a car for Rachel would be greatly appreciated. Some gave a little, some a lot, but I think everyone gave. George then went back to his brother and told him what he was able to collect. It was not the amount of the car's price, but his brother took it and gave George the car. Before George left the lot, his brother serviced it and made sure everything was in good order. To me, God's hand was all in this. Different people made suggestions on what we could do, and it all just fell into place. God's love was everywhere."

She continued. "On Wednesday, Adam Nelson's wife fell at home and broke her leg. She is to have surgery on Monday. Do you know that by the end of the day the ladies at McKay's had all decided on who would take food to them and on what day and who would be able to go over on the weekend and help with the housework, laundry, or anything else Adam's wife might need some help with. This is what makes me happy, helping people who are in need. This company is family. They have my heart."

"Rebecca, I know your parents are so proud of you," Mary said. "We all are. When Ms. Irene hired you, she picked the very best."

"Thanks, Mary, but both my parents are deceased," Rebecca

replied. "They were killed several years ago. I miss them so much, and yes they would be very happy."

"Oh, honey, I didn't know. I am so very sorry. I know you haven't ever mentioned them, and I didn't want to ask. I didn't know if you came from an abusive home or what."

"Oh, no. I came from a wonderful family. Both my parents were missionaries, and helping others has been instilled in me all my life. They both had such giving hearts, so full of love."

"That explains why you are the way you are," Mary said. "You have good genes and a heart full of compassion and love. We can talk more later—don't want you crying and messing up what little makeup you have on. Now, we were discussing jewelry, right? Let's go see Ms. Irene. She has a showcase of jewelry, and she will know just the right piece for you to wear. I must say, child, you could wear a feed sack and come out looking like a beautiful rose in full bloom."

Just then, Irene walked in. "There you two are," she said. "I was looking for you. Oh, Rebecca honey, you look just beautiful! But I think you need some jewelry to complete your ensemble. Come to my bedroom and let's see what I have that might give you the finishing touch."

Mary and Rebecca just looked at each other and smiled as they followed Irene to her room.

Irene opened her showcase of jewelry. What gorgeous pieces she had!

"Try these earrings on," she began. "With your hair up, you need something with a little dangle to it. For a necklace, let's see—yes, this one is perfect. With the neckline on your dress, you need something dainty, and this one will lay perfectly around your neck and not take away from your dress. I have a bracelet somewhere that would be perfect for your wrist. I know it's got to be here somewhere." She looked quickly through her case.

"Ms. Irene, what about this tennis bracelet?" Mary suggested. "It's not too wide, and with Rebecca's small wrist, it should complete her."

"Mary, I do believe you are right," Irene said as she pulled the bracelet out. She fastened it around Rebecca's wrist. "Now, let's see how you look, my dear. Phillip would be so thrilled if he could see you now. When you walk in tonight, you will certainly be turning some heads. All eyes will be on you, that's for sure."

Rebecca replied, "Ladies, the last thing I want is to be the center of attention. What about you, Irene? You look wonderful yourself! Besides, I could never keep up with you for you are such an eloquent lady. Phillip certainly picked out the right gown for you."

"Thank you," Irene said. "You're such a dear. Is Sammy ready with the car? It's so nice that he's driving us tonight so we won't have to worry with parking."

As Irene and Rebecca walked outside, Sammy smiled and said, "You ladies look magnificent, I'm so honored to be driving you tonight. Now when you are ready to leave just shoot me a text and I'll be right there."

Walking into the Winchester Opera House, Rebecca tried not to walk so close to Irene, yet she didn't want to get separated from her. Irene started introducing her to people as they walked through. Everyone seemed very nice and polite, but Rebecca was sure they could hear her heart beating since she was so nervous.

"Rebecca, my dear, I'm going to go look for our table," Irene said. "I'll be right back."

"Why don't you let me go look while you visit? As soon as I find it, I'll come back and let you know."

"That will be fine," Irene agreed.

Looking at first one table then another for their names, Rebecca felt so out of place.

"Hello," a man said. "You must be the new CEO at McKay's. Mark has mentioned you a few times. Rebecca, is that right?"

"Yes."

"Let me introduce myself. I'm Clay Fields. I work closely with

Mark and have been to his home many times, and you have never been there. I was beginning to think Mark had just made you up."

"No, he hasn't made that up," Rebecca replied. "It's nice to meet you, but if you will excuse me, I need to find Mrs. McKay. She is waiting on me."

"Remember, my name is Clay," he said. "Hope we get to talk more later."

Rebecca saw Irene and told her, "I found our table. Are you ready to go in and sit down?"

"Yes, but first let me introduce you to Lena Fields," she said, motioning to a woman standing next to her. "I've known Lena ever since she was a little girl. In fact, you were talking to her husband, Clay."

"Hello, it's nice to meet you," Rebecca said. "Do you know at which table you will be sitting?"

"Yes, Clay and I are sitting over to the left, a few tables from you and Irene," Lena answered. "It's so nice to meet you. Irene has told me so much about you and how dedicated you are to the company. She is very fortunate to have you."

Just then, Mark approached the group. "Excuse me, Mother, but everyone needs to get to their seats. We will be starting soon. Hello, Lena, how are you tonight?"

"Hello, Mark," Lena replied. "You look very handsome tonight, and I'm so excited to hear your speech."

"Well, this is all new territory for me, so hopefully it will all go well." Looking at Rebecca, he said, "How is Rebecca tonight?"

"I'm fine," she replied.

"Okay, I'm going to go find my seat, and I'll talk to you ladies later."

Mark turned to leave, but he turned back around, patted Rebecca on the back, and just smiled. Wondering what that was about, Rebecca followed Irene to their table.

As dinner was being served, Irene introduced Rebecca to the others at the table. Molly Stafford came over to the table to congratulate Irene on Mark's new adventure. She was so happy and excited for him.

As soon as the meal was finished, Bruce Stafford went up to the podium to say a few words and then introduce Mark as the new candidate for state senator. Mark's speech was about thirty-five minutes long. He certainly kept the audience's attention with the way he brought things about. People who didn't know him would have thought he was already the state senator.

As soon as Mark stepped down, people started gathering around him, shaking his hand, and congratulating him on how he was the right man for the position.

"Irene, I'm going to go to the powder room," Rebecca said. "I'll be right back."

Just before Rebecca made it to the powder room, Clay stopped her.

"Rebecca, why don't we go to dinner some evening, get better acquainted, and then take a nice ride somewhere?"

"Thanks, Mr. Fields, but I'll pass."

"Please call me Clay, and why would you want to pass?" he persisted. "You don't know me, and I really don't know you. We can go to any restaurant you want. We could have a wonderful time."

"Like I said, Mr. Fields, I'll pass."

"Do you mind telling me why?" he asked.

"Yes, I don't think your wife would appreciate it," Rebecca replied. "I met her tonight, and she is a very nice lady. I do not think she would approve."

"Oh, my wife does not need to know," he said quietly. "It could be our little secret. So what do you say—let's go out for dinner one evening. There is nothing wrong with having a meal together."

"If I should go out to dinner, I would not go out with a married man. Your wife deserves better, and you should be ashamed of yourself. Now, if you'll excuse me."

Turning, Rebecca went into the powder room. What nerve that man had! She wondered if this was the kind of life he lived. His poor wife, wondering if she knew what her husband was doing behind her back. Lana seemed like such a nice person.

As Rebecca was getting ready to leave the powder room and go find Irene, a lady about Rebecca's age came in. "Well, finally I get to meet you. You're Rebecca, is that right?"

"Yes. I'm sorry, I didn't catch your name."

"Lacey Stafford. My father is the one who introduced Mark."

"Oh yes, and your mother's name is Molly?"

Lacey said," Oh, I see you have already met her. We are all so proud of Mark. I'm hoping we will get married before the election, but with so much going on, it's hard to set a date."

Rebecca was taken aback. "You and Mark are getting married?" she asked.

"Yes. Do you mean neither Mark nor Mrs. McKay told you? I can't believe they have not said anything to you!"

Still in shock, Rebecca said, "No, it must have slipped their minds. I'm happy for you and Mark and hope everything goes well for you two."

Lacey went over to the mirror to touch up her lipstick. "Mark and I have been together for years and just recently decided we needed to get married. It would be a shame to have a little McKay before we tied the knot."

Even more shocked, Rebecca did her best to sound calm. "That's true. I do wish you both the best."

Rebecca needed to find Irene; she was so ready to go home. But Irene was busy going from one person to another, chatting away. Rebecca could tell by watching her that she was in her element. After another hour went by, Irene finally said she was ready to go.

As soon as they stepped outside Rebecca looked for Sammy. Sure enough, he was standing by the car, waiting for them. For Rebecca, he was a welcome sight.

As soon as they got home, Irene had to tell Mary all about Mark's speech, who was there, and who wore what. She went on and on, not leaving out anything. Finally, Irene said she was ready to turn in and would finish filling Mary in on the night's happenings the next day.

Rebecca told Mary and Irene good night, so glad to be going to her room. She sat down in her chair and began going over the evening in her mind. The guy named Clay was such a ninny. He, a married man, had asked her out to dinner with his wife standing not far from them. What kind of guys worked for Mark anyway?

Then there was Lacey Stafford. She was not someone she would have thought Mark would be seeing, but then she really didn't know what his type was. She wondered if they were not using protection, or was she trying to get pregnant? What an evening. Looking down at her wrist, she realized she still had on Irene's jewelry. *I had better take these pieces to her so she can put them away,* she thought. *I certainly don't want anything to happen to them.*

As Rebecca got to Irene's door, she saw that the lights were out and could tell she was asleep. *Oh well, I'll put them up and give them to her tomorrow.* As she started back to her room, she noticed a light on in the music room. Thinking someone had left it on, she went to turn it off. But just as she got to the door, Mark appeared. She nearly jumped out of her skin. She hadn't realized that Mark was home.

Putting her hands to her chest, Rebecca said, "Oh! I'm sorry. I didn't know you had come in. I saw the light on and thought someone had forgotten to turn it off."

"Sorry if I startled you, but I was hoping to get a chance to talk to you tonight. With so many people around, I never had the opportunity."

"Was there something you needed to tell me?'

"As a matter of fact, yes. I saw you come in with Mother, and I must say, you look so beautiful in this dress. It was very hard for me to concentrate on what I was needing to say in my speech because I couldn't help but look at you. Tonight, I could hear my mother's words very clear: 'Rebecca is a very special person.' She's right—you are a special person."

Taking in what Mark was saying, Rebecca didn't realize he had stepped closer to her. Suddenly, he took her in his arms and kissed her.

She pushed him away, hardly believing what had happened. Looking at Mark, she said, "Do all of the men in your campaign have no decency? How could you?"

She turned to leave, but Mark grabbed her arm. "Would you care to explain what you mean by that remark?"

"I'm sorry, I just imagined you to be on a different level than your so-called friends. Now if you'll excuse me, I'm going to my room."

Once inside her room, Rebecca wasn't sure how she felt. The evening had not turned out at all like she had expected. It was worse. How she wished she had never gone. She was so uptight that she knew this would be a long night. Taking a deep breath, she decided to shower, get ready for bed, and read her Bible. At least she knew God would not disappoint her.

Twelve

THE NEXT MORNING, REBECCA WOKE UP TO THE SMELL OF MARY'S good coffee. She got dressed and headed for the kitchen.

"Good morning, Ms. Mary," she said as she walked in. "Your coffee smells so good. I don't know how you make it, but it is so much better than mine."

Laughing, Mary replied, "Honey, you just put the grounds in the pot, add some water, and turn the pot on. It does its own thing."

"Maybe it's the way you do it, then. I don't know, but I do know it's the best around."

The doorbell rang, and Rebecca told Mary she would see who it was. Just as Rebecca got to the dining room doorway, she saw Mark opening the front door. Lacey came through the door, threw her arms around Mark's neck, and kissed him.

Rebecca thought back to the previous night, how Mark had kissed her, and now he was kissing Lacey. It just didn't add up. She turned, not saying a word, and hoped they hadn't noticed her. She went back to the kitchen.

"Who was at the door?" Mary asked.

"It was Lacey Stafford. I believe she came to see Mark."

"He's not asking her to stay for breakfast, is he?"

"I don't know, Mary. They were busy, and I didn't want to interrupt. Should I set another plate on the table?" Rebecca asked.

"For everyone's sake, I hope not."

"Why, Mary! What do you mean by that?"

"We will talk another time," Mary answered. "Don't want to say anything that might be overheard by the wrong set of ears."

Mark came through the kitchen door, and when he saw Rebecca, he looked straight at her and said, "You need to explain yourself."

"There is nothing to explain, Mark. Where's Lacey?"

"Trying to change the subject?" Mark said accusingly. "For whatever it's worth, Lacey had to leave. Now, I would appreciate it if you would be so kind as to answer my question."

"Like I said, there is nothing to explain. Actions speak louder than words."

Mark's cell phone rang, and he left the room to answer it. Rebecca figured it was probably Lacey, and she just wanted to get out of the house. She went to her room, put some things in a day pack, and dressed for riding. She really needed to get away and try to think.

As she was passing the kitchen on her way out, Mary called out to Rebecca, "Are you going somewhere?"

Rebecca stepped into the kitchen. "I just need to get some fresh air. I'll see if Sammy can saddle up a horse so I can go for a nice ride."

"Let me fix you a thermos of coffee and some muffins to take with you. You will appreciate it when you stop for a break."

"Mary, you are so thoughtful. Oh, would you do something for me? Don't tell Mark I have gone for a ride. I really want to be alone."

"Don't you worry, my dear," Mary said as she handed Rebecca the goodies. "I've got your back. Stay safe and enjoy the ride."

Rebecca saw Sammy working on a stall door.

"Morning, Ms. Rebecca," he called out. "How are you doing this fine morning? Did you enjoy yourself last night?" He continued before she could respond. "Ms. Irene certainly did. Say, you look like you're ready to go for a ride. Want me to saddle your horse up for you?"

"Yes, Sammy, that would be great, unless you're busy. Then I can do it."

"No, you won't. I saddle up the horses around here. That's my job, and you can't have it," he said with a smile. "You know, Ms. Rebecca, you are special. No one around here ever offers to saddle up a horse or brush it down after a ride. But you do. It doesn't matter what needs to be done, you just pitch right in."

"Sammy, it doesn't matter who you are, work is work, and no one should be above helping out," Rebecca replied. "Some jobs are clean, some boring, some stressful, and some dirty, but no matter what it is, we should never feel we are above doing it."

"That's why I like you, Ms. Rebecca. I feel very comfortable around you. You don't put me down or make me feel like I'm just the hired help or your slave. Say, what was the name you said you were going to give this horse?"

"Fairlight. Don't ask me where I got that name, but it seems to suit her."

"I'll make a sign to put up over her stall with her name," Sammy said. "Here you go. You have a good ride." He handed her the reins.

"Thanks, Sammy, and if Mark comes out and wants to know where I am, please don't tell him. I just need some time to myself."

"Is Mr. Mark bothering you?" Sammy asked.

"No, I just need to go for a ride. A lot has happened in the last little while, and I need to try to clear out my head if that's possible."

"Okay, you be careful and take care of yourself," Sammy said. "I won't tell Mr. Mark. You have a good ride."

This was what Rebecca needed, a gentle breeze blowing, the fresh smell of the outdoors, and as far as she could see, no homes or businesses, just wide-open fields. She had a favorite spot that was so peaceful and relaxing. She really needed to do this more often.

Finally, she spotted a big rock next to a tree. She secured the horse, spread her throw over the rock, and sat down to just take in the view of the hills and valleys before her. She felt close to God there. Even when she prayed, it was as if God was beside her. Taking her Bible from her backpack, she held it close to her, asking God to guide her to where she needed to read. She held the Bible out, and it fell open to Isaiah 55. She read through the verses and came upon verse 12: "You will go out in joy and be led forth in peace; the mountains and hills will burst into song before you, and all the trees of the field will clap their hands."

Rebecca looked around. Yes, she was in the spot God wanted her to be. Such peace came over her. The wind blew the pages of her Bible and stopped on Psalm 29. Wondering what verse may be there for her, her eyes stopped at verse 11: "The Lord gives strength to his people; the Lord blessed his people with peace."

She lay back and looked up to the sky, feeling so much peace come over her. She felt she could stay there forever. "God, grant me the serenity to accept the things I cannot change, the courage to change the things I can, and the wisdom to know the difference," she said aloud.

After a while, Rebecca decided to try one of Mary's muffins and have some coffee. She had forgotten she had not had breakfast, but her stomach was reminding her.

Back at the house, Mark walked into the kitchen. "Mary, do you know where Rebecca went?" he asked. "She was just here before I got that phone call."

"She's around here somewhere," Mary said vaguely. "Is there something important that you need to see her about right now?"

"She needs to explain something to me, and I have to leave this afternoon. I certainly would like to get this settled before I leave."

"Now, now, she'll pop in here soon," Mary replied. "This is the weekend, and I'm sure she is ready to have a nice quiet weekend away from work."

For some reason, something was eating at Mark. Something wasn't right about the previous night. He had not expected the response he got from Rebecca. Did something happen last night or had someone said something that upset her?

Going to his room to pack, he knew he needed to see Rebecca before he left. He heard a car outside and went downstairs to see if it was her. He reached the door and saw his mother coming in.

"Mark, dear, I understand you're leaving today?" she asked. "How long will you be gone?"

"I'm not really sure," he said. "By the way, have you seen Rebecca today?"

"No, dear, I left early this morning, and now I'm going to take a nap. With getting in late last night and leaving so early this morning, I am simply worn out. A good long nap is what I need. Have you asked Mary? If anyone would know, I'm sure she would."

"Yes, I've already talked to Mary," Mark replied, frustrated. "Mother, how did things go last night? Do you think Rebecca enjoyed herself?"

"She seemed to. I introduced her to a lot of people. Everyone was so pleased to meet her, and she seemed happy to meet them. Wasn't she just beautiful? Phillip made an excellent choice on her dress. When Rebecca walked in, every head turned, and all eyes were on her." Irene shook herself out of her memories. "Now, dear, if you'll excuse me, I really need to lie down. I'm not as young as I used to be, and eight hours of sleep at night is a must. Let me know before you leave."

Mark saw Mary dusting in the den. "Mary, has Rebecca said anything to you about last night?" he asked. "Did she say she enjoyed herself?"

"She was a little nervous about going, but we talked before they left, and I think she was okay."

"Why was she nervous?"

"What Rebecca told me last night, I don't feel I need to share," Mary replied. "It was nothing bad, but she has had a lot of adjusting to do since she came here. She has done extremely well and done wonders for the company, plus she has been a blessing for Ms. Irene and me. She is a very special person, and everyone who meets her loves her."

Mark grinned. "Funny, all I hear is how special she is."

"She is, Mark," Mary asserted. "You just have your mind preoccupied with other things and have not taken the time to get to know her."

"Well, I must finish packing," Mark said quickly. "Clay should be by in about two hours to pick me up. Have you seen my briefcase, by any chance?"

"I put it beside your closet door so you wouldn't forget it," Mary answered.

"Thanks, Mary. I don't know what we would do without you."

When he was finally all packed, Mark wondered if he should write Rebecca a note or maybe call her that night. That's not really what he wanted to do; he would rather talk to her face to face. After carrying his things downstairs and setting them by the door, he decided to check her room. Maybe she had come in and no one had said anything. He looked in from the door, but no, it looked the same as it had that morning. Looking at his watch, he knew Clay would be there soon. He took out his phone and tried calling Rebecca, but he heard it ringing and saw that she had left it on her nightstand.

The doorbell rang, and Mark knew Clay was there. He gave Clay his suitcases to put in the car and then went to tell his mother goodbye and that he would call her later that night. Mark didn't want to leave; he wanted to talk to Rebecca. What was it that he couldn't shake off?

"Mark, you had better not leave without giving me a hug, young man," Mary said from behind him.

"I would never do that," he replied as he hugged her. "Say, I never did find Rebecca. Would you tell her I will try to give her a call tonight?"

"Yes, honey, I'll give her your message," Mary said. "Now you be careful, eat well, and get plenty of rest. If you don't, you'll have ol' Mary to answer to."

"I'll do my best. See you in a few weeks."

Thirteen

LOOKING AT HER WATCH, REBECCA DECIDED SHE HAD BETTER RIDE back to the house. She had left her phone on her nightstand, and no one really knew where she was or could contact her. The day had turned out to be perfect, and she felt so much more relaxed. *This was a good decision coming out here,* she thought. She packed up but was in no hurry to get back, so she walked a good way leading the horse.

"Ms. Rebecca, you finally made it back," Sammy called out when she neared the stables. "I was beginning to get worried about you, especially since you were alone."

"I'm fine, Sammy, but thanks for caring about me. Would you like for me to brush the horse down before I go in?"

"That's my job, remember," he answered.

"That's right. I just want to help you and not cause you more work," she explained. "If you should ever need any help, you be sure to let me know."

"I will, Ms. Rebecca. Now you run along. It's past lunch, and I bet you're hungry. Ms. Mary has something good fixed. I can smell it all the way out here."

"Okay, okay, I'm going," Rebecca said with a laugh.

She walked into the house, and Mary said, "I was getting worried about you. Is everything all right?"

"Yes, it was a good ride, and the time alone helped me," Rebecca replied. "I really needed that. Mind if I raid the kitchen? I'm a little hungry."

"Help yourself," Mary said. "By the way, Mark has looked for you all day. Before he left, he said to tell you he would try to call you tonight. He wanted so much to talk to you face to face. I did not tell him you had gone for a ride. I kept my promise, but he did ask me about last night, whether you enjoyed yourself. He even wanted to know if anything had happened. *Did* something happen?"

"A couple of things didn't go well, but that's behind me now," Rebecca said unemotional.

"What kind of things are you talking about?"

"Oh, some things that I wasn't expecting. You could say they caught me off guard."

"Okay, you need to give here," Mary pressed. "I probably know a few of those people there last night. Maybe I can shed some light if you tell me what happened."

She hesitated, thinking about whether she should confide in Mary, for like Mary said, she probably knew most of the people who were there. What if they were friends of hers?

"Rebecca, what is said stays between the two of us," Mary assured her. "I promise you can trust me."

"Well, one thing that happened was this guy, who was truly a dunce, came up to me and asked me to have dinner with him sometime. When he told me his name, I wanted to slap him. Earlier that evening, Irene had introduced me to Lena Fields, who is a very nice lady and who is very much married to this so-called man who seems to enjoy lying and betraying her. He even said she wouldn't have to find out, that it would be our little secret."

"Honey, stay away from him," Mary said immediately. "He's a big flirt. Goes out with any woman that he can. Being married doesn't stop him at all. His wife, I'm sure, knows what kind of man she is married to. She just chooses to look the other way."

"I don't understand, Mary," Rebecca said sadly. "That's like Charlotte and Brad. What's wrong with these people?"

"Not everyone is like that, Rebecca. There are still a few good ones around. You just need to be careful."

"Let's just say I wasn't impressed at all last night," Rebecca commented. "I would have been better off staying home."

Later that night, as Rebecca stepped out of the shower, she heard her phone ring. Wrapping a towel around herself, she went to see who was calling. Sure enough, it was Mark. She decided to let it ring.

About an hour later, the phone rang again—still Mark. This time he left a message, which Rebecca deleted after she listened to it. She had no intention of returning his call. She lay on her bed with so many thoughts going through her head. Then she thought of Ray. She got up and opened a dresser drawer. Underneath some clothes was a picture of Ray in his military uniform and one of them on their wedding day. She went back to the bed and held the pictures close to her chest, letting her mind go back to when she and Ray were married and so happy. When Ray spoke about Rebecca to anyone, he always had so much pride and joy in his voice. Once, when one of the guys on base referred to his wife as his old lady, Ray became furious with him and told him he should never speak about his wife like that. He told him he should always lift his wife up and cherish her. Of all the years they had been married, Ray never spoke ill of her or made light of her to anyone. He was such a godly man who took his marriage vows very seriously. She couldn't imagine ever being treated the way Clay treated his wife.

Holding the pictures close, the next thing Rebecca knew, it was morning. Time to get ready for church.

After church and lunch, Rebecca decided to go into town for she wanted to fix up some trick-or-treat bags for the employees to take home to their children on Halloween. She found what she needed and headed to her car. Just as she opened the trunk, someone called out, "Hey, Rebecca!"

Looking up, Rebecca saw Lacey Stafford coming toward her.

"Fancy meeting you here!" Lacey said. "What's all this stuff? Planning a party?"

"Hello, Lacey. No, I'm fixing trick-or-treat bags for the employees to take home to their children for Halloween," Rebecca answered.

"You do stuff like that? Why?" Lacey inquired.

"Because I enjoy it, and the people at the company are like family to me. It's not much, but it's the thought that counts," Rebecca told her.

"Girl, you need to get a life," Lacey said smirking. "How boring can it be to sit around and fix trick-or-treat bags? Why don't we have lunch one day? You really need to get out and make some friends."

Rebecca replied, "Thanks, Lacey, but work keeps me busy, and I'm happy with what I do."

"Well, if you ever change your mind, let me know." Then, looking at her watch, Lacey said, "Oh, look what time it is. I must hurry. Mark will be calling soon, and I don't want to miss his call. Take care, Rebecca, and have fun with your trick-or-treat bags."

"I'm sorry if I have detained you, Lacey," Rebecca said as Lacey walked away. "Wouldn't want you to miss his call."

"Well, if I should, I can always talk to him tonight. He calls me at least three times a day to give me an update on his progress. He is just so sweet to me."

"It's been nice seeing you, Lacey. Do take care."

Driving down the road, Rebecca wondered, *Why would Mark call me while he's calling and seeing Lacey?* This just didn't make sense to her.

Mary met her at the door. "What have we here?"

"These are things for trick-or-treat bags. On Halloween, they will be passed out to the employees to take home to their children."

"Oh, Rebecca, what a great idea," Mary said enthusiastically. "Mind if I help you? This looks like so much fun."

"Sure! Two can work faster than one," Rebecca replied. "I wanted to do something that was simple, and this is the only thing I could think of. I'm sure the kids will enjoy the treat bags."

"It doesn't seem like Halloween should already be here," Mary said. "Next month is Thanksgiving and then Christmas. I need to start thinking about decorations and what to prepare for the dinners. What did you and your family do for the holidays?"

"We were usually in some overseas country doing mission work," Rebecca answered. "Most of the time we were able to receive gifts from different places in the States. A lot of churches made shoe boxes with gifts that they sent to us to pass out to the children. They were so appreciative of anything they received. At certain times of the year, the churches sent clothes, and we would help the people find some they could wear. We didn't prepare a big feast like is done here."

"Well, making these treat bags is an excellent idea. You have such a giving heart, always thinking of ways to help others," Mary said.

On Friday morning, Rebecca went in to work early to get her box of treats and everything else set up. At the morning break, she made an announcement that she was letting everyone off an hour early and said that, on their way out, those who had children at home should pick up a treat bag for each one. All the employees were so happy to get to leave early. This way, they could go home, have time to eat, and get their children ready to go trick-or-treating.

Rachel went over to Rebecca. "You are the greatest boss! You think of everything."

"Thanks, Rachel. By the way, how are you and Sarah doing?"

"Oh, she is doing wonderfully," Rachel said happily. "She is so proud of her room and her angel doll. She takes it everywhere with her, except to school. I still can't thank you enough for what you have done for us."

"Well, you are doing wonderful yourself," Rebecca said. "You have come out of your shell and blossomed into a beautiful person.

I'm sure the change in you has helped Sarah. What is she dressing up as tonight?"

"You must ask?" Rachel said with a laugh. "We found an angel costume, and she had to have it."

"Her outfit will be very appropriate for her. Please be sure to take a picture and let me see how beautiful she looks on Monday. Tell her I said hello and to have fun tonight."

"I certainly will," Rachel replied. "You have a good evening too, Ms. Rebecca."

After going back to her office, Rebecca couldn't decide whether to stay and work or go on home. She knew they would have no trick-or-treaters for they lived so far off the road. It was going to be hard this year because, for the past several years, she had loved giving out candy and seeing the kids all dressed up. The happiness in their faces brought her so much joy. Thinking about this, she decided to stay and work for a little while, anyway.

When she got home, she heard Irene talking on the phone. She heard her say, "She just walked in. I can't wait to tell her. She is going to be so happy."

Thinking she was talking to Mark, Rebecca now wished she had stayed at work a little longer.

"Oh, Rebecca, you are not going to believe what I must tell you!" Irene began excitedly. "Please come in and sit down. I am so excited! Oh, let me give you a hug for what you are doing. You are such a blessing!" Irene threw her arms around Rebecca.

"All I did was pass out trick-or-treat bags to the employees to take home to their children. It's really no big deal."

"Trick-or-treat bags?" Irene asked. "That's not what I'm talking about. I'm talking about that phone call I just received."

"What about it? Who was calling you?"

"Please sit down, and I'll explain. Do you remember asking me about adding on to the company? Putting in a day care, clinic, and gym? Well, I ran it by Joe Lewis, our new company attorney, and Mark. They did some research, drew up blueprints, contacted some architects, went to the city to see if this would pass the building codes, and all that stuff they must do. Everything passed, and when they told me the cost, I told them we could do it. Joe will contact you on Monday to go over the blueprints to see if you want to change anything since you were the brains behind all this. Well, what do you think, Ms. Rebecca Clark, CEO of McKay's?"

Shocked, Rebecca asked, "It's a go? You mean we can start making plans to add on and update the building? Oh, Irene, this is wonderful! It's a dream come true. Now I need to give *you* a big hug!"

With tears in her eyes, Rebecca felt like she was on cloud nine. She closed her eyes and said, "Thank you, Lord. Thank you so much."

Now she would have to wait till Monday to talk to Joe. Would Monday ever come? Then she happened to remember that Mark and Joe worked together in the same office on certain days.

"Irene, will Mark be at the meeting Monday, or will he still be traveling?" she asked warily.

"No, dear, he will still be traveling. I'm not sure when he will be home, and when we talked earlier, he wasn't sure either. But don't worry, Joe will guide you and answer any questions you have."

"I'm not worried," Rebecca replied. "Since Joe and Mark worked together on this, I thought Mark would want to be here when we go over the plans. But I'm sure Joe will fill him in on what's decided and get his input on it."

That night, Rebecca could hardly sleep. In her mind, she kept picturing what each area would look like—where doors needed to be, how the rooms for the children would be laid out, what kind of equipment to put in the gym, what kind of clinic would be needed for the employees and the children. She had thought about all of this when she first mentioned it to Irene and had only a rough draft drawn out, but now her dream was becoming a reality and she needed to really think it all through. There was no room for errors.

Monday finally came. Rebecca had all her notes and drawings

in her briefcase, ready to get started with this new project. She wondered if Joe had chosen a contractor or if she would have a say about it. She had so many questions for him and wondered if he would be coming by in the morning or not until the afternoon. As soon as she got to work, she informed Lynn that Joe would be calling and it would be a very important call.

Lynn buzzed her about an hour later and said Mr. Lewis was on the phone. He wanted to know if ten o'clock be a good time for him to meet her. Rebecca said, "That would be fine, and let him know I am looking forward to meeting with him."

Going back over her notes to see if she had left anything out, Rebecca was so deep in thought that she jumped when Lynn buzzed to let her know Mr. Lewis was there.

Rebecca met him at the door and asked Lynn to hold all calls till the meeting was over. Joe Lewis was a man of strictly business. He walked over to the table, laid out papers of all kinds, looked at her, and said," Are you ready for this big undertaking?"

"Yes, I am," Rebecca answered confidently. "I've never be involved in something of this magnitude, but I'm in it for the duration. By the way, for something this size, about how long will it take to complete it?"

"We were pretty sure Mrs. McKay was going to go for it by the way she talked when she came to see us, so we started making plans and getting things underway. As far as groundbreaking, we hope to start no later than the first of December."

"That soon? That's wonderful. When can we make an announcement to the employees? They are going to be so happy. This is a dream come true for me, and the employees will reap the benefits."

"You might want to discuss this with Mrs. McKay and see when she feels it would be best to make the announcement," Joe said. "Like I said, we hope to break ground December first if all goes well. Now, let me show you what all we have put together. We met with an architect, and these are the plans. Mark and I have been over them several times trying to draw out everything according to what you had roughly laid out. Look over this very carefully to make sure it's exactly what you want. Now is the time to make any changes."

"What are all these other sheets?" Rebecca asked. "They all look different."

"Each sheet represents something different, like where to put the heat and air ducts, alarm system, water pipes, electrical lines, plumbing. The list goes on."

"Well, that does make sense. I just hadn't thought about it. I did draw in bathrooms, windows, hallways, and where to put doors, but I hadn't thought about the alarm system, pipes, cameras, or any of that."

"That's why Mark and I have worked so closely with the architect. Between the three of us, we kept making changes till we felt it was a go. Now we need your approval since you came up with the idea."

They spent the next three hours going over page after page of drawings.

When they were satisfied, Joe said, "Rebecca, I'm going to leave all this with you. A Cecil O'Malley will be getting in touch with you; he is the contractor. Mark and I have talked to several contractors, and we feel Mr. O'Malley is the right one for the job. By the time this job is complete, you and Mr. O'Malley will be good friends."

Unsure how to take that comment, Rebecca thanked Joe for all he had done and walked him to the elevator.

Still thinking about how she should tell the employees, she called Irene. As luck would have it, Irene was in town and would stop by in about half an hour.

When Irene arrived, Rebecca went over what all Joe had told her and let Irene see the blueprints for herself.

"Irene, we need to let the employees know about the project, and I thought we could do a luncheon for Thanksgiving and announce it then. What do you usually do for the employees at Thanksgiving?"

"Well, my dear, I usually give them a ham and then at Christmas give them a turkey and a few days off with pay," Irene answered.

"Would it be all right to do a luncheon, say, have the food

catered, a buffet-style meal, and make the announcement? Then as they leave that day we could pass out the hams. Thanksgiving is always on a Thursday, so we could do this on the Friday before."

"I think that would be nice," Irene agreed. "It would certainly be a change and appropriate. What can I do to help?"

"Right now, I'm not sure," Rebecca replied. "I'm to meet with Mr. Cecil O'Malley, the contractor for the project. Let me meet with him and then I'll refocus on the luncheon. I may even put Lynn in charge of it. Would you mind working with her? She has proved to be outstanding when it comes to organization."

"No, dear, I don't mind at all," Irene said. "I do want to help any way I can."

Irene had already left when Mr. O'Malley came in.

"Excuse me," he said from the doorway. "I'm sorry I didn't make an appointment. I was in the area and thought I would take a chance to see if you could possibly meet with me. I'm Cecil O'Malley."

"Yes! Come in. I'm Rebecca Clark. Joe Lewis was here this morning and told me you are the contractor they've chosen."

"Did he leave the blueprints with you?" Cecil asked.

"Yes, he did. They are here on the table. We were looking over them to see if I was pleased with the layout, but I haven't fully studied it all. Are you needing them right away?"

"No, ma'am. I have a set of my own. I would like to go over some things with you, to make sure we are on the same page."

Cecil explained the plans in depth. It seemed to Rebecca that he didn't leave anything out.

After nearly two hours, he felt he had given her enough to think about, and they agreed they would meet again on Wednesday around nine o'clock.

As she gathered up all the papers, Rebecca's mind was overloaded. College had been a breeze compared to this. As she left her office, she stopped at Lynn's desk. "In the morning, we need to talk. There's something I need help on and could use your input."

"Sure, but are you okay?" Lynn asked, concerned. "You never took a lunch break today and have hardly been out of your office."

"Come to think of it, Lynn, I haven't had lunch," Rebecca said. "Maybe once I get home and eat, I can think a little more clearly."

"I ordered you a sandwich from the corner deli, but you have been so tied up, I haven't had a chance to give it to you."

"That was so thoughtful," Rebecca replied. "Where is it? I'll eat it on the way home. I feel a little out of sorts, and that's probably why." Lynn handed it to her. It was a sandwich from Granny's Deli.

Laying some money on Lynn's desk, Rebecca said, "You know I love her sandwiches. You are an angel. See you in the morning."

After dinner, Rebecca took out the blueprints, notes, and other drawings she had made. As she studied them carefully, it seemed the guys had covered everything she had written out that she wanted. She had wanted a covered area where parents could pull up to drop off the children in case the weather was bad. Employees with children would park in one area for the drop off, and those without children would park on the other side of the building and come through that entrance. She had forgotten to include water fountains, but yes, they had included them. She needed to let Irene see the plans and go over them with her. Besides, a fresh set of eyes might catch something she had missed. She took them into the living room, where they were sitting.

Irene and Mary studied the plans. Mary said, "Rebecca, it looks like everything has been covered. I can't wait to see it when it's finished. What do you think about the plans, Ms. Irene? I bet people will line up to come work for McKay's after it's finished."

"Not only did Rebecca have a great idea, seeing it on paper makes it even better," Irene said. "Mary, did she tell you what she wants to do for the employees for Thanksgiving? Those people will never want me to come back to work there. Rebecca has them all so spoiled, they would do anything for her."

"What else are you planning?" Mary asked.

"Well, I thought we would have a big Thanksgiving meal on

Friday before Thanksgiving, say, a buffet, and while they are eating, we can announce the new addition to McKay's. I will have a list of things that the new building will include and hope it will cover all the things I have heard them talk about. If they want to go to the gym, we will have one on site where they can go before or after work. It will have all the latest equipment, so when they want to work out, they won't have to rush to get to work on time, fight the traffic, or rush in the evenings to go to the gym. Day care will be right there, so they won't have to hurry to get to a day care or babysitter. If the child is sick, we will have a doctor in our clinic. No more having to leave work to take the child to a doctor, and the parent will be close by if they decide to go check on the child during a break. McKay's has a good name, and the people who work here are good people. So why not give them a little incentive? It will make things even better for them."

"Child, you amaze me," Mary said, shaking her head. "How do you store all the things you do in that little head of yours? When Ms. Irene hired you, she got a real gem."

"Thank you, Mary. You are so sweet to say that," Rebecca said softly. "I enjoy my work and doing for others. Thanks to Irene—she is making this dream become possible."

The next morning, Rebecca stopped off to pick up breakfast for Lynn and herself. Since she wasn't sure how long they would be tied up working on the Thanksgiving luncheon, she made coffee for them as soon as she got into the office.

When Lynn arrived, she buzzed Rebecca and told her that, as soon as she checked the messages and transferred all calls to Gloria, she would be right in. It didn't take her long, and as she walked into Rebecca's office, Lynn started laughing.

"What's so funny?" Rebecca asked.

Lynn held up a bag. "I stopped and picked up some breakfast for us this morning. I didn't know how long this would take, but from what you said last night, I thought breakfast might be a good idea."

Rebecca laughed. "Well, you know what they say: 'Great minds think alike.' We can have one this morning and eat the other for lunch. We'll just have two breakfasts today." She patted a stack of papers on her desk. "I'll explain some things while we eat, and I want your complete input. I know you have been wondering what's going on here in my office. What I am going to tell you must stay hush-hush, for a little while anyway. Basically, we are going to be adding on to McKay's, but not in the way you may think. I have the blueprints here to show you."

Rebecca went over the basic plans with Lynn, and then she said, "Now, this is where I need your help. We are thinking about having a buffet luncheon on the Friday before Thanksgiving, and that's when we'll make the announcement. Also, as they leave to go home that day, we will need someone at the door giving each of them a ham to have on Thanksgiving."

"Ms. Rebecca, this is wonderful!" Lynn gushed. "The employees are going to be so happy. You should save this for Christmas!"

"Well, we can't, because they hope to break ground December first. What I would like for you to do is call around and see who can cater the luncheon. We need the cost and the menu, which would be a Thanksgiving menu. Irene said she would love to help you in any way she could. Also, I prefer a buffet to a box lunch. Not sure how you will be able to arrange enough tables and chairs for the meal, but knowing you, you will find a way to make it work. If you need some privacy, use the back office to make phone calls or do whatever you need. If you need to leave work to check on things, make sure Gloria is here in the office to cover whatever may come up. Have I left anything out? I know this is all a short notice, but I believe it can be done."

"Don't worry about a thing, Ms. Rebecca," Lynn said confidently. "It will all be taken care of, and everybody will be so happy."

Wednesday's meeting with Cecil O'Malley went well. After it ended, Rebecca called Irene to fill her in.

"Rebecca, I was just getting ready to call you," Irene said. "My sister in Tennessee is not doing very well, so Mary and I are leaving tomorrow to go see her. Thought we would stay till Sunday and come home then. Her children will all be home for Thanksgiving, and we really won't get to spend any quality time together if I wait till then. Sammy will be here, so you won't really be alone. I'll have him come to the house and check on everything and you."

"Irene, don't you worry about me," Rebecca replied. "I'll be fine. Go and have an enjoyable visit with your sister. Besides, with all that's going on here at work, I have more than enough to keep my mind occupied. Have you heard yet from Mark? Do you know when he will be home?"

"No, dear. He is somewhere at a conference at a medical facility or something. I forgot what he said. Anyway, I don't think he will be home till late Sunday evening. He is so busy, I forget what hat he's wearing. I had just talked to my sister when he called, and my mind was not on what he was saying. Sorry."

"No big deal," Rebecca said. "I hadn't heard and thought I would ask."

Fourteen

ON THURSDAY AFTER WORK, REBECCA STOPPED TO PICK UP A PIZZA for dinner. As soon as she got home, she called Sammy to ask him to come up and join her. He did, and as they ate, he told her all about the horses and the work he had done that day. It seemed he never ran down, but then no one had ever really included him before. He said that after Susan left, things got better, but now he felt like part of the family. He had really changed and was a totally different person.

"Ms. Rebecca, I'm going back to my place," he said after they had talked a while, "but if you get scared or anything is wrong, you call me, and I'll be right up."

"Thank you, Sammy. I certainly will. Appreciate you looking out for me. I feel very safe with you around." That put a smile on Sammy's face. As he walked out the door, he turned and added, "Don't forget to set the house alarm when I leave."

"I'll be sure to do that," Rebecca said. "Thanks."

She had started cleaning up the kitchen when she heard a knock at the kitchen door. She opened it and saw Sammy standing there.

"I was listening, and you didn't set the house alarm. Also it's dark outside, and you shouldn't have opened the door like that when I knocked."

"You are so right, Sammy," Rebecca said appreciatively. "My bad. Again, I do appreciate you looking out for me. I'm going to set it right now." She closed the door and turned the house alarm on.

She heard her phone ding and wondered who was texting her. It was Sammy. "Thanks for setting the alarm."

Rebecca wondered, *How could anyone not like Sammy? He is such a sweetheart.*

Friday was an exhausting day, so Rebecca was glad when it was time to go home. Sammy called to tell her he was going to visit his friend Tommy for a little while and ask her if she needed anything before he left. She said she didn't. She had decided that, when she got home, she would take a nice shower, put on her PJs, find a good Hallmark Christmas movie, and just relax. It was going to be so nice to have a quiet, relaxing evening. She was not going to think about work or anything.

After her pleasant evening, Rebecca went to bed. Something woke her. It had been storming outside, but the storm had put her to sleep. She listened, and it sounded like someone trying to open the kitchen door. She sat up in bed, and everything was dark. She reached for her phone; it said the time was around one o'clock, but the clock on her nightstand was black. She tried to turn on the light on her nightstand—nothing. *The power must be out*, she thought. Quickly she texted Sammy and asked, "Are you home?"

Waiting and hoping that he had seen her text, she was relieved when he finally responded. "No. The storm knocked a tree down at the end of the drive here at Tommy's. We have been working trying to cut it up and move it. Are you okay?"

Not wanting to upset him, she replied, "I'm fine. Just checking on you. Stay safe."

Then she dialed 9-1-1. The operator finally answered, "9-1-1. Do you have an emergency?"

"Yes, this is Rebecca Clark," she said quietly. "I am home alone, and someone it trying to break in our back door. Can you send a police officer over to check it out?"

"I'm sorry, ma'am. There are several trees and power lines down on your road," the operator said. "I'll put this through, but keep in mind that it may be several minutes before anyone can get to you. The storm has really left a mess. Is there anywhere you can hide to be safe till the police can get there?"

"I'm not sure, but I'll try. Hope they can hurry." She hung up the phone.

She wasn't sure what to do. She could hear someone working the doorknob of the kitchen door. Easing out of bed with cell phone in hand, she made her way to the bedroom door. Whoever was trying to get in was having a very hard time. As she walked slowly toward the kitchen, she remembered the brass candlestick. She could use it as a weapon if she needed to. She picked it up and removed the candle. It was good and heavy, but hopefully she wouldn't have to use it. As she made her way to the kitchen, the back door finally swung open. From the best Rebecca could tell, there was only one person. It was still lightning outside, so she tried to get a glimpse of whoever was coming in. Suddenly, lightning flashed, and she heard a big thump. She froze, unable to move. She heard something that sounded like a moan but couldn't be sure. Clutching the candlestick tightly, she listened again. Her heart was beating so loudly that she knew whoever had come in could probably hear it. The best she could hear it still sounded like someone was moaning. Just as she stepped inside the kitchen door, the power came back on. She looked down at the floor and saw a man completely soaked and starting to get up.

With all her strength, Rebecca raised the candlestick to let the man have it. Suddenly, he stood and turned to face her. It was Mark!

"What are you doing with that candlestick?" he demanded. "Are you trying to kill me?"

"What are you doing home?" Rebecca yelled. "I was told you wouldn't be home till Sunday night! Don't you have a key to the house? And why didn't you come through the garage? Don't you know how to call and let someone know you are coming home?"

Mark was drenched. Water dripped all over the floor. Looking at Rebecca with irritation in his eyes, he said, "Trees are down everywhere, so I had to walk about half a mile to get here. Even if I had my car, the power was out, in case you didn't notice, so I still would not have been able to come through the garage. When I got here, I banged on the door, but no one answered so I had to hunt for the spare key out in the rain. When I finally made it in, I was so wet that I slipped on the floor and hit my head on the counter. Then the power came on only for me to find you standing over me with that brass candlestick ready to hit me! I've had a *wonderful* night, Rebecca. Hope yours had been just as eventful."

Feeling sorry for Mark, but also still mad, she asked how the kitchen light had come on because it was off when she went to bed.

"I probably turned it on out of habit when I stepped in here and it was dark," Mark reasoned. "Do you think I could bother you to go get me some towels? I would hate to track water everywhere."

As she turned to get him some towels, Rebecca thought about all he had said, and in a way, it struck her funny. Also, she took the time to call 9-1-1 to let them know what had happened and that she wouldn't need police assistance after all.

When she returned to the kitchen, she saw that Mark had removed his coat, shoes, socks, and shirt. She handed him the towels and said, "Do you think you could keep your pants on?"

He took the towels and replied, "Ma'am, there are some things you are not privileged to see, so I will be keeping my pants on as long as you are around."

Feeling her face turn red, Rebecca turned and went back to her room, leaving Mark to clean up his mess.

Feeling a knot on his forehead only made things worse for Mark. He thought, *She didn't even ask about my head, but then if she had used that candlestick I would have more than just a small knot. I would probably be dead. Doubt she would have even cared.*

After sunrise, Sammy knocked at the door. Rebecca let him in, and he filled her in on his night and how many trees had been blown down. After breakfast, he went outside to start cleaning up around the house. Having not heard from Mark, Rebecca assumed he was upstairs and had gone to sleep, so she went outside to help Sammy pick up branches and sticks. While they worked outside, Mark pulled in. Apparently he had gotten up and gone to get his car. He drove past them and parked his car in the garage.

Sammy and Rebecca kept on working for Sammy wanted everything to be in tip-top shape when Irene and Mary got home.

A few minutes later, another car pulled into the drive, and Lacey Stafford got out. Rebecca figured Mark had called Lacey to let her know he was home. *But he couldn't call me to tell me he was at the door last night?* she thought. Rebecca could feel her blood pressure rising.

"Morning, Rebecca," Lacey called out. "Why are you out here picking up this stuff? That's Sammy's job.

"Morning, Lacey. As you can see, there is quite a bit to clean up, way too much for one person. Would you like to help us?"

"Have you lost your mind?" Lacey squealed. "That's why we hire people like Sammy Newman! Why do you want to put yourself at his level?"

Rebecca's blood pressure hit an all-time high. "Lacey, maybe someday you will make it to Sammy's level," she retorted. "You know, miracles happen every day."

Lacey's face turned bright red at Rebecca's remark. "If you will excuse me, I need to see Mark," she said curtly. Turning, she walked to the front door.

"Ms. Rebecca, I appreciate you standing up for me," Sammy said quietly. "I know Ms. Lacey doesn't like me. She's nothing like you. She's a witch, and you're an angel."

"Oh, Sammy, if I had to choose between you and Lacey, you would win hands down." She leaned over and gave Sammy a light hug. "If she ever gives you a hard time, you let me know. I'll take care of it."

While waiting on Mark to open the door, Lacey saw Rebecca hug Sammy. When Mark opened the door, Lacey rushed inside and threw her arms around Marks neck. Trying to peel her off, Mark said, "Lacey, will you please refrain from hugging me? Is there something you need?"

"Yes, Mark," she replied. "I'm here about two things. First, I need a physical and want you to do it."

"I don't do physicals in my home," Mark answered. "If you need one, call the office and the secretary will schedule it."

"I did, and that bimbo scheduled it with your associate."

"That's because I asked her to, Lacey. Besides, have you forgotten that I haven't been at the hospital much here lately? Now, what was the other thing you needed to see me about?"

"Are you aware that Rebecca and Sammy are having an affair?" Lacey said accusingly.

"What did you just say?" Mark asked, surprised.

"It is true! Those two have a thing for each other. I saw it with my own eyes. Why, just a few minutes ago, they were hugging."

Leaning over close to her, Mark sniffed to see if Lacey had been drinking. "Well, I don't smell alcohol on your breath. Are you on any kind of medication?" he asked.

"What are you trying to insinuate?" she replied angrily.

"Lacey, you have said some foolish things before, but this must top them all."

"I'm telling you the truth! They were out front over near the driveway, hugging."

"I see," Mark said with a smirk. "You're jealous of Rebecca because she got to Sammy before you did."

"Mark McKay, how dare you say such a thing!" Turning on her heel, Lacey went out the door, slamming it as she left. She didn't say anything to Rebecca or Sammy as she got in her car.

Sammy called out, "You have a good day, Ms. Lacey." He knew that his speaking to her would just infuriate her further.

Fifteen

LATER, MARK CAME OUT TO HELP WITH THE CLEANUP. NO ONE
said a word about Lacey's visit or Mark's adventure of trying to get
in the house the previous night. The knot on Mark's forehead was
not bad, but it was sore to touch. After all the cleaning was done,
Rebecca changed clothes and drove to check on the plant. There
was no damage, but she did go in and reset the clocks that were not
hooked up to a generator. Then she drove out to check on Rachel
and Sarah. Pulling in the drive, she was pleased to see very few limbs
laying in the yard. She knocked on the door.

"Hello, Rachel," she said when the door opened. "Is this a bad
time for a visit? I wanted to check on you and Sarah. Have you had
any problems with the house after last night's storm?"

"No, come on in. We lost power, but other than that we are
fine," Rachel answered. "Sarah is at a friend's house playing. You
just missed her; they left about ten minutes ago. Would you like a
glass of tea or some coffee?"

"No, thank you. I just wanted to make sure all was okay over
here. How are you doing?"

"Ms. Clark, I'm so glad you stopped by. I have been wanting to
talk to you but hated to bother you at work."

"I told you to let me know anytime you needed to talk or
anything," Rebecca said reassuringly.

"Well, what I want to talk to you about has nothing to do with

113

work." Rachel was wringing her hands as she continued. "It has to do with me. Please don't get mad at me for what I'm going to tell you."

"It takes a lot to get me upset, and I think you know that," Rebecca said with a smile. "So tell me why I may possibly be mad at you."

"You know, you have a lot of books on the shelves here. One day when I was dusting, I picked up some of the books and flipped through the pages. I found a Bible that belonged to a Mamie Clark, according to the first page. On the next page, the marriage of a Ray Clark and Rebecca James was noted, but when I turned the page again, I saw the date that Ray Clark was deceased. I had no idea you were ever married or had lost your husband. I am so sorry."

"Oh, don't worry about it," Rebecca replied. "My being a widow is just something I don't go around announcing. I had a wonderful husband, but for some reason, God decided to call him home. But I wasn't left completely alone. Ray's mother, the Mamie Clark you mentioned, was just as wonderful. This was her house, and when she died, she left it all to me."

"She must have been a very special lady," Rachel agreed. "I have been reading her Bible, and she has notes all through it. Every night after Sarah goes to bed, I get her Bible out and read. Sometimes, it feels like someone is speaking to me when I read it. Do you think it is her?"

"No, Rachel, it's not Mamie. It's God speaking to you."

"I don't think God would want to talk to me," Rachel said, looking down.

We are not on good terms."

"Why do you say that? God speaks to everyone. The problem is that we often don't listen when he speaks."

"You don't understand," Rachel continued. "There was a time when I needed God so much, and he turned his back on me. He refused to help me, and I was desperate for help. After that, I was finished with God. He turned his back on me first."

"No, God doesn't turn his back on us," Rebecca said softly. "He is with us everywhere we go. Are you familiar with the Bible and the stories it tells?"

"Yes, I have heard all those stories. So what?"

"Rachel, when Jesus was born, he was born in no sin. He was sinless. Years later, he died for our sins. He was beaten beyond recognition and then nailed on a cross. I can't even begin to imagine the pain and suffering he went through. Here on earth, we all go through trouble and trails, but we haven't suffered what Jesus did, and he was innocent."

"You see, Ms. Clark, that's where you are wrong. I *have* suffered, and when I called out to God, he left me. He did nothing to help me."

"We all go through hard times, Rachel," Rebecca said. "What I have gone through may be different from what you have gone through, but both are bad. We don't get to pick the pain and suffering we face. What's important is how we handle the situation. Did it make you stronger, or did you become weaker? I'm sure Jesus didn't want to go through all he had facing him, but he did, and he did it for us. Have you talked to anyone about what you had to go through? Why do you feel you are on bad terms with God?"

"No, I'm too ashamed," Rachel murmured. "Well, I take that back. I told a friend once a little bit, but not much. It was just a very bad time in my life, and I can't forgive God for not helping me."

"Sometimes we go through things, and no matter how hard we try nothing goes right. Maybe it's not what we want, but God knows what is best. He can see on down the road, and we feel like our prayers are not heard when they are. If he answered our prayers the way we wanted, we would really be in a big mess. If you feel that someone is speaking to you when you're reading the Bible, it's God trying to get your attention."

"He had my attention and turned away," Rachel protested.

"Rachel, Luke 6:37 says, 'Judge not, and you will not be judged; condemn not, and you will not be condemned; forgive, and you will be forgiven.' We must forgive. If I had some ill feelings toward you and didn't ask you to forgive me, how could I pray and ask God to forgive me of my sins?"

"If I tell you what he did to me, will you promise not to tell anyone? I think then you will understand why God and I are not on good terms. I'm not one of his chosen people."

"Of course," Rebecca answered. "It helps to share our heartaches. You never know—someone may have experienced what you are facing and can help guide you to better understand your situation. Maybe I can help you see that God is always with us no matter what."

"I don't think you can change my mind," Rachel began. "You see, my parents—well, I really don't know who they are. I was raised by different people. I wasn't in a foster home, just raised by some of my parents' friends is all I know. When I graduated from high school, I wanted so much to go to college, to make something of myself. The only way that would happen was for me to get a job and work my way through, which I was determined to do. One night after a class, I was walking down the street to my room and stopped to fix a headset that I was wearing. A friend had let me borrow hers, and I think the battery had died. Anyway, a guy came up to me and asked if he could help me. I told him no, that everything was all right. Then two more guys came up, one on each side of me. They grabbed my arms, and someone from behind put tape over my mouth. They carried me inside the building we were standing next to. I was raped by all of them, kicked and beaten, and when I couldn't move anymore, just lying there, I could hear them laughing and saying all kinds of ugly things. I have no idea who found me, but I woke up in a hospital. My face was so swollen and bruised, and every part of my body hurt. I had some cracked ribs and a broken shoulder, and my left knee was bruised and swollen also. I was in the hospital for several weeks, and one of the nurses took me home with her till I could regain my strength and try to recover from the ordeal. When we were talking one day, I asked her about where I had been found. Those guys had carried me into a church and raped and tortured me there. *In a church*, Ms. Clark, God's house. Where was he when all of this was happening? Was God on a coffee break and didn't have time for me?"

"Rachel, I can't even begin to know how you felt, but you have to let go of that night," Rebecca said softly.

"That night I became pregnant and have no idea who the father is. Is that what God wanted for my life?" Rachel asked angrily.

"As bad as it all was—and I'm not saying what they did was right, for they all should have been punished—but through it all, you were blessed with a beautiful little girl. How many times have you said that Sarah is an exceptional child? No matter how bad things were with you two, she never complained."

"But there are times when I look at her and all those memories come back. She will always be a constant reminder of that terrible night."

"Don't look at it that way," Rebecca said. "Look at the blessing she is to you. If you didn't have her, you may have turned to alcohol or drugs while in college. Sarah may be what you needed in your life. Do you think Jesus was treated fairly? Do you think he wanted to be tortured? He even had to hang naked on a cross for all to see. Rachel, everyone goes through bad times; no one escapes. But we have choices. We can feel sorry for ourselves, stay mad at the world because things don't go our way, never smile, and become hermits. Or we can pray, ask God for guidance, and move on. If you don't, Rachel, your life will always be nothing but misery."

"I've hated God for so long and have no feelings for him," Rachel said, shaking her head. "You don't know the pain."

"You're right. I have no idea what you went through. When I was in college, at graduation time, I was so looking forward to seeing my parents and for them to see all that I had accomplished. Instead, I was given the news that they had been killed in an explosion at a mission site. Everyone was killed, and there weren't enough body parts to send back to the States for burial. Later, I moved to Texas and met my husband, only to give him up later to a car accident. God blessed me with a wonderful mother-in-law, but after my husband died, she was diagnosed with cancer. So I moved to Kentucky to be with her and help all I could. When she died, she left me this house and all that's in it. I had a couple of bad jobs before I was hired at McKay's, and I lived here till Mrs. McKay had me move in with her. I came very close to putting this house on the market, but for some reason it just didn't seem right. I'm so glad I kept it for now this is home for you and Sarah. All that happened was in God's plan. You must look at where you were and where you are now. It's not an accident; it's God doing his work. Can't you see how God brought us together?"

Looking down at her hands, Rachel didn't know what to say. Finally, she looked up at Rebecca. "I'm sorry you had to go through so much," she said. "I had no idea. You always seem so upbeat and happy, I would never have guessed you had lost so many loved ones. How can you go around laughing and smiling all the time? You seem like you don't have a care in the world."

"Well, I do, but again we have choices. Try to take the good out of things and leave the bad behind you. Count your blessings, not your heartaches. Rachel, would you mind if we prayed together? I don't want to push you if you're not ready, but I do think it will help."

"I can't pray," Rachel said. "I don't know how. Besides, I'm too afraid."

"What are you afraid of?" Rebecca asked. "Would you mind if I prayed and you just listened? You don't have to say a word."

"I guess that would be all right."

"Mind if I hold your hands? This way nothing can get in and only God's love will be in our circle." Rachel nodded.

As Rebecca took Rachel's hands, tears started flowing from Rachel's eyes. Rebecca started praying and could feel Rachel trembling. She knew God was among them, so she prayed as she was led. Then Rachel slid out of her chair and onto her knees, crying out for help. Rebecca knelt beside her and held her close, continuing to pray.

"Help me, Ms. Clark!" Rachel cried. "I don't know what to do. Do you think God can forgive me?"

"Oh, Rachel, God has never held anything against you. He has loved you and watched over you since the day you were born. He has been waiting patiently for you to ask him into your heart. You said God had forgotten all about you, turned his back on you when you needed him. Have you forgiven him for feeling that way? Because he has forgiven you for any wrong you have done."

Bowing her head and still crying, Rachel asked, "What do I say to him?"

"Talk to him just like you are talking to me. Ask him to help you, let him know you no longer blame him, ask for guidance to remove the bitterness you have been holding onto for so long and to replace it with love. He knows our hearts. He just wants us to talk to him and let him be a part of our lives."

"I feel so unworthy and ashamed," Rachel said. "How can I be sure he will forgive me?"

"Remember what I said earlier? Luke 6:37 says, 'Judge not and you will not be judged, condemn not and you will not be condemned: forgive and you will be forgiven.' Also, God doesn't go looking for those who think they are worthy of his love; he looks for those who feel unworthy. Would you like some time alone? I can go to another room or outside," Rebecca offered.

"No, I would feel better if you stayed close by."

Then Rachel tried to pray, but all she could do was cry. Rebecca put her arm around Rachel and prayed silently, giving Rachel some time to reach out to God in her own way. After some time had gone by, Rebecca put both her arms around Rachel and gave her a hug.

"Rachel, tears are a language that only God can truly understand. Your prayer life will get better in time, and I'm here for you anytime you need a friend," Rebecca said.

"You know, I never had a sister, but I feel so close to you."

"I never had a sister either, or a brother, but we feel close to each other because we are sisters in Christ. Those are the best."

"Do you think I will ever get to be like you?" Rachel asked.

"Like me? Why would you want to be like me?"

"You have it all together. I want to be like my new sister in Christ."

"Let me confess something. I have been envious of you, which I know is wrong, because you have a beautiful little girl. This is something God has not blessed me with yet, even though I dearly love children. To me, the greatest gift God can give a woman is a child. Having a child like Sarah would thrill me to death, but I must wait patiently till God sees fit for me to have one if that's in his will."

"I never thought of a child being a gift from God," Rachel said thoughtfully. "I have so much to learn. I want to be a better mother to Sarah. She deserves so much more."

"Why don't you come to church with me tomorrow morning? I can pick you two up and let you try the church I go to. Some of the people we work with attend, so you won't feel alone. If for some reason you don't like the church, I'll go with you wherever you want to go on Sundays till you find the right one."

"How will I know which one is right?" Rachel asked.

"Let God tell you. He is never wrong," Rebecca said confidently. "Are you going to be all right?"

"Yes, I do feel better."

"That's wonderful. Now, any book you find in this house, you are more than welcome to read. Something else to think about: try praying before you eat and before going to bed, and say a thank-you prayer in the morning before you two head out the door. This can really change things for you and Sarah. Enjoy it. Now, I'll see you two in the morning at eight."

"Ms. Clark, I just thought of something. I don't have a dress to wear to church," Rachel said.

"Just wear whatever you have. God doesn't look at what we wear. He looks at what we carry in our hearts."

With one last hug, Rebecca headed out the door, feeling as if she were on cloud nine.

Sixteen

As Rebecca backed out of the driveway, her cell phone started ringing. She looked down at her phone and saw that Mary was calling. She found a place to pull over and answered it. "Hey, Mary, how are things in Tennessee?"

"We are not in Tennessee," Mary began. "We came back home this afternoon. Ms. Irene wanted to check on things because we heard the storm was bad here. She was afraid there might be some damage to the house and no one would tell her till she got home. Ms. Irene had spoken to Sammy, but that didn't help; she had to see for herself. But that's not the reason I'm calling, Rebecca. Ms. Irene fell down the stairs. We think she missed the last two steps and hurt her ankle. Sammy and I have her in the emergency room and thought you might want to know. Tried calling earlier and all I got was your voice mail."

"I am so sorry, Mary! I don't remember hearing it ring, but then I was really busy. I'm not far from the hospital and should be there in a few minutes." She turned her car in the direction of the hospital.

As Rebecca walked into the emergency department's waiting room, she saw Mark at the nurse's desk looking at a chart. The elevator door opened, and Lacey came walking out. She went straight to Mark and put her arm through his. Rebecca thought, *You would never know she was huffed this morning by the way she is acting now*. Rebecca saw Mary look through the doors, so she went straight to her.

"How is Irene's foot?" Rebecca asked.

"She is in X-ray now. It's already swelled and bruised looking. Did you see Sammy? He just left to go back home."

"No, but I did see Mark and Lacey at the nurse's desk."

"What is she doing here?" Mary asked, annoyed. "That girl pops up out of nowhere and usually at the wrong time."

"Oh, Mary, here comes Irene now," Rebecca said. "Hope the news is good."

An orderly rolled Irene into the room and said the doctor would be right in to give her the results of her X-ray. Mary and Rebecca followed them into the room to wait with her.

Mark walked in and examined Irene's ankle. "Mom, I'll let the doctor tell you about your ankle, but don't give him a hard time, okay?"

"Now why would I give him a hard time?" Irene asked. "Is there surgery involved? You're a doctor. Why can't you just tell me what's wrong?"

"I'm just asking that you listen to him and not give him a hard time," Mark said. "I'm not the one treating you, and doctors don't just take over patients when they are being seen by another doctor."

Just then the doctor came in. "Mrs. McKay, I'm Dr. Brian Morris," he said. "Dr. William Ryan, the emergency room doctor who saw you when you first came in, asked me to look over your X-rays. I'm an orthopedic doctor, and he thought it best to put you in my care. I have good news and bad news. Which would you like to hear first?"

Irene replied, "The good news. That way maybe the bad news won't seem so bad."

"Okay, the good news is that it's not broken. The bad news is that you pulled the muscles and ligaments further than they like to be stretched. Nothing is torn, but still the muscles and ligaments do need to heal. So you will need to wear a boot for about six weeks. You don't need a cast on your ankle; you just need to wear a boot."

"What kind of boot are you talking about?" Irene asked.

"Well, it's not a designer boot, but it is black and will go with anything you wear," Dr. Morris said with a smile.

"Do I have to wear a boot on both feet?"

"No, just on your left foot. That's the one that was injured. I'll have the nurse come in and get you set up with your new boot. Also, you will need to wear it all the time, even when sleeping. Take it off only when you shower. I want to see you in my office in about two weeks to see how it is doing. I don't believe you will need any pain medication. Do you have any questions?"

"Why in the world do I need to sleep with it on?" Irene asked. "I'll be in bed, lying down."

"This is to protect your ankle. You might roll over and twist it or get up in the night and forget. You need that support for your ankle till it heals."

Irene looked at the doctor. "You are saying I have to wear it for six weeks? The holidays are coming up. What does it look like anyway?"

"The nurse will be right in to help you," Dr. Morris said, moving toward the door. "Mark, as always, it's good to see you. You make her follow the doctor's orders."

"Don't worry, Brian," Mark replied. "She will, or I'll have her put in the hospital where she'll be under surveillance."

Both doctors laughed, but Irene didn't seem to find any humor in the remark. Dr. Morris left just as a nurse walked in.

"Mrs. McKay, I'm nurse Lindsey, and I'm here to fit you for your boot," she said. "Let's try this one to make sure it's the right size. We don't want your toes hanging over the edge."

"Wait a minute," said Irene. "You expect me to wear that thing for six weeks? That's the ugliest thing I have ever seen! The doctor said it was black and would go with anything, but he didn't say it was humongous. No, I'm not wearing that thing. You can just take it back."

"Mom," Mark interjected. "You are going to wear that boot. It's for only six weeks, and people will understand. Remember I asked you not to give them a hard time. Let's cooperate and be nice."

"That's easy for you to say," Irene protested. "You're not the one who will be wearing it. Mark, the holidays are almost here! Nothing I wear will look decent with that thing. You need to be a little more understanding. I *am* your mother, after all."

"You have a choice: wear the boot and come home, or I'll talk to Dr. Morris and have you admitted to the hospital, where you will wear the boot and spend the holidays."

"You wouldn't," she said in disbelief. "Oh, go ahead and put that monstrous boot on then. I'm not happy about it, and I certainly don't like it."

Trying to come to Irene's rescue, Rebecca said, "You can wear a long, full skirt at Thanksgiving, and that will hide the boot. If you don't have one, I'll go shopping and find one. A long skirt and a colorful top would look nice"

"Oh, Rebecca, that might help," Irene said, a little happier. "Thanks. When we get home, we can look and see what I have. This is not going well for me at all."

Mary and Rebecca helped Irene into the car and took her home while Mark stayed at the hospital. After getting Irene home and settled in a recliner, Mary went to the kitchen to fix a quick snack for them.

Rebecca followed her into the kitchen. "Mary, would you mind if I asked you some questions? If I'm being nosy, just say so. I won't be offended."

"Rebecca, my dear, ask away."

"It's regarding Mark. Some things just don't seem to add up, and I'm a little confused. Well, really, I'm a lot confused."

Mark had just came in the back door when he heard Rebecca

mention his name. He decided to listen to what she was saying, so he stayed back where they wouldn't see him.

"I'll answer you the best I can, so go ahead. Fire away," Mary said.

"Well, when Lacey's name is mentioned, you and Irene seem to cringe. I don't understand why."

"That woman is evil," Mary said simply. "She is nothing but *trouble.*"

"Then why does Mark want to marry her?"

Looking at Rebecca with shock, Mary stopped what she was doing. "What did you just say?"

"I asked why does Mark want to marry her if she is trouble?" Rebecca said.

"Who in the world told you that Mark and Lacey were getting married?"

"Lacey did, the night of the dinner party when Mark gave his acceptance speech."

"Rebecca, that woman does not speak the truth," Mary said plainly. "Everything out of her mouth is nothing but lies. I wouldn't trust her as far as I could spit, and trust me that's not far. What else did that old witch tell you?"

"Oh, my, Mary! I have never heard you talk like that before. What Lacey told me seemed to be the truth. Besides, I have seen them kissing before."

"Correction. You might have seen Lacey kiss Mark, but honey, he did not return her kiss. She would like nothing more to get her claws in Mark and has been trying ever since Mark's wife died."

Rebecca paused. "I heard he was married but that his wife is gone now. May I ask what happened?"

"This is my opinion," Mary said. "Susan and Lacey are two of a kind. Mark learned his lesson with Susan. I know he won't go down that road again."

"What happened to her?" Rebecca pressed.

"She was killed in a car wreck. Trust me, Mark did everything he could to make her happy, but nothing pleased her. Lacey is a lot like that. No matter what she has, she always wants more."

"Then why does Mark let her kiss him or hold his arm?" Rebecca asked.

"She usually catches him off guard, and before he knows it, she's thrown her arms around his neck and is trying to kiss him, or if she thinks someone is looking, she slides her hands around his arm like they are together. He feels bad pushing her arm away when she does this, so if he sees her ahead of time, he tries to hide or get somewhere safe. He has told her to stay away, that they had no future together, but she won't listen. Mark doesn't want to be too cruel to her for her dad is Bruce Stafford. He's the one pushing Mark to run for state senator and who made a very large donation toward his campaign."

"Wow, this is all so hard to believe," Rebecca said. "Lacey can tell some convincing stories."

"Just what all has she told you?" Mary asked. "Come clean now. I've shared a lot here, so share away."

"Well, she said she would already have a ring, but with Mark's schedule they haven't had a chance to go pick one out. She's hoping he will surprise her and give her one by Christmas. Oh, and are you ready for this one? She is hoping to get married before the election because it wouldn't look good to have a little McKay before they got married."

"Mercy me, Rebecca. I need to sit down," Mary said. "I thought what Mark told me was a bit much, but I do believe this tops it."

"What did Mark say?"

"Well, Lacey came over this morning when you and Sammy were cleaning up outside from last night's storm. I don't know what was said, but Lacey came to the house and told Mark that you and Sammy were having an affair. She saw you two hugging right out front."

"What?" Rebecca said, outraged. "She told Mark that Sammy and I were having an affair? How dare she! Yes, I gave Sammy a hug, but it was after Lacey threw insults at him. She asked me why I was outside helping him, saying that he was hired to do such work and that I didn't need to put myself at his level. So I told her that, maybe someday, she *might* make it to Sammy's level. I even asked her if she would like to help us. You can imagine her response."

"I tell you, Rebecca, that woman is evil," Mary said.

"You know, Lacey and Clay need to get together. They are like two peas in a pod."

"Too late with that idea. Clay and Lacey have been slipping around for years. Those two deserve each other."

"I wonder if Lacey saw Clay talking to me that night and was upset that he was talking to me and not her?" Rebecca pondered.

"That's a good possibility."

"It really bothered me when Clay asked me to go out with him and then said no one would have to know about it," Rebecca said. "He is truly an all-out foolish man, as far as I'm concerned."

Mary stood up. "Well, I had better get this chicken salad sandwich to Ms. Irene before she comes looking for it."

"Here, I'll take it to her," Rebecca offered. "Then I'm going to turn in. It has been one long day." Rebecca left the kitchen and headed toward Irene's room.

"Here's your sandwich, Irene. Sorry it took so long to bring it to you, but Mary and I got to talking and time got away from us."

"Oh, that's all right, dear," Irene said. "I'm so frustrated with my new footwear that it has taken my appetite. I can't believe that little tumble I took messed up my ankle, especially here at the holidays."

"I will go look to see if I can't find you a lovely long skirt to wear that will cover up your new shoe. You must be careful, though, when you get up to walk."

"Rebecca, starting in December, we will be invited to several Christmas parties. I can't wear the same thing to every party! Some of the same people go to these parties."

"Do you remember what you wore to the parties last year?" Rebecca asked.

"Well, no, not exactly."

"Do you remember what the other ladies wore?"

"Some I probably would if I saw them, and some you just forget."

"I really doubt anyone will notice," Rebecca said. "You could always draw attention to your new footwear to distract from your dress or skirt."

"Rebecca, that is not funny," Irene chided. "I always take such pride in my clothing, especially when going to a party. By the way, what do you plan to wear to the Christmas parties coming up?"

"Well, since I haven't been invited to any parties, I don't think I will go."

"My dear, you must go!" Irene countered. "You're the new CEO of McKay's. A lot of single men will be there. You might need to call Phillip and set up an appointment with him to see what he can do for you. I have his number in the study."

"If I'm expected to be there, that's one thing, but don't get any ideas of playing matchmaker," Rebecca cautioned. "I'm just not interested. I have other things to keep me occupied, and I'm happy with my life just the way it is. Now if you will excuse me, I'm going to turn in for the night. Hope you sleep well, but if you need anything let me know."

Opening the side door, Mark walked into the kitchen where Mary was. "Mary, I overheard you and Rebecca talking," he said. "I didn't really mean to eavesdrop, but as I opened the door, I heard Rebecca mention my name, so I just stepped back with the door cracked open a little. I should have known Lacey had got to Rebecca and filled her with nothing but lies. That really explains some things to me."

"I'm not for people eavesdropping on other people's conversations, Mark, but this is an exception. I'm glad you heard. Rebecca was so confused about it all. You would think Lacey's parents would get her some help. There is no telling what lies that girl has told her parents over the years, and she seems to be getting worse."

"Having her committed would be a good start, say, for the rest of her life," Mark half-joked.

"Now, Mark, that is not a nice thing to say," Mary scolded him. "Lacey has a real problem and needs help. By the way, Rebecca knows you have been married. Why don't you tell her what happened before she hears someone else's version of it?"

"Because that's in the past, and I don't enjoy talking about it. It has taken a long time to get over all that. I put up a high wall between myself and everyone else, and I'm just beginning to let it down. Beside, getting a chance to talk to Rebecca is not easy."

"Are you seeing someone?" Mary asked.

"No. As much as you and my mother would like it, I'm still a little woman shy."

"Honey, not all women are like Susan. Take Rebecca, for example. She is nothing at all like Susan, while Lacey is a *lot* like Susan. You're a smart man. You can see who to trust and who not to trust."

"If I'm so smart, why in the world did I ever date Susan or ask her to marry me?" Mark asked. "She must be the biggest mistake I have ever made in my life, and don't say I was young and innocent at the time. She did a snow job on me, and I fell for it."

"Susan did a snow job on everybody, but finally her true colors came out and people felt so sorry for all of us. Don't judge others by Susan. You need to date and find someone who has the same goals in life that you do and loves you for who you are. Pray about it. Ask God to bring the right woman into your life."

"I have prayed, Mary, but so far, no luck," Mark stated, "When a woman touches my arm, it feels cold and I back away. Except for one—when she touched my arm, her touch was so warm."

"So, what did you do? Did you ask her out?" Mary asked eagerly.

"No, I don't think she is even aware of what her touch did to me. I might ask her out, but it depends on a lot of things. I'm going to go check on Mom. Thanks for listening, Mary."

Seventeen

On Sunday morning, Rebecca got up early so she could pick up Rachel and Sarah for church. She prayed all the way to their house, hoping Rachel would feel God's great love and power in church. The previous day had been such a big breakthrough for Rachel. Rebecca couldn't help but see God working in Rachel's life.

She arrived at the house, and as soon as she got to the door, Sarah opened it.

"Ms. Rebecca, Mama says we are going to church with you this morning," she said. "How do I look?"

"Sarah, you look beautiful! Is that a new dress?"

"Sort of. Someone gave us money for my birthday, and Mama let me pick out a new dress. I have worn it to school a few times. I really like it."

"You certainly have good taste in clothes," Rebecca said. "I might need you to go shopping with me sometime. Is your mother ready for church?"

Popping her head around the door, Rachel smiled and said, "Yes, I'm ready! Would you mind if I carried one of the Bibles from the shelf? There is one that I really like."

"Carry any that you want, Rachel. That's what they are there for. Everyone ready for church? Then let's go."

Back at the house, Mark went downstairs for his morning coffee and to check on his mom. Irene was still asleep, so he decided not to wake her. He went to the kitchen where Mary was and said, "Everyone must be sleeping in this morning. Just checked on Mom and she's asleep, and when I went by Rebecca's room, her door was closed so I take it she's still asleep too."

"Oh no, Ms. Rebecca left about forty-five minutes ago," Mary explained. "You have to get up early to get ahead of that girl! Are you hungry this morning?"

"No, not really," Mark replied. "Why did Rebecca leave so early? It's not a workday."

"She said something about picking someone up for church. She was certainly in a good mood and very eager to get going."

"Well, I won't be going to church this morning. I got a call from the hospital, and I have to go in. I promised to cover for a friend for the next few days." Mark started for the door. "Have a great day, Mary," he said. "I'll call later to check on Mom."

After church, Rachel got into the car and said, "Church was good today, Ms. Clark. What the preacher talked about this morning, I had read about this week, but he talked about things that I didn't see when I read it. He made it so much easier to understand. How did he do that?"

"It takes hours of reading and praying," Rebecca answered. "You keep reading, praying, and believing, then before you know it, God will open your eyes to see things you never saw before. You are on the right path. Stay with it."

"Mama, I like the church a lot," Sarah spoke up,. "Do you think we can go again with Ms. Rebecca?"

"There you go, Rachel," Rebecca said. "God may be working on Sarah also. I don't mind at all coming by to pick you both up on Sundays. It would really be my pleasure."

"If you are sure you don't mind, that would be great," Rachel said. "To be truthful, Ms. Clark, I'm anxious to hear what he has to preach on next Sunday."

"That's great. Now, how about some lunch? My treat. Sarah, you pick out a place, and then we can go back to your house. Upstairs in the attic are some things to decorate the house with for fall. We can get those things down and get your house ready for Thanksgiving. I also believe there are some Christmas decorations and possibly a tree. We can look at them and decide if they are still worth using."

"You mean we will have a Christmas tree in our house this year?" Sarah asked excitedly. "We have never had a tree before! Mama, do you think we could put one up if there is a tree?"

"Sarah, calm down," Rachel said, laughing. "Ms. Clark said we could look, so just wait and see."

Sarah ate her lunch so fast; all she could talk about was finding a Christmas tree in the attic. As soon as they got home, she changed her clothes and was ready to see what they could find in the attic. She didn't even know the house *had* an attic. Rebecca pulled the door down so they could go up the ladder. Sarah stood back as she watched the door come down and was so amazed. All three then went up the ladder to see what they could find. The boxes were dusty, but all were labeled to indicate what they contained.

Rachel found several boxes that were labeled "Fall." "Should I open them?" she asked.

"Sure. Like I said, some you might can use, and some we may need to throw away." After a moment, she added, "Rachel, why don't you call me Rebecca. I know I'm your boss at work, but we are much closer now. We are like family."

"Oh, Ms. Clark, I appreciate that—I mean, Ms. Rebecca." She smiled, and tears welled up in her eyes.

"Here it is," Sarah said excitedly. "Look! A box that says 'Christmas tree' on it. I found it! Can we open it up?"

"Sarah, calm down," Rachel said. "We don't need a tree now. When we do, Ms. Rebecca can come back over, and we will go through the Christmas things. Let's take one holiday at a time."

"Mama, we could put it up and decorate it and just not turn the lights on," Sarah said. "We've never had a tree. They are so pretty. What do you think, Ms. Rebecca?"

"That's between you and your mother," Rebecca said. "She's the boss, not me."

"But you're Mama's boss!"

"Only at work," Rebecca explained. "Here at your house, she's the boss."

"Mama, what do you think? Can we?" Sarah pleaded.

"I guess it will be all right. But we can't turn the lights on till after Thanksgiving. The rest of the house, we will decorate for fall."

"Thank you, Mama! This is going to be a fun day."

They spent the rest of the day decorating for Thanksgiving throughout the house, except for one area, where they put the tree up. Sarah carefully placed the ornaments on the tree as high as she could reach. When the tree was finished, Rebecca and Rachel helped Sarah up a ladder to place a fiber-optic angel on top. Rachel turned the tree on to see how it looked, and Sarah stood in awe.

"It's beautiful. Our very own tree, and it's beautiful! The angel is smiling down on us, Mama. She's happy too."

"Now that everything is all decorated, I think I will go home and let you two enjoy it," Rebecca said. "It's been a fun day."

"Ms. Rebecca, thank you so much for all you have done," Rachel said. "Thank you also for taking us to church this morning. We really enjoyed it, and we would like to go again next Sunday."

"That's wonderful. Next Sunday it is. I'll be by to pick you ladies up at the same time as today."

Sarah ran over to hug Rebecca. In her ear, she whispered, "Thank you for making everything so special. I love you."

Rebecca whispered back, "I love you too."

On the way home, Rebecca felt so happy that Rachel was getting her life back an on the right track also that Sarah was enjoying life the way a child should.

When she got home, she went to check on Irene. She found her in her bedroom trying to walk without the boot on.

"Irene, what are you doing?" she exclaimed. "You know you are supposed to wear the boot!"

"Oh, I came in here thinking no one would come in. I just wanted to see if I was able to walk without that ugly boot on, but it's not going to happen. Too much pain when I put my weight on it."

"What would you have done if I had been Mark?"

"Dear, thank goodness you weren't," Irene sighed. "He would still be giving me the third degree. Don't say anything to him about this. I'm not up to one of his doctor lectures."

"If you promise not to try this again for several weeks," Rebecca said. "I'll go this week and look for a long skirt to hopefully cover up the boot, but there's nothing I can do to cover up the cane or your limp."

"Oh, I hope to be able to walk without the cane by Thanksgiving," Irene said, "and maybe my limp won't be as bad. By the way, you have been gone all day. Is everything okay?"

"Yes, it is. I will fill you in on all that's been going on later. Right now, I'm going to turn in. Lynn and I have a lot to do this week to get ready for Friday's Thanksgiving meal at work. Sleep well, and leave the boot on." Rebecca headed to her room.

The next morning, Lynn was already at the office when Rebecca came in.

"Good morning, Ms. Rebecca," Lynn said. "I'm going through everything to see what's left to be done before Friday. Can you believe the holidays are almost here?"

"Yes, stores are already decorated for Christmas. As soon as we finish with Thanksgiving, we might as well go ahead and decorate the place for Christmas and start planning what to do for the employees."

"They are going to be so excited about expanding the building and all the details you will be sharing with them. You are going to have to come up with something big for Christmas to top Thanksgiving."

"Maybe I shouldn't tell them everything on Friday and save some announcements for Christmas," Rebecca said, thinking out loud. "I could say we are expanding McKay's and will be breaking ground December first. Then, at our Christmas dinner or party, whatever we decide on, I could go more into details on what all the expansion will include. Oh, by the way, I didn't tell you. Irene will not be able to help you with Thanksgiving on Friday. She fell Saturday and stretched the ligaments in her left foot and ankle, so now she is in a boot. She is going to be fine; she is just so upset to be wearing an unstylish boot over the holidays. Even though it is black, it still doesn't go well with her clothes."

Lynn said, "Oh, bless her heart. I can see why she is so upset over wearing an orthopedic boot. She is such a classy lady, everything must match, and nothing is ever out of place. I'm sure she feels it really clashes with her wardrobe. How long will she have to wear the boot?"

"If she takes care, she should be out before the first of the year," Rebecca explained. "I caught her trying to walk without the boot on, which of course she couldn't. That boot and her pride don't go together." Rebecca went into her office to get to work, and Lynn followed.

After several hours, Lynn said, "Okay, Ms. Rebecca, we have put in a good day's work, and I think we are all set for Friday. Why don't I start tomorrow working on something for Christmas? Do you have any ideas yet?"

"No, I don't. So much has been going on lately that coming up with a few things for Thanksgiving has been a miracle," Rebecca said. "Lynn, I don't know what I would do without your help. You are a gift to me, and I want you to know I truly appreciate you. If I ever fail to say thank you, please know you are a blessing to me."

"Ms. Rebecca, this is the best company I have ever worked at.

All the employees get along so well, and they care for one another. You don't see that just anywhere anymore."

"You are right. All the employees seem to care for one another in such a loving way. This is a very special company, and I'm so proud to be a part of it. Now, go home and get some rest for who knows what we will get into tomorrow. I have some filing to do, and then I'm out of here myself."

Rebecca gathered up the stack of papers to be filed, went over to the window, and let her mind drift back to the weekend. So much had happened—the storm, Lacey, Rachel turning her life over to the Lord, Sarah, and Irene. What a packed weekend it had been! She wondered what would happen next. Talking to herself, she said, "Now if I don't stop letting my mind wander, I'll never get this filing done." When she went to the file cabinet, she had another thought: in a few weeks, she would be pulling files to get ready for the end of the year.

A knock on the door brought her back to what she was supposed to be doing.

Rebecca said, "The door is unlocked, Lynn. Did you forget something?"

The door closed, and the voice she heard wasn't Lynn's. Turning around, she wished she had locked the door when Lynn left.

"Mark, what are you doing here?" she asked.

"I have been wanting to talk to you for a good while, so catching you here after work seemed like the perfect chance," he said. "We won't be interrupted by phone calls since they have already been transferred to the after-hours line, and all the employees are gone, so no one will be knocking at your door. Now, if you will have a seat, I would like to have your undivided attention for a few minutes."

Unsure what all Mark felt he needed to talk to her about, Rebecca took a seat at her desk. This way, they had some space between them.

"I don't bite, Rebecca," he teased. "Why don't we sit over here on the couch where we will be more comfortable?"

Rebecca did not really want to move from the desk, so she waited till Mark sat down before she chose her seat.

Mark could tell she was very tense, so he didn't push her about where she sat.

"There is a lot I feel we need to discuss about Saturday night. I don't make a habit of listening to other people's conservations, but what I heard helped explain a lot of things."

"You listened to my private conservation?" Rebecca asked.

"Yes, and as I just said, what I heard really helped me understand why you keep avoiding me and why you reacted the way you did the night I tried to kiss you," Mark said. "Rebecca, there is nothing between Lacey and me. As Mary told you, I'll do anything to avoid her. She is like a pain or a disease that won't go away."

"Lacey did tell some very convincing stories, except for the one about Sammy and me. That was just plain cruel."

"That's how I feel about all her wild tales. When I tried to kiss you that night, you thought I was seeing Lacey and also trying to make a move with you. I'm not that kind of guy. Mary told you my wife was killed, but let me explain about my wife. When we were dating, she was a totally different person. She knew I was studying to become a doctor, and we had discussed the long hours that I had facing me. Still, she wanted to get married, and the sooner, the better. That was my first mistake. While I was going to school and spending sleepless nights studying, she was out on the town partying. After I became a doctor and went into practice with a friend here in town, she started taking trips abroad. Her trips became longer and longer over time. Of course, I was told of things she was doing, and spending my money was one of them. I tried talking to her when she was home, but it did no good. I didn't want a divorce; no one in the family had ever gotten one, and I didn't want to be the first. One day, Susan texted me that she was coming home, and she wanted to make sure that her car and her room were ready for her. So I made plans to take her to a play in New York and then out to dinner at a nice restaurant. I even ordered flowers to be sent to the house, hoping to earn some brownie points with her. I thought maybe I could get her to stay and be a wife to me instead of jetting all over the world."

Mark leaned back in his chair, remembering that day and the conversation Susan and he had had.

"Mark, are you okay?" Rebecca asked.

"Yes, I was just remembering that day. I had my schedule cleared for that afternoon, came home early, and got ready to take her out. I had left a note on her dressing table about the plans I had made, so I assumed everything was a go since she hadn't called. When I came out of the bedroom, she was coming out from her room, all dressed up. I was thinking she was going with me. But when I walked over to her, she just brushed by me without saying a word. I asked her where she was going, and she looked me straight in the eye and said, 'Anywhere you're not going.' When I asked her if she was going to New York with me, she broke into a big laugh and asked if I really thought she would go anywhere with me. She informed me that she would rather go out alone than be seen in public with me. Then she went back into her room, picked up the flowers I had sent to her, and beat them over the stair rail and walls, saying, 'This is what I think of you! Do you understand?' She left in her car to go meet her lover. About an hour later, a police officer came to the house to tell us that Susan had been in a car wreck. Her car had gone under a tractor-trailer rig, and any part of her body that wasn't severed had been crushed. I never really grieved the loss of Susan. For one, she was very seldom home, and when she was we always argued over something. We weren't happy, and the truth is that we were only husband and wife for about a month after we married."

"I know you said you didn't want to be the first in the family to get a divorce, but how did you tolerate all this?" Rebecca asked. "Did you have your own lady friends?"

"I kept thinking she would get it all out of her system and settle down. No, I never had any lady friends on the side. Had plenty of opportunities, but I couldn't do to her what she was doing to me.

It was so hard, but I had Mom and Mary always telling me that, whatever I did, I should not take a woman out because, if Susan found out, she would use it against me and possibly try to slander my career. I worked all hours, even went to law school at night, thinking it would help me understand a few things about the law in the medical field. I had plenty of time on my hands, so why not?"

"Do you like being an attorney better than a doctor?"

"At first, I thought I did, but being a doctor is more rewarding," Mark answered. "I cut back on my days in the medical field and started spending more time in the law office with Joe Lewis. Then Bruce Stafford, who is a patient of mine, started talking to me about running for state senate. He hooked me up with certain people who would be helpful to me, and that's how I met Clay Fields, the guy you think is such a dunce."

"Oh, he is in my book," Rebecca scoffed. "Do you know him well?"

"No. Bruce introduced us; his family has known Clay and Lena for years. As you know, Lacey and Clay know each other quite well. Anyway, that's where I am at the present. I'm not comfortable with running for state senate. The I more I got into it, the more I realized the job is not for me."

"Have you told Bruce this?"

"No, not yet. He and Molly have been out of town, and this isn't something you discuss over the phone. When Bruce first approached me, I was very hesitant, but he kept saying this would be good for me and I would be good for the people. He had me going to different places to talk to people -for lack of a better term—to *groom* me and prepare me. At first, this seemed like the right thing to do." He paused and took a deep breath. "Now, you know all about me. Do you think I'm such a bad guy after all?"

"Mark, I never said you were a bad guy," Rebecca said. "I said it was wrong to be engaged to one person and kissing another. I had no idea she was lying the whole time."

"So does that mean that, if I tried to kiss you again, you would let me?"

"I'm not committing myself to anything,." Rebecca said blushing.

"But there is still a possibility for a kiss, especially if we are not at the house where you can get your hands on that brass candlestick of Mother's," Mark joked.

"Sorry about that, but both times you came in unannounced, and I was scared. The candlestick was the first thing I came across that looked like it could be used as a weapon. Just for the record, always make sure that Irene, Mary, and I know when you are going to be coming in at an odd hour of the night."

"You mean, 'let *you* know,' for you're the only one who goes for a weapon."

"Like I said, for your own safety, it would be wise of you to let us know. Besides, I have no desire to be responsible for your death due to your negligence."

"So, no matter what, it's going to be my fault?"

"Sounds good to me," Rebecca replied with a smirk.

Mark laughed. "Okay, now, you have never really talked much about your past. So what all has been going on in your life?"

"I can assure you that my life does not have a Lacey in it, or at least it didn't till I met Clay Fields. I do apologize for treating you so badly, although Lacey certainly pulled one over on me. Will you forgive me?"

"Yes, I will. Shall we start over and be friends instead of enemies?" Mark asked.

"That I will agree to. Now, not to be rude, but if you will excuse me, I really would like to go home sometime tonight, but until this filing is finished, I'm not going anywhere."

"Can I be of help to you since I'm the reason your work isn't finished?"

"Thanks," Rebecca said, "but only one person can work in the filing cabinet at a time."

"Mind if I wait on you? Then maybe we could go to dinner somewhere."

"Oh, you don't have to wait on me. I do appreciate the offer though."

"Are you afraid of being seen out with me?" Mark asked sincerely.

Surprised, Rebecca answered, "No. Why would you think that?"

"Good. Then I'll call and make reservations while you file. I'll relax while you work."

"Suit yourself."

Rebecca had really wanted to go home, but since they had gotten off to a bad start and he was Irene's son, she felt she at least needed to try to mend their relationship.

About an hour later, she said, "Okay, it's all finished. What time did you make reservations for?"

"Seven o'clock, so you finished in time," he replied. "Would you like to ride with me? I can bring you back here to pick up your car after dinner. It's on the way."

Rebecca thought for a minute and said, "Sure. It would make more sense to take one car."

After turning everything off and locking up, they went out to Mark's car. When Mark started to open the car door for Rebecca, he leaned over and kissed her. Then he took her in his arms and kissed her again. As much as Rebecca hated to admit it, being in Mark's arms with him kissing her made her feel so alive. She could feel herself sinking into his arms.

He pulled back and looked at her. "This is the way it should have been the first time I kissed you. I have wanted to hold you in my arms so many times. We are definitely off to a better start this time." Taking her in his arms again, he kissed her with more passion than before.

Dinner went much better than Rebecca had expected. Mark was so easy to talk to; he had a way of holding her attention. She thought back to the night he had given his acceptance speech. He had very seldom looked at his notes, and his voiced flowed so easily.

She was so grateful he didn't bring up her past during dinner. She had avoided the question earlier at the office and still did not want to talk about it. She realized they both had been through some very hard times.

Eighteen

ON FRIDAY MORNING, LYNN AND REBECCA WERE BUSY GETTING everything ready for the employee luncheon. They had put up decorations, making the cafeteria area more appealing and hopefully more enjoyable. The food came, and soon everything was all set. When the first group of employees came in, they were so surprised.

"Ms. Rebecca, this room does not look like the same room!" Emma exclaimed. "This is so nice. Thank you for doing this for us."

"You are most welcome, Emma. I'm glad everyone likes it," Rebecca replied. "I can't take all the credit. Lynn did a lot of this. I feel more like her helper. By the way, how are things with Rachel?"

"Oh, she is a totally different person," Emma said. "None of us knows what has happened to her, but it's a big change. She changed when Sarah had the big birthday party and they got to move into the house. That was the beginning, but this past week, it's like she has blossomed. She's so much more outgoing, and she smiles a lot, a big difference in her. She's no longer the poor-pitiful-me person."

"That's wonderful news. She just needed a little help to pull her out of her shell. That will help Sarah too."

"Don't mean to interrupt," another employee said, "but, Ms. Rebecca, you have done wonders here today!"

"Why, thank you, Tom. I was just explaining to Emma that Lynn did the bulk of it. I approached her with the idea, and she took off with it. She is truly my right hand."

While everyone was eating and having a good time, Rebecca took the microphone.

"May I have everyone's attention? So glad to see everyone enjoying themselves, but we have a few announcements to make. You can eat while I talk. First, be sure you let Lynn know how much you have enjoyed today, for she is the one who put the bulk of this all together. If you would, let's give her a big round of applause." She paused for everyone to clap. "Now what I am getting ready to tell you, please don't go out on the floor and share with those who have not eaten yet. We don't want to spoil their surprise. Lynn and I have done a little decorating in this room, and everyone has been so very pleased with it. A little sprucing up helps. Well, while I have been here, although you may not realize it, I have listened to comments you have made. To some it was just a comment; to others it was a big deal. I took those comments and put some things together. Starting December 1, we are going to be breaking ground to add on to McKay's. You are going to see a lot of construction going on around here, but in the long run, it is going to be worth it. That is all I will tell you for now. Come Christmas, I will share more information on what you can expect. You are going to be so surprised and happy. Also, today when you leave to go home, we will be passing out hams to everyone at the door. Enjoy your lunch, and may all of you have a wonderful and blessed Thanksgiving."

Everyone began talking, trying to figure out what was going to be under construction. A lot of questions were asked, but no one knew the answers.

When the last shift of employees had eaten, Rebecca and Lynn were worn out. They had very little food left over, so Rebecca gave it to Lynn to take home so she wouldn't have to cook that night.

"You know, Lynn, for a little while, I was so afraid we were going to run out of food," Rebecca commented. "We need to make Christmas a little more special and increase the amount of food available. Those men can really eat."

"Did you notice that some of the women didn't do so bad

themselves? I think tonight would be a good night to take one of those long, soothing baths."

"Not a bad idea. I have some lavender salts I could sprinkle in my bath. I'm ready to go home now, thanks to you. My lavender salts are calling my name."

As soon as everyone had left, Lynn and Rebecca closed the office, thankful that the next week was only a three-day workweek.

"Rebecca, is that you?" Mary called from the kitchen when Rebecca walked in.

"Yes, Mary. How are things going with Irene?"

"She wants to see you. All she has talked about is the Thanksgiving party at the company. She is so upset that she had to miss it. She is in the den."

Rebecca thanked Mary and then went to the den. "Irene, I understand you want to see me."

"Oh, Rebecca, please sit down and tell me all about today. How did it go?"

"It went well," Rebecca began. "We took pictures before and during the luncheon. In the announcement, I only told them we were adding on to McKay's and that, at our Christmas get-together, I would fill them in a little more about what was going to be taking place. Lynn pointed out that, if I told them everything now, I would have a hard time topping it at Christmas, so I decided to give out a little information at a time."

"That was a smart idea," Irene agreed. "What are your plans for Christmas?"

"Well, we haven't gotten that far yet. We just had Thanksgiving. Here's my phone—you can look at the pictures on there. I'm going to take a nice long, hot, lavender bath."

"Go right ahead, dear. I'm sure you have earned it."

Rebecca made her way to her room to relax.

A few minutes later, Irene heard the door open again. "Mark, is that you?" she called. "Come in here for a minute and look at the pictures Rebecca took at the company party today. Those people just love her."

"Where is she?" he asked.

"Oh, she went to take a long, hot bath. She was worn out. Sometimes I think she puts in too many hours at work. Do you know she still hasn't hired anyone to fill Charlotte's position? She's doing that job plus everything else. She is the CEO; she should delegate more of the work."

"Why won't she hire someone?" Mark asked.

"I think she is still finding things Charlotte either didn't do or messed up. She says she will start interviewing when the time is right."

"Can I borrow Rebecca's phone for a minute?"

"What are you up to?" Irene asked.

"Let's do a selfie and some individual shots. That way, the next time she goes to look at her pictures, she will have plenty of photos of us."

"Mark, you have a mean streak in you. What do you think she is going to say when she finds out?"

"Hopefully, we won't be around!" Mark said with a laugh.

They had just sat down to dinner when Rebecca's phone rang. She answered it without even noticing that the wallpaper picture on her phone had been changed. It was Rachel.

"Ms. Rebecca, I hate to bother you and want you to know how much we appreciate the ham you gave us today, but I have never cooked a ham before and don't know what to do."

As Rebecca tried to give her instruction, Irene picked up on what they were talking about.

"Rebecca, my dear, ask Rachel if she and Sarah would like to come over and have Thanksgiving lunch with us. Tell her to bring the ham, and Mary can work with her on it so they can have ham to eat next week."

Rebecca passed on the message and added, "We will have plenty to eat and would enjoy the company."

"Oh, I didn't call to get invited over!" Rachel exclaimed. "I just need some help with the ham."

"Rachel, if Mrs. McKay invites you and Sarah over, then you need to come," Rebecca said with a laugh. "We will see you both on Thursday for lunch." She ended the call and set her phone down. "Irene, that was very kind of you to want to include them next Thursday. They will be here."

"Well, I had a motive for wanting them to come. Bruce, Molly, and Lacey will be here also."

"Really," Rebecca said, unamused. "Think I'll call Rachel back and tell her I will come to her house, and we will cook there."

Mark piped up. "Do you mind if I go with you?" They laughed.

"Mark, you are not going anywhere, and neither are you, Rebecca," Irene ordered. "If I must sit through Lacey being here, so can you two."

"Fine, Mother, but I will let them know at work that, if they need a doctor, I will be available."

"You had better be here," Irene replied. "We can't entertain all three of them. You can at least talk to Bruce."

"I would rather not—not on Thanksgiving Day, anyway."

"What do you mean?"

"I'll explain later," Mark said.

"I would help you both out," Rebecca spoke up, "but Rachel and Sarah will be here, so I'll be tied up with them. Maybe Mary could help you out. She can handle Lacey."

"See, Mother? Problem solved. Thanks, Rebecca."

"No, the problem is *not* solved," Irene persisted. "Mark, I expect you to be here. I would hate to have to put this boot to good use."

"That's it!" Mark exclaimed. "Use the boot on Lacey. It certainly can't hurt, and it just might do a little good."

At that, everyone broke out laughing.

That night after Rebecca got ready for bed, she opened her phone to set the alarm for the next morning. What was Mark's picture doing on her phone? Then she looked at all of her pictures. There were shots of Mark, Irene, Mary, and Sammy. Then she noticed some others of Tilley, Mark's horse, and Fairlight. Yes, Mark had had her phone. Who else would take a picture of that brass candlestick? But how had he gotten it? She shrugged and lay down to finally go to sleep.

"Good morning, Rebecca. Are you feeling rested after a good night's sleep?" Mary asked when Rebecca walked into the kitchen.

"Yes, the bath helped relax me, and when I lay down, I was out like a light."

"I meant to tell you," Mary added, "the pictures you took yesterday at the company luncheon were so good. Everyone was smiling and seemed to be having a good time."

"I do think they enjoyed themselves. I think I'm going to go for a ride this morning. It is such a beautiful day. Better enjoy it while the weather is nice." She left the house and headed for the stables.

As Sammy was saddling up Fairlight, it dawned on Rebecca that she hadn't shown the pictures to Mary. *So how did she know about them?* she wondered.

"Sammy, did Mark come out here yesterday and take some pictures?"

"Now, Ms. Rebecca, you know I love this family, and there are some things I just can't talk about," Sammy replied.

"I totally understand, Sammy, and I'm sorry. I should have known not to ask a question like that. I need to go back in the house for something. I'll be right back." She walked quickly back to the house and found Mary again.

"Mary, you said you saw the pictures of the luncheon yesterday," Rebecca began. "Who showed them to you?"

"Mark did. He was going around taking pictures and showed me the ones of the luncheon. Why?"

"Would you help me with something?"

"If I can," Mary replied. "What can I do?"

"This is my phone that Mark used yesterday," she said, holding out her phone for Mary to see. "Here are the pictures he took, and he even changed the wallpaper. On Thanksgiving Day, can you help me get his phone? I'm going to take pictures of Lacey and fill his phone up good."

Mary laughed. "Girl, you are out to have some fun! But when he finds out those pictures are on his phone, I wouldn't want to be you. I'll do what I can to help you."

"Thanks, Mary. I think it's only fair to pay him back, especially with his favorite person."

Thanksgiving Day was going to be a busy, and fun day. If only Lacey were not coming. Her very presence put a lot of stress on everyone. That's just how things are when she is around.

Rachel and Sarah arrived around ten thirty, and Sarah and Mark hit it off right away. It seemed that they had been friends forever, but Sarah was one of those who had a lovable personality and made friends so easily. At noon, Bruce, Molly, and Lacey came. Tension was on the rise as soon as Lacey walked in. Mary, true to her word, was able to get Mark's phone for Rebecca and handed it to her. As they went in to sit down for lunch, Lacey went over to Mark and took his arm.

"Are you Mark's girlfriend?" Sarah asked.

"No, she's not," Mark answered. "*You* are my girlfriend. Can I have the pleasure of sitting beside you at lunch?"

"Yes, you may," Sarah replied. "Where will Mommy sit?"

Lacey spoke up. "She can sit next to Rebecca. Mark has two sides. You can sit on one side, and I'll sit on the other. We can share him."

"So, you *are* Mark's girlfriend?" Sarah asked again.

Mark said, "Everyone here is our friend." Then he added quietly, "Some more special than others."

Mary came in with a big platter of turkey and ham to put on the table. "Well said, Mark," she commented.

"Irene, what in the world happen to your foot?" Molly asked.

"Oh, I had a little fall, but to hear Mark and the others tell it, I nearly lost my leg. They won't let me do anything, and I must wear this lovely boot for six weeks. Rebecca went and bought me this skirt, hoping to cover the thing up a little."

"With the way you were sitting, I didn't notice it till you stood up and started walking," Molly said. "Don't feel bad. I had to wear one once. It was a royal pain. We were in Hawaii on vacation, and I fell the first day there. Couldn't go swimming or do hardly anything. Bruce finally rented a motorized wheelchair for me to get around in. At least you are home and not on vacation. They said I could use crutches, but that wasn't going to happen. I would end up in a body bag before it was all over, and no telling how many people around me would be injured."

"I appreciate that, Molly," Irene said. "I have griped and complained ever since they put this thing on me. How did you fall in Hawaii?"

"Coming down some steps. I apparently missed a step and fell down the last three or four. I pulled some ligaments in my foot and ankle, and putting weight on it was so painful. I don't know why it had to be at the beginning of our vacation and not at the end."

"That's exactly what I did. I pulled the ligaments in my foot and ankle. Did it take the full six weeks for it to heal?"

"For me it did, but then I really didn't do what I was supposed to do. Bruce fussed at me all the time. Take my advice and do what the doctor says, and you might get out of it sooner."

Irene glanced over at Mark but never said a word.

Soon everyone was seated, and Lacey made sure her chair was as close to Mark's as possible. After the blessing, Bruce started in on politics. This gave Rebecca the perfect opportunity to snap a few pictures without Mark's noticing. As soon as lunch was over, Sarah wanted to play some board games.

Lacey walked over to Mark," since Rebecca and Sarah are going to play games, why don't we go for a walk?"

"Sorry, Lacey, but I'm going to play board games with the gals," Mark answered.

"Mark, that's for kids and so boring. We could go for a walk and maybe do some fun adult things."

"Sorry, but I made Sarah a promise."

Lacey turned and went into the kitchen, where she found Mary and Rachel with their heads together.

"What are you two doing?" she asked.

"I'm showing Rachel how to fix a ham and make other dishes," Mary answered. "Care to watch? We might even let you do some cooking."

"No, thank you," Lacey snipped. "That's what servants are for."

With nothing else to do, Lacey went into the living room to see what the others were doing. She took a seat near Molly, Bruce, and Irene, but she was bored to death. She could hear Mark, Rebecca, and Sarah laughing over some silly game. For the life of her, she couldn't figure out what enjoyment they got from them. Finally, Clay texted her. She told the others she was going for a walk since it was such a beautiful day. Instead, she walked down to the end of the driveway, where Clay picked her up. Later, she texted Molly to let her know she was out with friends and would be home later.

Bruce and Molly left about two. Sarah didn't want to go home then because she was happy playing games and having fun. Finally, about five, Rachel and Sarah left. The house phone rang, and it was for Mark. One of his patients was sick, and the hospital needed him to come in. He left to take care of it.

The next morning, Rachel dropped Sarah off with Rebecca so she could go shopping and get some Black Friday deals. Rebecca had told her to bring Sarah over so they could do some fun things while she did her Christmas shopping. While the two were playing games, Mark came in.

"Mr. Mark, do you want to play games with Ms. Rebecca and me?" Sarah asked hopefully.

"Not right now, but I do need to borrow Rebecca for a few minutes. She won't be long."

"Oh, Mark, I'm sure it can wait," Rebecca said. "Sarah doesn't get to come over very often, and we need to make the best of this time."

"Does that mean you can play games with us then?" Sarah asked.

Mark thought a minute and said, "I have a better idea. How would you like to go ride a horse?"

"I've never ridden a horse before!" Sarah said excitedly.

"Then let me change clothes, and we will go out back and let you pet one, maybe even sit on one to see how you like it."

"Can Ms. Rebecca come with us?"

"Sure. I'll be right back," Mark said.

"Are the horses really big, Ms. Rebecca?"

"Some are of good size. What you need to start out with is a pony, something more your size."

A minute or two later, Mark came back in. "Okay, are you ladies ready?" he asked.

"How big are the horses?" Sarah asked. "Do they bite?"

"Come on out to the barn and tell me what you think," Mark said. "We have one that we call Tilley; that's my horse. The other one's name is Fairlight, and that one is Rebecca's."

Holding on to Rebecca's hand, Sarah just wasn't sure about horses. As they walked into the barn, Sammy came out. "Hello! Now who is this little darling?"

"My name is Sarah. What's your name?"

"Everybody calls me Sammy. It's nice to meet you, Ms. Sarah. I bet you want to see the horses."

"Only if Ms. Rebecca is with me," Sarah said.

"Sammy, would you mind bringing Fairlight up for Sarah to pet", Rebecca asked?

When Sammy brought Fairlight over to see Sarah, she gasped and grabbed hold of Rebecca's hand. "She is so big!" Sarah said.

Rebecca went over and started petting Fairlight. "Here, would you like to feed her a sugar cube?" she asked.

Slowly, Sarah took the sugar cube and held it up to the horse.

"Just lay it in the palm of your hand and let her lick it up," Rebecca trying to encouraged her. "Don't pull away. Just open your hand and she will take it."

Carefully, Sarah walked up to Fairlight with her hand open. When Fairlight bent down to take the sugar cube, Sarah gasped, afraid to move.

"She didn't hurt me! It tickled my hand," Sarah exclaimed.

Reaching up, Sarah started to pet her. Mark picked her up so she could rub the horse's back. After a few minutes, he sat Sarah on the horse. She held onto Mark's arm, unsure if she was safe. Sammy took the reins and led Fairlight around the barn while Mark walked alongside, holding onto Sarah.

"You are doing such a great job, Sarah," Mark said. "How would you like for Sammy to put a saddle on her so you and Rebecca can ride together?"

Sarah looked at Rebecca and said, "That would be good."

Sammy saddled up both horses, and soon they were riding around slowly in the fields.

"Ms. Rebecca, this is fun," Sarah said. "We are so high up."

"Anytime you want to go riding, you and your mom can come over and Sammy will fix you up," Mark said. "But make sure Rebecca or I are here to ride with you."

"This is so fun. I can't wait to tell Mama about this. Thank you, Mr. Mark. This is as much fun as playing games."

Rachel called about four o'clock to say that she was heading home to unload her car, then she would come pick up Sarah. Rebecca told her she would bring Sarah home and that she would stop and pick up something for dinner.

After taking Sarah home, Rebecca got home about seven. As she started to her room, Mark walked up and said, "Now that you're home and alone, you have some explaining to do. I know I put pictures on your phone as a joke, but the pictures you put on mine—they were not a joke. Of all people, why would you put Lacey's picture on my phone? You know how I feel about her!"

"It was mean of me, but I did do it as a joke," Rebecca said, smiling. "She is head over heels in love with you, and I'm sorry you ended up sitting by her at Thanksgiving lunch."

"You know when she left to go for a walk? Well, she walked down to the end of the driveway, only to be picked up by Clay," Mark said.

"How do you know that?"

"Sammy was coming home from one of his friends' house and saw her get in the car with Clay. That woman has one thing on her mind, and she doesn't care if anyone gets hurt." He paused for a moment. "Lena went to visit her family for the week, so I'm sure Clay took Lacey back to his house."

"I'm sorry, Mark. I do know how much you detest her, but honestly, I did it as a joke."

"Well, to make it up to me, it will cost you a kiss, and I would like to collect it now."

Rebecca leaned over and kissed him on the cheek.

"No, no, that's not a kiss. I had a kiss like *this* in mind." He took Rebecca in his arms and gave her a kiss that caused her heart to race, and her body felt like it was going to melt.

Mary came around the corner and saw the two embraced. Slowly, she backed up so as not to be seen. She thought, *Yes! Just maybe those two will start dating.* She wanted very much to tell Irene, but she thought she had better wait to see just where things were going with them. She couldn't think of anyone better for Mark than Rebecca.

Nineteen

REBECCA WAS LOOKING OVER HER CALENDAR FOR THE MONTH OF December. It was going to be a busy month—construction starting, party planning, parties to go to, Christmas shopping, decorations to put out, plus everyday duties at work. Rebecca was so grateful for Lynn and her willingness to help; she really needed to do something special for her.

"Morning, Ms. Rebecca," Lynn said when she entered. "Are you ready for this hectic month?"

"Morning, Lynn. I was just looking over the calendar and all this month holds. As you know, I'm going to need your help to make it through all this. In fact, I think there need to be two of each of us."

"I'm here to do whatever needs to be done," Lynn said. "If I need to work late or come in early, just let me know."

"I don't want to take advantage of your willingness. You have a life outside of this office."

"Actually, I knew this was going to be a busy month, so this weekend, I got most of my shopping done, plus my tree and decorations are all up at home."

"My goodness!" Rebecca said. "You had a busy weekend. I would say you needed to come back to work to rest, but with all we must do here, that's not going to happen."

Lynn laughed. "So, where do we start? On my way to work this morning, I was wondering what you have in mind for the company

155

Christmas party. Also, if my memory is correct, the decorations we have here are in bad shape. Mrs. McKay was sick last year from October thru January, so we just used what we had and didn't say anything. When she was able to come into the office, she felt so bad that I don't think she even noticed what was decorated and what wasn't."

"Okay, tonight after work, I'll go shopping for decorations," Rebecca said. "I'll walk through and make a list of things we need. And if you can think of anything that needs replacing, write it down."

"Tony is out of town this week," Lynn said, "so if it's okay, I'll stay over tomorrow night and start decorating."

"He's out of town a lot. Are you ever able to go with him?"

"I could, but while he's at work, I would be by myself all day," Lynn said. "Sometimes he has late meetings, and I would just as soon be at home. I keep hoping he will have to go to New York for a meeting, but so far that's not happened."

"Why do you want to go to New York?" Rebecca asked.

"I've never been, and since we don't have any children yet, I thought it would be nice to go. It's on my bucket list. So is Niagara Falls."

"With as much as Tony travels, does he mind going on a vacation or taking a trip?"

"No, when we go away like that, he has two phones, a work phone and his personal phone. He leaves his work phone and laptop at work. He needs the break, and he told them that. Even if we don't go anywhere and stay home, he won't bring them home."

"That's good. Irene has an office set up at home, so when I'm not here, I can still work from there. It has its good points and bad." Rebecca paused a moment. "Okay, let's put our heads together and see what all we can come up with. Tomorrow, don't wear anything nice. Come dressed very casually since we will be decorating."

The next day, Rebecca arrived with many decorations. Sammy

had come with her to the office to bring some trees that she had bought to decorate.

"Rebecca, did you buy out the store? Oh my, we are going to have fun tonight putting this all together."

"I took pictures of different areas and shopped according to what I thought would work," Rebecca said. "I felt like a kid in a candy store. Also, Sammy will be coming by tonight to bring us dinner. Mary is making some homemade soup and said she would send him over with some."

After everyone was gone for the day, Lynn and Rebecca started on the decorations. They didn't notice that anyone had come in till they heard someone say, "It's looking good." Both Lynn and Rebecca nearly jumped out of their skin.

"Mark! What are you doing here?" Rebecca asked.

"Mary sent you both some of her soup and a jug of tea. I didn't tiptoe in, just opened the door as usual. You two were so wrapped up in decorating that anyone could have walked in on you."

Rebecca looked at Mark and said, "I thought Sammy was coming over."

"He was going to, but I volunteered to bring it and thought you might need someone with muscles."

Lynn chuckled. "Are you saying, Mr. McKay, that Rebecca and I are not strong enough to handle putting up decorations?"

"No, of course that's not what I meant," he backtracked. "Besides, an extra set of arms can come in handy at times."

"Okay," Rebecca began, "while Lynn and I take a dinner break, you can finish up this room. We will be back in about thirty minutes." They left to enjoy their dinner.

Looking at all the decorations laying around, Mark had no idea where to start, but he had to do something, even if it was wrong. When the women came back, they looked at what Mark had done.

"Not bad," Lynn remarked. "Do you help Irene put up Christmas decorations at home?"

"No, she and Mary do all that. Sometimes they get Sammy to help. Is it that bad?"

Rebecca laughed. "No, but we were going to do it just a little differently."

"Ms. Rebecca, while you and Mr. McKay work on this room, I'm going to take these decorations and work in the break room. Maybe he could put the trees up for us before he leaves tonight."

"Would you mind doing that?" Rebecca asked Mark. "We have different sizes, and they all go in different areas."

"For you, my dear, I'll put the trees anywhere you like, but it will cost you," Mark said with a grin.

"Mark, we are at my office! How can you say that?"

"I'm just asking for a kiss. Besides, Lynn is in the break room. She will never know." Taking Rebecca in his arms before she could say anything, he kissed her. Just then, Lynn came in.

"Do you have any scissors? Oh! I'm sorry," she said, flustered. "I didn't mean to interrupt. I'll look someplace else."

Rebecca pushed away from Mark. "I should have stopped you," she said.

"But you didn't. Admit it, Rebecca. You enjoy our kissing as much as I do. Do you think I can't tell when we are kissing that you are enjoying it?"

Rebecca didn't answer. "No more kissing while I'm at work. Understand?"

"Then as soon as we are finished and go home, we can pick up where we left off."

"No, we don't need to be kissing at home either. Someone might see us."

"Why are you afraid of someone seeing us?" Mark asked. "Kissing is normal. Are you ashamed of us?"

"No, I just feel uneasy about kissing in public," Rebecca said.

"Excuse me, but in case you haven't noticed, we are not outside. We are in a building where only one other person is. And at home, what we do there is our business. I enjoy holding you in my arms. It feels so right."

Turning every shade of red, Rebecca was not sure what to say. Finally, she muttered, "We had better get these trees put together and decorations finished."

Finally, at one o'clock in the morning, they had everything done. As much as Rebecca hated to admit it, having Mark around had really helped.

After locking up, Mark walked to the car with Rebecca. "Want me to drive?"

"Where's your car?" she asked.

"I had Sammy drop me off so we could ride home together. Hope you don't mind."

"Here's the keys." Rebecca was so tired that she wasn't about to put up an argument. If fact, she was glad that Mark was driving. When they got home, he went around to help Rebecca out.

"You are so tired, Rebecca. Why don't you sleep in tomorrow?"

"Because Lynn is just as tired, and she will be there early in the morning."

Mark held her close to him and could feel her relaxing in his arms. He was falling in love with her, and he wondered if she felt the same way he did.

The next morning, Rebecca arrived at work expecting to see Lynn at her desk. It was very unusual for her not to be there for Rebecca was about twenty minutes late herself. Rebecca's cell phone rang, and it was Lynn.

"I'm so sorry I'm late," she said, panicky. "I overslept. I'll be there in about fifteen minutes."

"Lynn, don't rush," Rebecca said. "I just got here myself. If you feel anything like I do, you are dragging today, so just take your time."

"Okay, thanks, but I still can't believe this has happened!"

All the employees were so excited as they came into work. They couldn't believe how festive the outside and inside looked. It seemed to put everyone in the Christmas spirit.

As she was trying to stay awake, Rebecca's phone rang again.

"Rebecca, it's Phillip. Your evening gown is ready, and it will be shipped out today. It turned out beautiful, and I know you are going to enjoy wearing it. How is Mrs. McKay? She told me about her accident."

"Oh, Phillip, that is wonderful! Mrs. McKay is doing fine. But having to wear a boot during the holidays has really set her back. Thank you so much for asking about her. I'll let her know."

"If you need anything else, let me know," Phillip said. "In fact, I took the liberty of making another gown in case you decide you might need it. It's totally different from the last two, and I think you will fall in with love it. Just let me know. If you decide you don't need another one, it's no problem. With New Year's Eve just around the corner, the gown will certainly sell."

"Thank you, Phillip. To be honest I haven't even thought about New Year's Eve yet. I'll check with Mrs. McKay to find out what they normally do. All of this is so new to me."

"Totally understand," Phillip said, "but know you are taken care of in case you need another gown. You have a great day, and I hope to hear from you soon."

"Thanks, Phillip, and blessings to you."

As she hung up, Rebecca thought, *New Year's Eve. Hadn't even thought about going to a party, but I'm sure the McKays will either have one or go to one.* She needed to call Irene and find out what all was expected of her regarding the holidays. She dialed the number.

"Irene, good morning. How are you feeling today?"

"Rebecca, my dear, I was feeling very well till a few minutes ago," Irene said. "I got up out of bed and thought I could make it to the bathroom without that boot, but I hit my ankle on a chair as I was limping across the room. Now it's giving me a fit. Other than that, I'm okay, I think."

"Oh, no! You know that boot is to be on your foot even when

you sleep," Rebecca said. "I'm not going to fuss at you because the pain you are in speaks for itself. Now, my reason for calling—with December almost here, can you tell me what parties you feel like I need to go to? Do you host any parties at the house?"

"We used to host parties, but now we just go them," Irene said. "The Staffords always have a big Christmas Party and New Year's Eve party at their house. Of course, we always go. Then we usually have a small party for the company, and Mark always has a little party for his staff. The church puts on a small play on Sunday night before Christmas, the widows of the church have a little party, and different groups in the church have little get-togethers. I think that's all. Did you want to host a party here this year?"

"No, this is all new to me, and I wasn't sure what was expected of me. Thank you for your help, and do put the boot on. You know that if you reinjure it, you will have to face Mark."

"Don't remind me. He offered to help me up this morning before he left for work, and I wouldn't let him. Please don't say anything to him. His doctor speeches are not on my list of things I want to deal with today."

"I won't say a word. So Mark went in to work this morning?"

"Yes, he wasn't his usual peppy self. Must have had an emergency at the hospital last night that kept him up. Usually when he works late, one of the other doctors covers for him the next morning."

At the hospital, a nurse came to Mark's office door. "Dr. McKay, your patient is waiting on you. Did you forget?"

"Sorry, I'm a little tired today. Can't seem to get myself going."

"Hot date last night, doctor?" the nurse teased.

"No, not hardly, Paige. I was helping a friend last night and got home late. What is my schedule like today anyway?"

"You have a full schedule, and as of right now, you are behind. Your patients are sick and really need to keep their appointments. Would you like me to get you an energy drink? That might help."

"No, I'll get going," Mark replied, "but if anyone cancels, don't fill the opening. Be sure to pass that along to the reception desk."

"Dr. McKay, you've lost sleep before and worked just fine," the nurse said. "Are you coming down with something?"

"No, just a lot on my mind. I'll be fine. Now, which room do I need to go to first?"

Twenty

THE STAFFORDS' CHRISTMAS PARTY WAS ONE REBECCA REALLY wasn't looking forward to. She knew Lacey would be there, and there was a good chance Clay would be also.

"Rebecca, Ms. Irene is ready if you are," Mary said when she popped her head in. "Oh, my, your gown is so pretty. I love that burgundy color on you, and velvet is perfect for this time of year. I like the way it fits at the top, and it's so flowy at the bottom. The sleeves are so different. I don't think I have seen sleeves that come down to a point over your hand. But I do believe you could wear a sack and make it appealing. "

"Thank you, Mary," Rebecca replied. "Will I be driving, or will Sammy drive us?"

"You ladies are in luck. You will be chauffeured by the good doctor, Mark."

"I didn't realize he had made it home yet," Rebecca said.

"Oh, when he came in, he was in a dead run to shower and get dressed. He's ready and waiting on you ladies."

Rebecca walked out to find Irene talking to Mark. "Irene," she said, "did Phillip make your gown?"

"Yes, he did. He called to let me know he had spoken to you and wondered if I needed a gown. I told him about my lovely boot, and he promised to take care of everything. I really like the way he put this together. He knows I like jackets, but to put the gold, red, blue, and green together like he has is beautiful. The long black velvet skirt covers my boot, but I must remember to put my good foot forward. See, on this foot my shoe matches my gown. Phillip truly came through for us."

They all climbed into Mark's car and headed for the party.

Bruce and Molly greeted the guests as they came in, making everyone feel welcome. Irene soon found a group of her lady friends to talk to, and Mark went off into another area with some men. Rebecca found herself wandering around and walked into a room that was very different from the rest of the house. The room was filled with antiques, some Rebecca was familiar with and some she had no idea about.

"So, I see you found Mama's antique room?"

Rebecca spun around. "Hello, Lacey. Yes, this room is amazing. Where did Molly get all these things?"

"Oh, some are from her mother and some her grandmother. I don't know what she sees in these old things. I told her that, when she is gone, I will take them outside and burn them."

"Lacey, these things are rare and probably worth a lot of money. Surely you wouldn't want to get rid of them."

"My taste in homes, decorations, and men are much different than yours, Rebecca. I personally like the finer things in life."

"I like nice things too, but I don't think you realize the value of the things in this room. And you're right that your taste in men is different from mine. I don't go for men who are married, and I do believe you do. Now if you will excuse me." She walked toward the door.

"Rebecca, I believe you are the one who prefers the hired help, men with no class," Lacey shot back.

Rebecca stopped. "I look for love and men who are godly, but then you wouldn't know anything about that, would you." She left the room.

Rebecca went looking for Molly to talk to her about her antique room and hopefully lose Lacey. *Maybe she went looking for Clay,* she thought.

She saw Molly and approached her. "Molly, I just saw your antique room. It is just wonderful. Sometime, I would like to come over when you have some spare time and let you tell me all about that room. I could spend hours looking at all that you have."

"Oh, my dear, that's so kind of you," Molly replied. "As soon as the holidays are over, I will give you a call and you can come spend the day with me. When I get started talking about my antiques, I sometimes don't know when to hush. Lacey thinks they are ratty old things and wants nothing to do with them. I have quite a few things that were my mother's and grandmother's. I also have things that my great-grandmother used. Yes, I will certainly give you a call."

"I look forward to it. Don't mean to keep you from your other guests, but I'm so glad I happened upon your precious room. I better go check on Irene and see how she is doing."

"We have been talking, and she seems to be doing better with her boot, steadier than before," Molly said. "She was even telling the other ladies about her designer boot. When she found out I had gone through the same thing, it helped her. I know exactly how she feels. That boot is a royal pain, to say the least. We will talk soon, Rebecca, and I hope you are enjoying the party."

The room seemed more crowded than before. Irene was still chatting with her friends, so Rebecca thought she would look around some more. A door that was slightly open led to a patio, and she thought she would step outside for a few minutes. Just as she walked out onto the patio, Clay walked out behind her.

"Well, Rebecca, are you enjoying the party?"

"I was," she said dryly.

"Do you always have to be so short with me?" he asked. "Why do you not like me? I haven't done anything to you."

"As I told you before, you are a married man. That alone draws a line between us."

"If you would just lower that wall that you have built up, you might find I'm not such a bad guy after all. Lacey tells me you have a thing for Sammy, Ms. Irene's groundskeeper and whatever else he does. Honey, I have a lot more to offer than he does."

"That's a matter of opinion, Clay."

He walked closer to Rebecca. "Are you that desperate for a man?" he said quietly. "I bet Sammy had never been with a woman till you came along."

With that comment, Rebecca turned to slap Clay across the face, but he grabbed her arm.

"You make me sick," she spat out. "If you were the last person on earth, I still wouldn't want anything to do with you."

As she tried to pull away, Clay grabbed her arm even tighter. "Nobody tries to slap me and just walks away." He pulled her close to him, and she fought back. About that time, a strong arm pulled Clay back and shoved him. Clay lost his balance and hit the corner of a concrete bench. Rebecca turned to see Mark standing there.

"Clay, don't you ever touch Rebecca again," Mark growled. "Do I make myself clear? She will not be one of your little puppets. I know Lena is out of town. What's wrong with all your other so-called lady friends?"

The side of Clay's face was beginning to throb. When he reached up and touched his face, he realized he was bleeding.

"Mark, you are going to regret this. I have the power to make you big in politics. You will never make it on your own. I will see to that!"

"Apparently, Bruce hasn't told you?" Mark replied.

"Told me what?"

"Why don't you make yourself useful and go talk to Bruce," Mark said dismissively.

Clay gave Rebecca a harsh look and told her, "Your watchdog here won't always be around, if you know what I mean." He then turned to Mark. "By the way, you just wasted your time defending her. If you have thoughts of having her for yourself, you're too late. She hangs out in your barn with the stable boy and gets it on with him."

In two steps, Mark grabbed Clay's jacket with both hands. "As much as I would like to punch you in the nose, I'm not going to stoop to your level. I have no desire to have your blood on my hands. You are not worth losing my medical license or my testimony over," he said in his face. "I gave you fair warning about Rebecca. Keep your thoughts and comments to yourself also. You have no business saying things that are not true."

"That's how little you know," Clay scoffed. "Lacey told me what she saw, so apparently you don't know what goes on behind your back."

"Clay, you know Lacey. I can't believe you can be so naive as to listen to and repeat anything she says. By the way, your jaw is not broken. It just feels like it."

Trying to pull himself together, Clay headed toward the bathroom to clean himself up. Blood had gotten on his shirt and pants.

"Are you okay, Rebecca?" Mark asked.

"Yes, I'm fine. I'm so glad you came out when you did. Thank you. How did you know we were out here?"

"I saw you slip through the doors, and then in a few seconds, I saw Clay go out. Just to be on the safe side, I came over and looked out to make sure you were all right. That's when I saw Clay grab your arm. Are you sure he didn't hurt you?"

"No, I'm fine. I'm just so grateful you were here."

"Are you ready to go home, or would you rather stay a while longer?"

"It depends on Irene. I don't want to leave if she is not ready. She seems to be enjoying being with the other ladies."

"I'll go check on her and see what she says. Would you feel more comfortable coming with me, or will you be all right here by yourself?

"I think I'll go in but stay back while you talk to her."

Mark made his way over to his mother. "Excuse me, ladies," he said. "Don't mean to interrupt, but I wanted to check and see how my mother is doing."

"Oh, Mark, I was wondering where you had gone off to. I had Molly look for you, but she couldn't find you. If you and Rebecca are ready, I'm ready too."

"I'll have Rebecca come over to help you while I go get the car and bring it around front. Ladies, it's good to see you again, and I hope you have a Merry Christmas."

He motioned for Rebecca to come over, and then he went out to get the car. Once they were home, Rebecca helped Irene to her room.

"Did you have a good time tonight?" Rebecca asked her.

"Yes, dear, I did enjoy it. I didn't walk around very much because I didn't want to draw attention to my boot, but it was good to talk to my friends. We managed to catch up on all that has been happening. I hope you enjoyed yourself."

"I stumbled across Molly's antique room. It's amazing. She told me to come over after the holidays and she would give me a tour of the room and tell me about the things in it. Did you know Lacey dislikes the antiques?"

"Honey, that girl is so ungrateful for all she has," Irene said. "I know Molly must be heartbroken over the way Lacey is. Bruce and she deserve a child who's loving, kind, and appreciative."

"Irene, Lacey has the things of the world on her mind. She only wants the finer things in life, she says. She should count her blessings for what she has for there are so many people who would love to have one fourth of what she has." Rebecca shook her head. "Before I turn in, is there anything I can help you with?"

"No, dear, I'm going to change and go to bed. As much as I enjoyed this evening, I'm glad it's over. Hope you rest well, and I'll talk with you tomorrow."

The house lights were all out as Rebecca started toward her room. She figured Mark had already turned in, but just as she got to her door, he spoke.

"Mind if we talk for a few minutes?"

"What are you doing in the dark?" she asked. "You know what happens when I get spooked in the dark."

"You are not near the candlesticks, which is in my favor," he teased. "No, I wanted to talk to you about tonight."

"Did you get a chance to talk to Bruce about dropping out?"

"Yes, he understood, but he wasn't happy. But that's not what I wanted to talk about."

"Oh, about Clay?" she asked.

"No, about us. When I saw him grab your arm, I became furious. I couldn't get to you quick enough. I don't want anyone near you or to ever harm you. I have very strong feelings for you and am wondering where I stand. What are your feelings for me?"

Dropping her head, Rebecca wasn't sure if she was ready for this. Was she ready to make a commitment? She knew how she felt whenever Mark held her close to him or kissed her. Her heart felt like it was going to beat out of her chest.

Before she could say anything, Mark spoke. "I guess you don't feel the same way I do. I'm sorry if I have pushed myself on you. I will back off, Rebecca."

"Mark, don't. I do have feelings for you. I'm just afraid."

"What are you afraid of? Has someone in the past hurt you so badly that you're afraid to let someone in your heart? If so, I totally understand."

"Yes, but not in the way you're thinking," Rebecca said. "I really don't want to talk about it, at least not now. Mark, I'm grateful for what you did tonight. I knew then that your feelings for me were more than just friendly. Before, on that night when you helped Lynn and me with the decorations, I gave a lot of thought to what you said. I wondered how much you really cared for me, and tonight you showed me."

"Rebecca, you mean so much to me. Holding you in my arms and feeling you melt when I embrace you, I don't want to let you go. Let me hold you close. Let me feel the tenderness of your lips."

As Mark took her in his arms, Rebecca knew she loved him and didn't want to let him go. But she was afraid that if she let Mark into her heart, something would happen to him. She loved her parents deeply, Ray had been her world, and Mamie Clark was more than a wonderful mother-in-law—she had been her best friend and like a mother to her—yet God had taken them to heaven. She wasn't mad at God for all that had happened. But where was her faith? Should she take a chance on Mark? *Dear Lord, please guide me and show me what I need to do.*

Meanwhile, Irene had decided she needed a little snack and went into the kitchen to see what she could find. She heard voices and went to see who was talking. With the moonlight shining through the window, she could make out two people standing close together. Just as she realized who it was, she saw Mark kiss Rebecca. It was not a quick kiss, but one with passion. She knew there was something special between the two of them.

Twenty-one

Lynn had finalized all the details for the company Christmas party. She went over everything with Rebecca to make sure nothing had been overlooked, and they agreed it should be a big hit.

"Lynn, why don't you take tomorrow off from the office and make sure everything is on schedule at the clubhouse? The employees will be getting off an hour early to get ready for the party, so hopefully no one will feel rushed or stressed."

"That's great," Lynn said. "Thank you. I'm glad it's going to be casual. Everyone signed up and is bringing either their spouses or whoever they are dating. Rachel is coming with Emma and Frank because she didn't know anyone to bring."

"Who is watching Sarah for her?" Rebecca asked.

"You're not going to believe this, but Mark is watching Sarah. They are supposed to have a dinner date and see a movie, wherever Sarah wants to go. He seems to have really taken to that child."

"She is a lovable child. Rachel doesn't realize how lucky she is to have her. Even though they had basically nothing, she did teach Sarah manners, and she is always so polite. If you tell her that she can't have something or do something, Sarah just says, 'Okay' and goes on. If I ever have children, I pray they will be just like Sarah."

"Oh, I agree," Lynn said, "but with our luck, we wouldn't be so fortunate. Tony has told me a little about his childhood. He gave his parents a hard time, and I'm afraid ours would be like him."

The next day, Rebecca went through the plant talking to the employees, and everyone seemed excited about that night. So many told her they had never had anything like this before at McKay's, and they said they were glad it was casual and that it wasn't just for employees. Of course, some asked questions about the construction. The weather had been good, and the workers were moving right along. Rebecca asked them to wait just a little longer.

The night of the party came, and everything was going perfectly. After everyone had eaten, Rebecca got up to give a little talk.

"First, I want to thank everyone for coming out tonight. Hope you enjoyed your meal and fellowshipping with people you see every day but don't really get to talk to. Everyone has been asking about the construction. If you will all look to this wall, I will share some slides on what will be taking place. As we go through them, I will explain everything to you. Like I have said before, your comments have not been brushed aside. They were taken very seriously."

Rebecca explained each step in the project, and the last few slides, showing completion and how McKays would look when completd. Everyone was so excited. They couldn't believe what all she was having done for them. Adam Nelson and George Clure both stood to praise Rebecca for her great interest in the company. They said they had never worked for a boss who cared so much for her employees and treated them with the respect that she had.

When the night was coming to an end and people began leaving, Lynn made sure they each had a turkey to take home and reminded them that, when they received their pay checks, it would be a little bigger than usual. This was to help them make it through the company's shutdown over Christmas.

Mark and Sarah came in just as Rachel, Emma, and Tony were about to leave.

"Mama, Mr. Mark took me out to eat, and then we went to the

movies," Sarah told her. "We also got to go Christmas shopping, but I can't tell you what we bought. It's a surprise."

"Sounds like you had a good time tonight," Rachel said. "Did you thank Mr. Mark for a good evening?"

"Yes, I did. Mama, do you think Mr. Mark could be my daddy? I have so much fun with him, and I don't have a daddy like the other kids do."

Rachel paused for a moment. "Sarah, that's not possible, but when he has some time, you can go see him. He's a doctor and takes care of sick people, so he is really busy."

"He told me tonight that I can call him anytime," Sarah said. "He gave me his phone number."

"Yes, you can call him, but not every day," Rachel cautioned.

"Mr. Mark, thank you again for all we did tonight," Sarah said. "I had a great time. I really do like you. You're the best, even if you can't be my daddy."

"Sarah, you call anytime," Mark replied. "If I can't talk to you right then, I'll call you as soon as I can. Since we had so much fun tonight, we will have to go out again. Would you like that?"

"Yes, I would, Mr. Mark. When I go home tonight, I'm going to tell my angel doll all about tonight. She will help me with my wishes. Ms. Rebecca got her for me, and I talk to her a lot. She really understands."

Rachel cut in. "Sarah, tell everyone good night. It's getting late. You have probably talked Mr. Mark's ears off tonight." She turned to Rebecca. "Thank you for this evening, and I'm looking forward to our new building. It's all so exciting."

"Rachel, don't forget," Rebecca said, "you and Sarah are invited to come over on Christmas and spend the day with us."

"Mama, do we get to go over to their house on Christmas? That's going to be fun!"

Rebecca leaned down and took Sarah in her arms. "You don't have to come early. I know you will want to see and play with whatever Santa Claus brings you."

Sarah smiled. "That's okay. Santa always runs out of things by the time he comes to our house. Mama said that he tries to get to all the houses, but it doesn't always happen. So we can come over early if it's all right. Maybe I can help Ms. Mary again in the kitchen like I did at Thanksgiving."

"Well, now, Sarah, you have moved," Rebecca said, "and I bet this year, he will be able to make it to your house."

"Do you really think so?"

"I'm pretty sure. When you go to bed on Christmas Eve, be sure to put a glass of milk and some cookies in a dish for him. He likes that."

"Wow, I bet *that's* why he hasn't stopped. We never put anything out for him. Mama, did you hear? We must put out milk and cookies for Santa."

"Yes, Sarah, I heard. Don't worry, we won't forget. Now we really do need to go." Rachel held Sarah's hand as they walked to their car.

When everyone had left, Rebecca turned to Mark. "So, you had a big date tonight! I do believe you impressed her."

"It's not hard to impress Sarah," Mark said. "It did break my heart when she said Santa Claus never came to her house, that he ran out of toys by the time he got there. She seemed okay with it, though."

"Well, you must realize that Rachel and Sarah had very little," Rebecca replied. "The house they are living in now is just a modest little house, nothing fancy, but to them, it's a mansion. When Sarah gets something, she is so grateful and takes such good care of it."

Mark nodded. "Tonight, when we went shopping, I asked her if she would like to pick out a Christmas gift for her mama. Her response was, 'Is it very expensive? Could I afford it?' How many kids do you know who would ask a question like that?"

"She is one in a million," Rebecca agreed. "I hope Rachel makes her Christmas morning really special this year."

As they were leaving, Lynn came up to Rebecca. "You are the

best. I just opened the Christmas card you gave me. I don't know what to say."

"You don't have to say anything," Rebecca said. "You have earned your gift, and I hope you and Tony have a great time."

Mark asked, "What kind of gift did you get, Lynn? Must be a nice one by the look on your face."

"She gave us tickets to fly to New York! We get to stay four days. We will be there for New Year's Eve, and we also get to see a play. It's just wonderful. This is a dream come true. I can't wait to get home to tell Tony. Thank you again, Ms. Rebecca. I'm so happy and excited, I'm about to cry."

"Lynn, you are the best, and I didn't want you to think I was taking advantage of you. Enjoy, and when you come back, tell me all about it."

"Oh, I certainly will! Have a good night."

Twenty-two

ON CHRISTMAS MORNING, WHILE REBECCA WAS DOING HER morning devotions, her cell phone rang.

It was Sarah. "Ms. Rebecca, he came!" she exclaimed. "Santa came to our house last night! He didn't run out of toys this year. He brought me a bicycle. It's so pretty! Mama said she would teach me how to ride it. He left some games and a doll and dollhouse."

"Sarah, that's wonderful!" Rebecca replied. "I had a feeling he would come this year. You have some presents under our tree too, so you and your mom come whenever you want. And thank you for calling and telling me your good news. I'll let the others know."

Saying a pray of thanks, Rebecca felt tears roll down her cheeks. Sarah reminded her of the children in the camps on her mission trips, so thankful for anything they could get.

By ten o'clock, Rachel and Sarah were knocking on the door. Sarah was so excited as she came in, telling everyone what she had under her tree that morning. They had brought gifts for everyone, and she had to call out the names as she placed them under the tree very carefully. Finally, Sammy came in, and they decided it was time to open the gifts.

Mark said, "Sarah, I was not able to wrap my gift to you. It was just too big."

Everyone looked at Mark, not knowing what he was talking about—except Sammy.

"I'm going to put this blindfold on you and take you outside, okay?" Mark said. When it's time, I'll take the blindfold off."

Everyone followed Mark and Sarah, eager to see what the gift was. Once they were outside, Mark took off the blindfold, and Sarah gasped.

"Is it mine?" Sarah squealed. She ran over to the pony and gave it a big hug. It was a Shetland pony. "What's her name?"

"She doesn't have one yet," Mark answered. "You have to decide what name to give her."

"I'm going to call her Beauty because she is beautiful. Sammy, where is Beauty going to live?"

"She is going to live right here with Tilley and Fairlight," Sammy answered. "I'll take good care of her, and when you come over, you can take her for a ride and then help brush and feed her."

"I'm so glad she won't be alone," Sarah said. "She will have a daddy and mama to look out for her. Can I brush her now or feed her?"

Sarah didn't want to eat lunch when everyone else went in to eat. All she wanted to do was stay with Beauty. Rebecca went out to the barn later to check on her, to see how it was going.

"Sarah, I do believe you like your gift from Mr. Mark," she said.

"Oh, I do. Last night, I held my angel doll real close to me and asked her if Santa Claus could come by my house. I asked if I could have just one present; it didn't matter what. She heard my prayer, Ms. Rebecca. My angel doll heard me. She gave me so many presents."

"It was your prayer and your faith, Sarah. God heard you and knew what was in your heart."

"My angel doll listens to what I say to her and takes it to Jesus," Sarah said. "In church, my teacher said we all have an angel to watch over us. She is right. When we go to church on Sunday, I'm going to tell her about my angel doll."

Rebecca knew that, in time, Sarah would come to see that she was talking to Jesus herself, not the angel doll. Sarah had faith, strong faith.

Rachel called to Sarah, "It's time to go home."

"Mama, I just want to spend a little more time with Beauty," Sarah protested. "She might miss me when we leave."

"She will be fine," Rachel said. "Sammy will be with her, and so will the other horses. You can come back again soon to see her, I promise."

Sarah hugged Beauty one more time, and as she walked away, she kept waving, saying, "I'll be back, Beauty."

Rachel said, "Mr. Mark, I'm sorry we have stayed so late. Sarah is really taken with Beauty."

"You are fine, Rachel, and anytime Sarah wants to come over, give Sammy a call to let him know you're coming. I had no idea she would be so excited over the pony when I got it. I have loaded all your gifts in the car for you. We certainly have enjoyed you two today, and I'm sure we will be seeing you both very soon."

"Thanks, Mr. Mark."

"Bye, Mr. Mark," Sarah said. "Don't forget to check on Beauty for me."

As Mark walked into the house, Rebecca looked at him and smiled.

"Well, you made one little girl very happy this Christmas. After seeing the pony, she completely forgot her other gifts. She is always smiling, but today, her smile said it all."

Mark looked at the Christmas tree and said, "I had no idea she would take to the pony the way she did. But that little girl deserves to have a very special Christmas, and I do believe she had it this year. Look at all the years her birthday and Christmas went by and she got nothing, yet she never complained."

"I know exactly what you mean," Rebecca said. "It's so easy to want to spoil her, and she is so appreciative of whatever she gets. You can't help but love her."

"Have you ever wanted children of your own?" Mark asked.

"The thought has crossed my mind, and if that day should

come, I would want a child just like Sarah. Maybe someday God will grant me that blessing. If not, I'll just spoil Sarah. How about you?"

"There was a time I had thought it would be nice to have children, but with Susan's lifestyle, I soon changed my mind." He thought for a moment. "Oh, by the way, thank you for the briefcase. You must have seen the one I had been carrying."

"Yes, it did look like it needed to be replaced. And thank you for the earrings. You spent way too much on them, I'm sure."

"I noticed you never wore diamond earrings, so I thought it would be safe to get you a pair. They look very nice on you. Why don't we go raid the kitchen? I'm sure Mary has something unhealthy to snack on."

With Mark so close to her, Rebecca knew her feelings for him were growing stronger. He was so thoughtful and caring. What was not to like about him? Like Sarah, he was easy to care about and to love. Yes, she loved him, but was she ready to admit it to him? Where was her faith? What was it the Bible said in Matthew 8:26? "Oh ye of little faith, why are you so afraid?" She had faith, but was it enough? Why was she not able to be upfront with Mark? Maybe the problem was that she had never told him about her past. He had been upfront with her; she needed to do the same. She had to be honest with him and not keep things from him. If he knew, then hopefully he would understand why she had been afraid of letting him into her heart.

"Excuse me," Mark said, interrupting her thoughts. "I hear my phone beeping. Let me see who it is." He went to the table and picked up his phone. "Just what I thought. You will have to raid the kitchen by yourself. I must go to the hospital."

"It's Christmas," Rebecca said. "Are you on call?"

"I'm covering for another doctor who wanted to go out of town. I was hoping it would be a quiet Christmas, but at least it's at night and wasn't earlier in the day. I'll see you later, and tell Mom I got a call." He leaned over and gave Rebecca a quick kiss before leaving.

A few minutes later, Irene came into the kitchen and found Rebecca looking in the cabinets. "Needing a snack before bed, my dear?"

"Well, Mark got a call from the hospital and had to leave, so I was left to raid the kitchen by myself. Are you hungry too?"

"I just need a little something. Nothing heavy." Irene sat at the table. "Rebecca, if you have a minute, I would like to talk to you."

"Sure. Is everything all right?"

"That's what I wanted to ask you," Irene began. "I have noticed you and Mark here lately. Anything special between you two?"

Not sure what to say, Rebecca dropped her head. If she couldn't admit her feelings to Mark, how could she ever tell Irene?

Irene broke the silence. "Sit down, dear. I have something to tell you. I don't mean to bring up any bad memories, but you have been through a lot, just like Mark, Rachel, and Sarah. We all go through hard times. Some of the things you have been through I wasn't aware of till you came here. Do you remember when your husband passed away?"

"How did you know about that?" Rebecca asked, stunned.

"That evening, you came out of the emergency room and walked over to a bench and sat down. You were heartbroken. A lady came up to you, sat down beside you, held your hand, and did her best to console you. She quoted some scripture to you."

"Yes, but how do you know all this?"

"Rebecca, my dear, I was that lady. I put my arms around you and tried so hard to comfort you. You told me that Ray was your life and you loved him with all your heart. You asked how you could possibly give him up when you were trying to start a family and had so much going for you. My heart went out to you because, about a year before that, I had lost my husband. I knew exactly how you were feeling."

"You were that lady?" Rebecca asked. She shook her head in wonder. "I have often wondered who she was, where she went. You said some very kind things and words that I thought about later. I had no idea it was you."

"When you sent your resume in and I saw your name, I wondered if it was you or someone with the same name. But when you walked in that day, I recognized you right away. I knew then you were the one for the job. God had brought us back together. But I have noticed you and Mark lately, the way you look at each other, the expressions on your faces when the other walks in the room. Honey, it's time to put the past behind you and move on. Ray loved you for what time he could. Now it's time to let someone else love you."

"I know what you're saying," Rebecca replied. "I'm just not sure I'm completely ready."

Irene continued. "I didn't know about your parents or Ray's mother till after you moved in here. Rebecca, God never takes away without giving back. We get comfortable with the way things are sometimes and have difficulty making changes. But changes come for a reason. We just need to rely on God for direction. I know you know all this, but sometimes it takes hearing it from someone else.

"And you can't judge Mark by what Ray was like. They are two different people. After my husband passed, about a year later, Molly tried to set me up with a man about my age. He had lost his wife and was so very lonely. He was nice in every way, but he wasn't Charles. Molly had to point it out to me that, when we talked, I always brought up Charles and didn't realize I was comparing this man to my late husband. It's hard to let go, but dear, it's time. I'm not saying Mark is the perfect guy for you—there may be someone else for you—but until you see them for themselves, you will never be able to get close to them. Think about what I've said for you may see why you're unable to move on. Don't get me wrong. I would like nothing better than to see you and Mark together, but this is something only you can decide."

"What did you ever do about the man you were talking about? "

"I had said some hurtful things to him before Molly had a talk with me," Irene answered. "By the time I realized she was right, he had decided to move away to be closer to his daughter. The move was good for him; Molly told me he found a nice lady and was very happy, and I am happy for him. You could say my loss became her gain. That's why I am telling you this. Don't be like me and make mistakes you will regret later."

"Thanks, Irene. I'll think about what you have said," Rebecca replied. "And I can't get over the fact that you were the lady that night at the hospital. You said something shortly after I came to work here that made me think of her, but I brushed it off for I just knew there was no way you would have known her. I thought it was just a coincidence. I'm glad God brought us back together. He does work in mysterious ways." Rebecca leaned over and gave Irene a big hug. "Good night, and thanks for the talk," she said.

After Rebecca left the room, Irene wondered if she had overstepped her bounds, but she did it for Rebecca's sake. She knew all too well what she was going through. She closed her eyes and said, "Dear Lord, please open her eyes and guide her."

As she closed the bedroom door behind her, Rebecca still couldn't believe Irene was the helpful lady the night of Ray's accident. She wondered at how her journey in life had made a complete circle. Was Irene right about what she was doing? Was she comparing Mark to Ray? Is this the reason she was holding back? Was she afraid she might lose Mark like she lost Ray? Standing next to her bed, she fell on her knees. "Oh, precious Lord, I need guidance. Please open my eyes and my heart that I may do what's right." With that, the tears seemed to overtake her.

Twenty-three

Molly called Irene a few days after Christmas to remind them of her New Year's Eve party and wanted to make sure they were coming.

"Let me get back with you on what Rebecca and Mark plan to do," Irene told her. "Mark may still be on call for his friend. I'll call you back at least by tomorrow." She ended the call and went to find Rebecca.

"I just got off the phone with Molly," Irene said when she found Rebecca. "Do you plan to go to her New Year's Eve party?"

"I had first thought I might, but Rachel wants to go out with Emma and Frank, so I thought I would keep Sarah for her," Rebecca answered. "Rachel hasn't had much of a life in years, and she could really use this time."

"Rebecca, you are so thoughtful, but its New Year's Eve! Wouldn't you like to go out with friends?"

"No, I would rather be with Sarah. Just let Molly know I have already made other plans and they can't be broken. Thank her for the invite. I'm sure she will have a houseful of people and I won't be missed. Are you going to go?"

"No, her Christmas party was enough for me," Irene replied. "I visited with a lot of my old friends, so I'm good for a while. I need to check with Mark to see if he's working or will be off."

"With neither one of us going, I bet he won't go. He would have to work hard all night to keep Lacey away from him."

"He probably would go to the hospital even if they didn't need him," Irene agreed.

"I'm going into town," Rebecca said. "Do you need anything?"

"No, but thank you. Have you checked with Mary?"

"Oh, yes, she gave me her grocery list, so I'll be gone a while. By the way, how is your foot? Noticed you have the boot off."

"Yes, the doctor said it was healed and I didn't have to wear it anymore. What a blessing," Irene said with a sigh. "When I left his office, I left that lovely boot with him. Hope I never have to see or use one again."

Mark came home around one that afternoon.

"I am tired," he told Irene. "Going to take a shower and go to bed. Do you need anything, Mom?"

"Have you been up all night and morning?"

"Yes, there was a bad eight-car pileup on the interstate about one this morning. I was just getting ready to come home when the call came in. I'm glad the office was closed today."

"Oh, Mark," Irene said. "Molly called and was wondering if you are planning on going to their New Year's Eve party."

"Is Rebecca going?"

"No, she is going to be watching Sarah so Rachel can go out with some friends."

"Then no, I'm not going," he answered. "Besides, I may be at the hospital. Hopefully, it will be a quiet New Year's Eve. If so, I might just invite myself to be with the girls. But that's between us, Mom."

"My lips are sealed," Irene replied. "Now go get some rest."

New Year's Eve looked like it would be a quiet evening at the McKay home. Sammy went over to a friend's house, and Rebecca went to Rachel's to take care of Sarah.

Mary asked Irene, "Would you care for some popcorn while we watch a movie?"

"That sounds good. I'm going to let you decide what movie we will watch." She turned to Mark, who was standing in the doorway. "Say, Mark, are you going to join Mary and me for a movie tonight?"

"I might hang around for a while," he answered.

"Are you still planning on crashing the girls' get-together?" Irene asked.

"Mr. Mark, you're not going to go over to Rachel's, are you?" Mary said. "Why don't you stay here with your mama and me? We can enjoy a good movie and popcorn together."

"You know you both are my two favorite ladies ..." Mark began.

Mary interrupted. "Two favorite ladies, my foot. I know who has top priority in your life!"

"You do? How did you find out?" Mark asked.

"Ever since you got Sarah that pony, she has won you over. Your poor mama and I are now in second and third place."

"Oh, Sarah," Mark said. "Yeah, right."

"Who did you think I was talking about? Are you holding something back from your mama and me? If so, spit it out."

"No, Mary, it's Sarah. She is just so adorable. Anyway, I will have some popcorn and hang around for a while. I promise."

Mary got up to make the popcorn. "While I'm gone, why don't you find a good movie for us?" she said to Mark. "Nothing scary, and no war movies. You watch him, Ms. Irene." She headed for the kitchen.

"You know, Mama, Mary can get a little bossy at times," Mark said with a grin.

"I almost burst out laughing when she was talking about the favorite person in your life. You were thinking Rebecca, and when she said Sarah, the look of shock on your face was priceless."

"I think I had a good comeback. Mary is none the wiser."

"Don't be so sure," Irene cautioned. "Mary has been with us

since you were little. She knows you all too well. I could almost see her mind working, putting things together."

"You haven't said anything to her, have you?"

"I don't have to. All we have to do is watch you and Rebecca."

Mary walked back into the room. "Mark, the hospital just called on the house phone," she said. "They have been calling your cell phone and can't reach you."

"Oh, my phone is in my room on the charger," he replied. "They didn't say what they needed, did they?"

"She just said they needed to speak to you."

"Guess I had better go call them. Don't eat all the popcorn while I'm gone." Mark walked quickly to his room.

"Mary, that's a big bowl of popcorn!" Irene commented. "Do you really think we can eat all that during one movie?" They started munching on it.

Mark ducked back in the doorway. "Well, ladies, looks like it's going to be just the two of you. Some guys got into a big fight, and several got stabbed. I have no idea how long I will be gone. Happy New Year to you both, and I'll probably see you next year."

"Sorry you must go, but Happy New Year to you, son," Irene said.

Mary called out, "Happy New Year, Mr. Mark!"

Rebecca and Sarah went out to eat and then brought home some goodies to snack on while playing games and waiting for the time the ball would drop. By eleven o'clock, Sarah was sound asleep. She had tried so hard to stay awake but just couldn't make it. Rebecca left her on the couch and thought, *Just before the ball drops, I'll wake her.* About a quarter before midnight, someone knocked on the door. Rebecca peeped out the window to see who it was, and there stood Mark on the porch.

Opening the door, Rebecca asked, "What are you doing here?"

"Trying to get here before the ball drops so we can all be together to bring in the New Year," he replied. "Where's Sarah?" he asked as he stepped inside.

"She's on the couch asleep. She fought to stay awake but lost. Thought I would wake her so she could see the ball drop." Rebecca went over to the couch as Mark shut the front door. "Sarah, it's about time. You need to wake up."

Sitting up, Sarah was so drowsy that her eyelids just didn't want to open. Finally, Mark was able to wake her. He held Sarah in one arm and put his other arm around Rebecca just as the ball started to drop.

Sarah became wide awake then. She had never seen anything like it! When the crowd yelled, "Happy New Year," she got so excited. She hugged and kissed Mark and Rebecca. Then, realizing Mark hadn't been there earlier, she asked, "When did you come in?"

"I just got here. Wanted to spend it with you and Rebecca," he answered. "Hope you don't mind."

"No, I don't mind. I love you and Ms. Rebecca. You're my family."

Finally, they were able to get Sarah in bed. Then Mark took Rebecca in his arms.

"Now, for that New Year's kiss."

Around seven in the morning, Mark's phone began vibrating in his pocket. Waking up, he realized he was still at Rachel's, sitting on the couch with Rebecca sleeping in his arms. As soon as he moved, she woke up. The hospital was calling again, needing Mark to come in. Rebecca went to her phone and saw that Rachel had texted her, stating that it was late when they got back to Emma and Frank's house so she would just stay there. She would be home sometime that morning.

"Hate to leave you, but I must go," Mark told her. "Send me a text when Rachel gets home, and when you're ready to leave, maybe we can meet somewhere and grab a bite to eat."

"Sounds good," Rebecca said. "Mark, thanks for coming over last night."

"I just wanted to be with you. That's all I could think of while I was at the hospital. I love you so much."

Taking her in his arms, he never wanted to stop kissing her.

"I had better go. See you in a little while, I hope."

"Mark," Rebecca said confidently, "I love you, too."

Mark turned back around. "Oh, Rebecca. I was so afraid you didn't have the same feelings for me that I have for you." He took her in his arms again, and this time their kiss seemed different.

"Can I have a hug too?" Sarah asked, just walking into the living room.

"You most certainly can," Mark said. "Come here. I've got to go to the hospital to work. Did you know today is a special day? I don't know when I have been so happy."

"Did I do something to make you happy, Mr. Mark?"

"Yes, you and Rebecca both did. You two are my new favorite people." He hugged her and then said, "Now, I must go." He opened the front door and stepped outside.

"Mr. Mark really did seem happy," Sarah said to Rebecca. "What did we do?"

"You could say we all just love each other," Rebecca answered with a grin. "Why don't we get you dressed and go visit Beauty? I bet Ms. Mary may even have something good to eat."

"Yes, that would be great," Sarah agreed. "Can I tell her and Ms. Irene about seeing the big sparkly ball drop last night? That was so cool."

"Yes, you can. Beauty might even enjoy hearing about it. While you get ready, I'm going to text your mom to let her know where we are going, and I'll send Mary a quick text that we will soon be on our way."

Once they got there, Sarah had to tell everyone, even Beauty, about watching the ball drop on television. Sammy let her ride

Beauty, which only added to her excitement. By the time Rachel came to pick her up, Sarah was asleep on Rebecca's bed.

"Sorry I'm so late getting her," Rachel said apologetically. "Frank, Emma, and some others and I all went out and had a really good time. Thank you so much for watching her. I won't do this to you again."

"Rachel, anytime we can watch Sarah, you know we will. She is no problem, and I'm glad you had a good time."

The rest of the day passed uneventfully. It was getting late and Rebecca hadn't heard from Mark, so she decided she would shower and go on to bed. She could feel the effects of being up late the night before.

"Rebecca, Rebecca, can you hear me?"

She turned over in bed, and there stood Mark. "Mark, is everything all right?"

"Yes, I'm sorry it's so late," he said, "but I just had to see you before I went to bed. Since you told me last night that you loved me, that's all I have thought about. I just need to hold you in my arms for a few minutes and kiss you. I love you so much."

"Oh, Mark. I do love you," she replied.

They held each other for some time before Mark finally released his hold of her.

"I had better go," he said. "You sleep well, and I'll see you in the morning. I love you."

After Mark left, Rebecca could still feel his arms around her. Yes, this was right. She was ready to move on, and Mark was the one.

Twenty-four

January was a cold, snowy month. Everyone was ready for spring, including the construction workers. Everything was on schedule, which was good. Some of the McKay workers went outside and made snow people, even decorating them. The local paper sent someone out to take pictures, and a TV news crew even came and put it on the local news. The interviewer asked one of McKays employees what the McKays would do for February.

It was getting close to Valentine's Day, so Lynn and Rebecca decided to give each employee a small box of candy as they left. Some said they would save theirs for their spouses, some saved them for their children, and some started eating the candy right away. Not sure what to get Mark, Rebecca decided on a gift card for a massage. When she got home that evening, she was met with a dozen red roses in a vase with baby's breath all through it. They were beautiful.

"Well, Rebecca," Mary said, "looks like someone has been nice this year."

"Aren't they just beautiful?" Rebecca swooned. "I like where they are on the living room table. It's a perfect spot. Let me put my things away and I'll come help you in the kitchen."

When she opened her bedroom door, there sat a dozen yellow roses. "Oh, my. These are beautiful also," she said to herself. "Mary," she called out, "when did all these flowers come in?"

"Just a little while ago. Ms. Irene and I looked at the cards, and they both had your name on them. We thought for sure we would see our names on at least one," she teased.

"I'll share, Mary! I'll leave them out where everyone can see them. They are too beautiful to put in a room where they can't be enjoyed." She looked at her phone. "Excuse me a minute. Sarah is calling."

"Hello, Sarah," she said. "How are you today? And oh, happy Valentine's Day!"

"Ms. Rebecca, guess what?" Sarah said excitedly. "Mr. Mark sent me flowers and a big box of candy! Some guy brought them to the house a few minutes ago. I have never had flowers or candy in such a big box. Mama and I opened the box of candy, and there are so many kinds! We each took one, and it was so good."

"That is wonderful!" Rebecca said. "Mark must really like you. He got me flowers, but I didn't get candy."

"I'm sorry," Sarah said sweetly. "You can come over and have some of mine. It's a really big box and in the shape of a heart."

"Did it have a card?" Rebecca asked.

"Yes, it said 'To my littlest sweetheart. Love, Mark.' I'm his sweetheart!"

"Yes, you are, and a beautiful one at that."

"Mama also gave me the box of candy you sent me. Thank you."

"You are most welcome," Rebecca said, "but my little box is probably small compared to what Mark sent you."

"Mama told me it's not the size that counts; it's the thought."

"She is so right. Sounds like you will have enough candy to eat on for a while." She looked toward the door when she heard it open. "Sarah, do you want to talk to Mark? He just walked in."

"I called him first," she said. "I was so excited, and I wanted to thank him. Mama says I must go now. I love you! Bye." Rebecca said goodbye and put her phone down.

When Mark walked in the door, Mary was in the kitchen cooking. She said, "Well, I know a little girl who is very happy right now. Mark, that was so thoughtful of you to remember Sarah."

"Yes," Mark replied, smiling, "Sarah called me while I was driving home. She was so excited about the flowers and candy."

"You mean you sent Sarah flowers and candy but your poor mama and I didn't get anything?"

"Oh, Mary, you know I would never forget you two." He reached into a bag he was carrying. "Here, I have something for you and something for Mama."

"Did I hear my name?" Irene asked as she walked in. "What did you get your mama?"

"A red rose and candy," Mary answered. "Mark, you are a dear."

"See, Mary? He does care about us," Irene joked.

Rebecca walked into the kitchen to find Irene and Mary smiling. "Well, I just got off the phone with Sarah, and she sounded as happy as you both look. Rachel sent me a picture of Sarah with the flowers and candy that Mark sent her."

With a sparkle in his eyes, Mark said, "As much as I care for you ladies, right now I need to take this dear lady from your presence. We have dinner reservations, and we don't want to be late."

Rebecca turned to Mark and said, "I was just getting ready to help Mary."

"Mama can help Mary," he said. "You are going with me. See you two later." He led her by the arm out of the kitchen.

"Where are we going?"

"You will see. It's someplace I don't think you have been."

"What about what I'm wearing?" Rebecca asked. "You haven't given me a chance to change."

"You always look good no matter what you have on."

"Well, thank you, but for some places you need to dress a little better than others."

"Don't worry, you are going to be fine," Mark assured her. "Trust me."

Getting into the car, Rebecca wondered how her hair and makeup looked. She really wished he had given her just a few minutes to freshen up.

It was a nice drive, and Rebecca was sure she had never been in that part of town. Soon they pulled into a small parking lot.

"All right, here we are," Mark said. "I made reservations, so we won't have to wait." They walked inside and were seated immediately.

"This is a really nice place," Rebecca commented. "It's nice and warm too. Did you request a table by the fireplace?"

"Yes, I did. I also took the liberty of ordering our dinner for tonight so we wouldn't have to sit and wait. As you can see, the place is packed."

"Mark, you must have made reservations a month ago to get this table." She was impressed.

"The night you told me you loved me, I started making plans for a lot of things, this being one of them."

"Oh and the flowers—did I thank you for them? They are both so beautiful."

"Only the best for you," he said. The waiter approached the table, and they sat back in their seats. "Here's our dinner," Mark said. "Hope you enjoy it."

Rebecca took a bite and closed her eyes. "This is so good. Have you eaten here before?"

"Some of the doctors met here for a seminar not long ago, and I was impressed with the food and the way the place is laid out. I knew I had to bring you here."

"You have never said anything about your talk to Bruce. How did he handle your decision to not run for office?"

"I think he knew it was coming. We had a good long talk, and all went well. We are still friends, and I don't regret my decision at all. Practicing medicine was my first dream, and going to law school was good. I enjoyed it, and the education has come in handy for me. Joe Lewis and I have been friends for years, so if I ever wanted to, I could work with him. He calls every now and then to run things by me, just to see what my response would be."

"That's good. Bruce and Molly are such sweet people."

"Yes, but please, don't mention their daughter. I'm enjoying my meal. Please don't ruin it."

Smiling, Rebecca said, "No problem."

When they finished their meals, the waiter came over to the table to clear away the dishes. Then he turned and placed a covered dessert in front of them.

"Oh, I don't think I can eat anything else. Could you possibly put this in a to-go box?" Rebecca asked.

"I'm sorry, madam, but we don't have to-go boxes. Hopefully, you will enjoy what Mr. McKay picked out for you tonight." He turned and walked away.

"Mark, would you like to have at least half of my dessert?" she pleaded. "Dinner was so good that I really don't think I can eat much more."

"Why don't you see what's under the lid before you decide to share it?"

Raising the lid, she saw a piece of paper. It said, "You have a surprise at home. Are you ready to go?"

"What's at home?" she asked. "Did you get more flowers?"

"If you're ready, then shall we go find out?"

When they walked into the house, Rebecca saw that candles had been lit and music was playing softly in the background. Mary and Irene were nowhere to be seen, and on the table in the foyer near the front door was a huge arrangement of flowers. As she looked around, she noticed smaller vases of flowers sitting everywhere. She walked over to the large arrangement of flowers and leaned over to smell them. It was all so breathtaking. Looking at Mark, she said, "This is worth coming home for! Thank you. It's all so romantic."

"You need to look closely at the flowers," he suggested.

Taking a closer look, Rebecca wasn't sure what he was talking about.

"Here," Mark said. "This rose looks very special."

She looked at the rose but still didn't know what was so special about it. Then she saw that, around the stem, was a ring. Mark removed the ring and then got down on one knee.

"Rebecca, will you marry me?"

For a few seconds, Rebecca couldn't speak. Tears filled her eyes, and her heart beat so fast. Finally, she managed to say, "Yes." She was trembling all over. Then Mark placed the ring on her finger and took her in his arms.

"I love you, Rebecca, and I don't want to waste another day without you," he said. "We can have a big wedding or a small one. It's your call; just don't put it off too long. I'd marry you tonight if I could."

"Oh, Mark, I love you too," she said. "I haven't even thought about a wedding. I've done good to let you know how I feel. This is all so sudden!"

"I was sure you felt the same for me as I felt for you, but I needed to hear you say it. When you did, I couldn't think of anything else but to make you mine. I have waited so long for the right woman to come into my life. You have no idea how hard I have prayed for God to send me the perfect wife."

"Are you sure I'm the one?"

"Yes, I'm very sure," Mark said. "I asked God to show me, and he did. I won't say how I know—that's between God and me. I know you pray about everything, and that says a lot for you. Rebecca, whatever you want, I'll do my very best to give it to you. The family already loves you, and this will make them all very happy."

"Where is Irene and Mary?" Rebecca asked.

"I asked them to go see a movie for a few hours. I wanted it to be just us here."

"Mark, life with you is going to be just wonderful. You think of everything."

"I try, but staying ahead of you might be a little challenging. I'm ready to take it on though."

Just then, Irene and Mary came in. Looking around, Irene said, "Oh, my! Look at all the flowers. What's going on?"

"Mama, I just asked Rebecca to marry me, and she said yes," Mark answered.

Both ladies rushed over to Rebecca, wanting to see the ring and both talking at the same time.

Rebecca asked, "Did either of you know about this?"

"No!" Irene exclaimed. "Mark said he was sending us to the movies for Valentine's Day."

"Then who fixed the house up with the candles, music, and flowers?"

"I did, Ms. Rebecca," Sammy said from the doorway. "Mr. Mark texted me from the restaurant saying about what time you two would be home, so I dropped Ms. Mary and Ms. Irene off at the movies just to make sure they were out of the house and then came back to put the flowers out."

"Sammy, I had no idea you were in on what Mark was up to. No wonder Irene and Mary were so surprised! This evening has been full of surprises. Whose idea was it to put the ring on the rose stem?"

"That was me," Sammy said. "Mr. Mark wanted to do something different yet special. Knowing how you enjoy flowers, I suggested this way. He liked it, so here we are."

Rebecca looked at Mark. "How did you know which rose to pick?"

Sammy spoke up again, "He knew to go for the one in the middle or the tallest rose. Men do work together on things, Ms. Rebecca."

She laughed. "Well, Sammy, you certainly outdid yourself this time," Mary said. "This calls for a celebration. I'm going to the kitchen to see what I can find."

"Rebecca, welcome to our family," Irene said, beaming. "Finally, I'm going to have a daughter-in-law to brag about. Correction—I'm going to have a beautiful *daughter*, who I am already proud of."

She looked at Mark. "Oh, by any chance have you thought about a date?"

"Personally, I would like to get married tonight, but I know that's not possible," Mark replied.

Irene chided him, "Mark, this is a wedding we are talking about! It takes time to plan one. You just can't do it overnight."

"Okay, I'll give you ladies till the end of February to get everything planned. There are three of you, so that should be no problem."

"Don't be ridiculous. For a doctor, sometimes I wonder about you," Irene said.

"Now, Mama, I know what I want, and I want to get married as soon as possible. I'm not getting any younger, you know."

"Well, you and Rebecca need to talk and let us know what you decide." Turning to Rebecca, Irene said, "Good luck, my dear." She headed to the kitchen to help Mary.

Mark took Rebecca in his arms, pretended no one was around, and kissed her like there was no tomorrow.

Twenty-five

AT WORK THE NEXT MORNING, REBECCA WASN'T SURE IF SHE should tell the workers or wait till they saw the ring on her finger. Lynn came in with some papers for Rebecca to sign, and right away, she saw the ring.

"Ms. Rebecca! Did you get a ring last night?" she asked.

"Yes, Mark asked me to marry him," she said, smiling.

"Wow! I must say, he certainly has good taste in jewelry. That is beautiful. How do you feel?"

"Overwhelmed. He said he was ready to get married last night! I'm not sure when the date will be."

"Mind if I share the news with the other workers?" Lynn asked.

"No, I don't mind. They are going to find out soon enough."

At the midmorning break, Lynn got on the intercom to make her usual announcements. "May I have everyone's attention?" she began. "I have a very important announcement to make. Our lovely and wonderful boss, Rebecca Clark, is engaged to get married! No date has been set at this time. Thank you."

Rebecca went out to Lynn's desk. "Lynn, that's not exactly what I meant when I said you could share the news with the others!" She laughed.

"I just thought it would be better to make one announcement, plus this way you would know exactly what was said."

"If I didn't think so much of you, I would disown you right

now," Rebecca teased. "But I guess you're right. Might as well get it out in the open."

All day, Rebecca tried to stay away from as many workers as she could. Those she did encounter wanted to see the ring and asked so many questions. Finally, the day was over, and she was ready to go home.

Mark had a late meeting to attend, so Rebecca figured she would enjoy a nice, quiet evening at home. But as soon as she walked in the door, Irene and Mary wanted to show her some wedding gowns they had been looking at online, as well as invitations, wedding cakes, and more.

By the time she went to bed, her mind was spinning. Rebecca prayed that the next day would be better.

The next morning, Rebecca went in to work early. She called Lynn on the way and told her she would be bring in breakfast.

When she arrived, Lynn was already there. "Ms. Rebecca, are you all right? You look tired. What's wrong?"

Rebecca set the breakfast down on Lynn's desk. "When I got home last night, Irene and Mary had been busy all day looking at wedding dresses, invitations, and cakes. I'm not sure what I want. I appreciate their help, but I don't feel like I will have a say about any of it. I don't want to hurt anyone's feelings, but right now, I'm ready to elope."

"You can't do that!" Lynn protested. "This is a big day for you and Mark. You are going to make a beautiful bride. Let everyone get a chance to see that." She paused for a moment. "Thanks for breakfast. I'd better get back to work. I'll try to keep things quiet for you and handle as many of the calls I can."

"Thanks, Lynn."

In her office, Rebecca stood looking out the window, unsure what to do. She needed to talk to Mark, but then, she didn't want to seem ungrateful for what his mother and Mary were trying to do.

Soon, Lynn burst into Rebecca's office. "Ms. Rebecca, I'm sorry to bother you, but there's been a terrible accident."

"Where? What happened?"

"One of the workers was in a bad wreck this morning and died."

"Oh, no! Do you know who it was?"

"It was Rachel Mills."

Shocked, Rebecca just stood there.

"Frank called Emma, and Emma told me," Lynn added. "Are you okay?"

"This just can't be true," Rebecca said, horrified. "I just spoke to her the night before last. Mark had gotten Sarah some candy and flowers for Valentine's Day. Rachel had taken some pictures of Sarah and sent them to me." She gasped. "Sarah! What will happen to Sarah? Lynn, I have to leave. Did Emma say where they had taken Rachel?"

"No, she was crying. I think Frank was coming to get her. You know, they were all very close."

"That's fine. I've got to leave." She rushed out the door.

Traffic was still backed up in the area, and Rebecca had to take a different route to get to Sarah's school. She went into the school office, explained why she was there, and asked if she could talk to Sarah's teacher. She didn't want Sarah to find out at school. While she waited, her cell phone rang. It was Mark.

"Rebecca, I have some bad news," he said.

"I heard. It's Rachel. I'm here at Sarah's school, hoping to talk to her teacher."

"It was a bad wreck," Mark said. "Four people have died, and there were six cars involved. Rachel is almost unrecognizable. She was pinned in the car, and another car landed on top of hers. Whatever you do, don't bring Sarah to the hospital. It's not a good place to be right now."

"Okay, thanks." She hung up.

"Ms. Clark, did you need to see me?" the teacher asked as she walked in.

"Ms. Reagan, yes. I do apologize for just showing up like this. I have some very bad news. Sarah's mother was killed this morning on her way to work. From my understanding, there were six cars involved, and four people died. I don't want Sarah to find out about her mother here at school."

"Oh, I agree. I am so sorry, even more so for Sarah," Ms. Reagan said. "Since things have improved with Ms. Mills and Sarah, Sarah has become even more delightful to be around. Her happiness is breathtaking." She thought for a moment. "Would it be all right if I kept her here at school and then took her home as usual? She usually stays with me till Rachel comes home. This way, she will have as normal of a day as possible. I have an assistant here with me today, and I can keep Sarah with me to avoid her having contact with others. We don't do this often, but Sarah is ahead of the class, so I'll let her help with other things to keep her busy."

"That would be great. I'll pick her up at your house." Rebecca pulled out a business card. "Here's my number. Just text me."

"Ms. Clark, what will happen to Sarah? She has had such a rough life, and now this. That child doesn't deserve all that she has been through."

"I agree. Sarah has no family. It was just her and her mother. But I intend to do all I can to keep her out of a foster home. I have a friend who is an attorney. Hopefully he can be of help."

When Rebecca got back into the car, she wasn't sure what to do first. She couldn't believe that Rachel was gone. Maybe Lynn knew something more or could offer a suggestion.

She called Lynn and told her she had just left the school after talking to Sarah's teacher. She added that any of the employees who were very close to Rachel or good friends with her could go home if they wanted. It wouldn't count against them. "I need to talk to Mark about my options for getting Sarah," she said. "I can't stand the thought of her going into a foster home."

Lynn asked, "Do you think you will get to talk to him? Is he not tied up with the wreck at the hospital?"

"Yes, but I've got to get through to him somehow before school is out. I'm headed home right now. Call if you need me."

As Rebecca walked in the door, Mary was surprised to see her.

"Rebecca, what's wrong? Why are you crying?"

Irene came in at the same time and went straight to Rebecca. "My dear, whatever is wrong?"

"It's Rachel," she said weakly. "She was killed in a wreck on her way to work this morning."

Both ladies were in shock.

"According to Mark, there were six cars involved and four people died," Rebecca added. "I just can't believe this has happened." I went to the school to talk to Sarah teacher and we agreed to keep her there and let her have as normal a day as possible. I plan to pick her up this afternoon. Some way, I've got to figure out how to keep Sarah. I don't want her going into a foster home or a children's home."

"Oh, Rebecca, I totally agree," Irene said.

"I also plan to move out, to move back into my other house."

"Why do you want to move out?" Irene asked. "Why can't you bring Sarah here?"

"I just don't think it would be right to disrupt your home with a child. Besides, Sarah has gotten use to that house, and she may feel more at home there."

"Rebecca, I will not stand for this talk about moving out. This house is plenty big, and we will choose a room for Sarah and fix it up any way she wants. Now, no more talk about that," Irene said. "It will do her good to leave that other house and be around all of us."

Mary went over to hug Rebecca. "Remember, she has Beauty here," she said softly. "That will help her too."

"Thank you, Mary. I hadn't thought about Beauty."

Mary asked, "Do you need help bringing Sarah's things over?"

"I need to take her home first and talk to her. I'm not sure how she will react, and I think it would be best if she was at home. I sent Mark a text asking how I could go about getting custody of Sarah but haven't heard anything. I'm sure that, with the wrecks, he's very busy."

"Would you like me to fix you something to eat?"

"Thanks, but I'm just not hungry," Rebecca said. "I'll be in my room if you need me."

Closing the door, Rebecca went to her favorite spot and knelt. Her heart was so heavy. "Lord, please help me find a way to get custody of Sarah. I love that child as if she were my own. Please help me."

Soon, Mary knocked on Rebecca's door. "Ms. Rebecca, I'm sorry to bother you, but Joe Lewis is here to see you."

Trying to pull herself together, Rebecca walked out to the foyer where Joe was.

"Hello, Joe. How are you?"

"Rebecca, Mark called me and filled me in on what all has happened this morning. Does Sarah know about her mother?"

"No, I plan to tell her this afternoon, after school. Do you know if Rachel had a will?"

"Yes," Joe said. "Right after Christmas, she made an appointment to see me. She wanted to fix up a will in case anything should ever happen to her. She has it at her house somewhere."

"What does the will say?" Rebecca asked.

"We need to find it and go over it together. That's all I can say for now."

"Okay, I have some time before I pick up Sarah. I'll go over and see if I can find it. Do you want to come with me?"

"Sure. I would like to be there when you find it for I'm sure you will want to see what it says," Joe replied.

Going into the house was hard for Rebecca. She remembered that, when Mamie had died, she had to come back to this house alone. Why was this happening again?

"Rebecca, do you have any idea where Rachel may keep her files?"

"No, I don't. Let's start in her room and go from there."

After looking for thirty minutes, Joe found the right file folder. "Here it is. Let's sit down, and I'll go over it with you."

As Joe started reading the will, Rebecca could feel the tears trickle down her cheeks. What would she say to Sarah? How would she take it? She snapped out of her thoughts when she heard Joe say her name.

"What did you say?"

"Rachel left you full custody of Sarah," he repeated.

Rebecca had planned to try to get custody of Sarah but had no idea that Rachel had already taken care of it. She was honored that Rachel thought that much of her, to entrust her daughter to her. Her tears were overflowing. Joe read the rest of the will, but Rebecca could only remember that one thing he read.

Finally, he said, "I will need you to come down to the office. There is some paperwork we need to do."

"Yes, of course," she agreed. "I'll call and set up an appointment."

As Joe was leaving, he turned and asked, "Are you going to be all right? You realize you will be taking on a big responsibility. You have a company to run, you will be a single parent, and you have never had children."

"When my parents were alive, they were missionaries," Rebecca answered. "I've been around lots of children of all ages."

"Yes, but this one is twenty-four-seven, three hundred sixty-five days a year. It's a big difference."

"It's okay," she assured him. "I love that little girl and have said I hope to someday have one just like her. So now I do. At the factory, we are having a day care set up, so I'll be like the other workers putting it to good use."

"You really need to give this a lot of thought," he said. "Call in a few days and we will talk more then."

"Thanks, Joe," Rebecca said as he left.

As Rebecca looked around the room, she remembered the day Rachel had told her about her past and why she felt God had turned his back on her. That very same day, Rachel allowed God back into her life. Now she was with her heavenly father. Oh, how thankful Rebecca was for that precious day and time she had had with Rachel.

It was nearly time to pick up Sarah, so Rebecca knew she needed to pull herself together and fix her face. "Dear Lord, please give me the right words for Sarah, and please comfort her in a very special way. I know how I felt when I was told my parents were killed. She is just a child, where I was an adult. The pain is so deep." She took a deep breath and headed for the car.

As soon as Rebecca knocked on Ms. Reagan's door, she answered. Ms. Reagan invited her in. "Sarah is in the kitchen having some cookies and milk," she said quietly. "She knows nothing. Ms. Clark, I have been praying for you and Sarah ever since we talked. May God's blessings be with you both."

"Thank you, Ms. Reagan. We are going to need all the prayers we can get. I have a hard job facing me, but Sarah is the one I worry about. It's just been her and her mother all her life, until recently, and it's not been that long since they have let others into their life."

Sarah came into the room where Rebecca and Ms. Reagan were talking. "Ms. Rebecca, I thought that was you. Can we go to your house so I can see Beauty?"

"We will go later, I promise, but we need to go back to your house first," Rebecca said as calmly as she could.

"Okay. Bye, Ms. Reagan. See you tomorrow."

As soon as they walked through the door, Sarah went to the kitchen, looking for her mother. Then she called out, "Mama, where are you?"

"Sarah, come here and let's talk," Rebecca said.

"Where's Mama?" she persisted. "She is always here when I come home."

"Honey, you know how you talk about your angel doll? How you say she hears your prayers?"

"She does. She's the best angel doll ever."

"Well, everyone has an angel that watches over them, no matter what age they are," Rebecca said. "Do you remember your teacher in Sunday school at church talking about heaven?"

"Yes, Ms. Betty said heaven was a beautiful place and one day we would all go there. She said everybody in heaven was happy, no one was ever sick, and when we go to heaven, we will get to see Jesus. She said Jesus lives in our hearts and he is filled with love."

"She is right. You said your teacher told you one day we would go to heaven?"

"Yes, she did," Sarah confirmed.

"We never know when Jesus is going to take us to heaven. We all go at different times, and we never know how we are going to go. When he takes a loved one, we miss them because they are not here with us, but they go to heaven to be with Jesus. And when we die, we will get to see them again. Do you understand what I'm saying?"

"Why don't we all go together?" Sarah asked.

"When a person dies, that means the work God wanted them to do here on earth is finished, and then they go to heaven to be with him. God puts us here for a reason, and only he knows when he wants us to come home to heaven. If I should die today, you may not die for many years."

"That's because my work isn't done."

"That's right," Rebecca said.

"What kind of work am I supposed to do? Will he tell me?"

"Yes, if you listen to him. Praying is very important, and so is reading your Bible. God doesn't talk to you like the way we talk. He speaks to you in other ways. As you get older, you will understand this better."

"Is God talking to me now?" Sarah asked.

"God loves you very much. He loves us all. But when things happen, we don't always understand why, but we must trust God to help us through those bad times in our lives. When we face bad times, God will send someone to help us. Do you remember when your friend Brooke at school lost her puppy?"

"Yes," Sarah said sadly. "Somebody ran over it and killed it. She cried and cried."

"She was hurting because she lost her puppy, and she loved her puppy very much. Then later, do you remember what happened?"

"Madison's dog had puppies, and she gave Brooke one."

"That's right, and then Brooke was happy again," Rebecca said. "But she still remembered her other puppy and still loved it. That's the way it is when we lose someone we love. God brings someone into our lives to make us happy and to help us not be sad anymore."

"Like when you helped Mama when I was sick? We got this house, and I had the best birthday party ever. Mama used to lay beside me and cry at night, but when we moved in here, she stopped crying. She said you were the best angel ever. Are you Mama's angel?"

Fighting back tears and trying to stay calm, Rebecca could feel herself shaking. This was much harder than she thought.

"God used me to help you and your mama, for which I am very grateful. I had a home that no one was using, and you two needed a home. That's how God works."

"Can we go to your house now so I can see Beauty?"

"Sarah, what I have been trying to say is that God sent an angel down this morning to take someone we love to heaven to be with him."

"Who?"

"The angel reached down and gave your mama a big hug this morning, and then they went to heaven." Rebecca studied Sarah's face.

"Mama went to heaven this morning?" she asked.

"Yes, honey, she did."

"But I didn't tell her bye, and we always tell each other bye when we leave."

"Your mama didn't know God was going to send an angel after her this morning," Rebecca explained. "But she did tell you goodbye when she dropped you off at school. I bet she even told you she loved you."

"But if Mama went to heaven, she's not coming back, is she?"

"No, honey, she's not. But one day, when it's our time to go to heaven, we will get to see her then."

Sarah thought a moment. "Will I stay here by myself?"

"No, Sarah, I thought you could come to my house and stay with us. Mark, Irene, Mary, and Sammy will all be there. Would you like that?"

Dropping her head, Sarah said, "Okay."

"Why don't we go into your room and put some things in a suitcase to take to our house, and then later we can come back and get more."

"We don't have a suitcase," Sarah said. "We always put our things in a bag."

"Then we will get a bag."

Sarah got up and slowly walked to her room. When she got to the doorway, she stopped and looked around. She walked over to her angel doll, picked her up, and just held her. She didn't move.

Rebecca came with a bag. "Sarah, here's a bag. What would you like to take with you?"

"It doesn't matter," she replied. "Whatever you want me to have."

Rebecca went through her things, picking out what she thought Sarah might want with her.

"All right," she said when she was finished. "Do you see anything I forgot that you would like to take?"

"No."

Sarah was going into a shell, and Rebecca wasn't sure what to say or do to help her at this point. She knelt down and put her arms around her.

"I know this is hard to understand, but I am here for you."

The drive over to Rebecca's was quiet. Sarah held her angel doll and looked out the window, never saying a word. Rebecca hoped Sarah would be able to adjust without too much difficulty.

As they walked into the house, Mary and Irene were waiting on them. When they saw Sarah, their hearts broke.

"Sarah, my dear, may I hug you?" Irene asked.

Not really looking at her, Sarah softly said yes. As Irene hugged her, Sarah said so quietly, "My mama went to heaven."

Fighting back tears, Irene held onto Sarah a little longer, not sure what to say. When she did let her go, Mary went over to hug her. She said, "Sarah, we are all here for you, and we love you so very much."

All that Sarah could say was thank you.

Rebecca took Sarah in her arms. "Would you like to look at the bedrooms and see which one you might like?"

"Can I sleep in your room with you?"

"Yes, you can, honey," Rebecca answered as she stood up. "Why don't we go and put your things in our room?"

Sarah turned and walked toward Rebecca's bedroom, still not saying anything. Sarah's whole world had been turned upside down, and everyone knew so many things must be going through her mind. She was surely wondering what she was going to do without her mama.

Mark came home a little early to see if he could talk to Sarah. When he saw her, he knew she was going to need to talk at some point. She just sat and stared out into space. He picked her up in his arms, and she put her arms around his neck and lay her head on his shoulder. He sat in a chair for over an hour holding her, and not a word was spoken. Finally, Rebecca came in the room. "Sarah, would you like to get ready for bed?" Still not speaking, Sarah got down from Mark's lap and went to the bedroom.

"Mark, what can I do for her?" Rebecca asked. "She is going into a shell."

"Be patient with her," he replied. She has had a lot dumped onto her plate today for a seven-year-old. She will talk when she's ready. Just make sure that what you say to her is very positive." Rebecca nodded and turned to join Sarah in the bedroom.

As they laid down, Sarah snuggled very close to Rebecca, hugging her as if she was worried she was going to leave. As they laid there, Rebecca softly said a prayer. Still, Sarah never moved.

Twenty-six

THE FUNERAL WAS KEPT SMALL AND SIMPLE FOR SARAH'S SAKE. Rachel's injuries were so bad that the casket could not be opened for viewing, which made it even harder on Sarah. She wanted so much to see her mama. Rebecca talked with Ms. Reagan, and they agreed that Sarah needed to stay home for a few days to adjust to her new home and all that had happened. Ms. Reagan also wanted some time to talk to her students about what Sarah was going through so that, when she came back, hopefully, things would go much more smoothly for her.

Five days had passed, and still Sarah only spoke when asked a question. She ate very little, mostly looking out into space holding her angel doll. Sammy came in and asked, "Ms. Sarah, would you like to help me brush down Beauty?"

For a few moments, Sarah did not respond, but then she finally said, "Okay." As they went out to the stables, she didn't have any excitement about her. Usually, she was so bubbly and happy to see Beauty. But that day, she just drug along. Finally, she went to Sammy and said, "I really don't want to brush her anymore. Can I go back in the house?"

"You sure can," Sammy said. "I thought you might want to spend some time with Beauty. She enjoys it when you brush her."

Sarah just stood there. Sammy took her by the hand and walked her back to the house. As they were walking in, Rebecca pulled up in the car. Seeing Sarah, she thought sure the child was going to cry. So instead of going in the house, Rebecca approached her and held out her hand.

"Sarah, would you like to go for a walk? It's so pretty out today." Taking Rebecca's hand, Sarah still didn't say a word. As they walked across the field, Rebecca stopped and sat down in the grass.

"Sarah, would you like to talk?" she began. "I know what it's like to lose a mother. I lost mine several years ago. In fact, I lost my mother and my dad at the same time."

Looking at Rebecca, Sarah asked, "Did your mama tell you goodbye before she left you?"

"No, I did not get to tell either one of my parents goodbye. I was in college in Colorado, and they were overseas doing mission work. The place where they were was bombed, and everyone was killed. I hadn't seen them in about a year, and they had planned to come see me graduate, but they didn't make it. It hurt when I lost them, especially when I lost them both at the same time, so I really know how you feel."

"I didn't know you lost both your daddy and mama," Sarah said thoughtfully. "So, you didn't get to say goodbye either?"

"No, I didn't. I wanted so much to tell them I loved them and was going to miss them, but I didn't get to."

"Did you talk to your angel doll?"

"No, I didn't have one," Rebecca answered. "But a lady came and offered me a job, so I moved and made new friends. Keeping busy helped me. I still cried at times over losing them, but as time went on, it got easier. Now when I think of them, I smile for I know they are in heaven, and I am so grateful I had them for what time they were here. They taught me things that I will never forget."

"I don't want to forget my mama." Sarah said quietly.

"Oh, Sarah, you won't. And look at you. Your mama has taught you so many things. You do great in school, and at church the teachers brag on how well behaved you are and how quickly you catch on. Your mama taught you manners, she worked with you when you had schoolwork, and look what a great reader you are. Your mama helped you every night in reading. You are the wonderful person you are because of your mama. She will always live right here in your heart."

"Does your mama live in your heart?"

"Yes, she does," Rebecca said, "but God has also sent some wonderful people into my life for whom I am so grateful. If my mama hadn't died, I would have never moved here, and then I wouldn't have met you. Now, I can't imagine not having you."

"So God took your mama away and gave me to you?"

"You could say that. I filled my mama's heart and she filled mine, so when she went to heaven, I needed someone to fill my heart with love. And God knew you could do that."

"Did I not fill Mama's heart with love?"

"Yes, you did. You filled your mama's heart, and she filled yours. With both of our mamas gone, we need each other. God picked out the very best when he sent you to me. I love you, Sarah, with all my heart, and I'm so proud of you. I know I won't do all the things right like your mama did, but I want to try."

"So, do I call you Mama?"

"Honey, you can call me Mama or Rebecca, whatever you are happy with. I'm going to love you either way."

"What are you going to call me?"

"I will call you Sarah. When we are out around people, I will tell them you are my beautiful daughter."

With that, Sarah smiled. "I have a new mama, and I love her."

The two hugged and rolled around in the grass, laughing and having fun. Rebecca knew that Sarah would have some bad days ahead—that was to be expected—but for now, she was going to enjoy the happiness they both had.

Instead of eating at home that night, Rebecca and Sarah went out. Rebecca texted Mary that they would be home later. The two had so much fun, and Sarah started to seem like herself again. When they got home, Sarah went to take her bath and get ready for bed.

In the meantime, Mark had come in and was talking to his mom and Mary.

As soon as her bath was over, Sarah went to the living room where they were. When she saw Mark, she ran over to him and said, "Guess what? I have a new mama. It's Mama Rebecca."

They all stood in shock at how alive Sarah was. They didn't know about the talk Rebecca and Sarah had had, but it had done wonders for Sarah. It was as if the whole room lit up.

On Monday, Sarah went to school and told the class about her mama, Rachel, going to heaven, and then she told them about God giving her a new mama whose name was Rebecca. Ms. Reagan was so impressed with Sarah and how well she handled questions the others asked her. They did very little schoolwork that day for Ms. Reagan thought it would be good for the other kids and Sarah to talk about what Sarah had been through.

Rebecca went into work that Monday also. Everyone was so happy to see her. Emma came up and asked, "How is Sarah?"

"To be honest, at first, she went into a shell," Rebecca answered. "Then a few days ago, we had a talk, and with the help of our good Lord, she is doing good right now. How are you doing?"

"I'm doing okay," Emma answered. "Rachel and I had become so close working side by side every day, getting together on the weekends. When she first came here, she wouldn't talk to anyone, and then she became my best friend."

"Any time you want to come by and see Sarah, come ahead. But if it's too much for you …" Her voice trailed off. "Well, you are welcome any time."

"Thanks, Ms. Rebecca. I'm doing a little better. It's just going to take time." Emma smiled and turned to go back to work.

The elevator doors opened, and Lynn walked into the office. When she saw Rebecca, she went around her desk and gave her a big hug. "Oh, Ms. Rebecca, it's so good to see you back at work. How are you doing?"

"Right now, I'm doing good," Rebecca said. "When Rachel died, it was terrible. Sarah's heart was so broken, and to see her like that, our hearts broke. I don't think I have ever felt so helpless, but God worked his miracles, and things are so much better. I'm not sure how long it will last for I'm sure Sarah will have a few down times, but God will get us through them. How is the new building coming along?"

"Whenever you're ready, we can walk over and look. You are going to be so surprised! Oh, and you're going to be so shocked when you see all the papers waiting for you. I did what I could, but it's still stacked up."

"That's all right. I'll work on it later. Let's walk over now." The two headed for the elevator. "You know, when we first started planning for the addition, I never dreamed I would be using it myself. When school is out, I'll bring Sarah over."

"You're right," Lynn said. "You were thinking of the employees here, not yourself. Sarah would have been coming here anyway, but with Rachel. Who would have ever thought it would happen like this?"

Rebecca just shook her head. "Have you already looked everything over?" she asked. They exited the elevator and began walking toward the new building.

"Yes, you are going to be so pleased. This was a wonderful idea to add on to the company. They should be finished in just a few weeks. We also have a doctor who will be here and two nurses who will be rotating. We've gotten approval for certain medications to keep on site, and we have hired a man and a woman to work as trainers in the gym."

"My, you have been busy!" Rebecca replied. "I believe you could run this company yourself."

"Not hardly," Lynn scoffed. "Mark has helped. He said he knew you had too much on your mind so he stepped in to do what he could. He knew what questions to ask in the medical area and what we needed. I just took notes and did what I was told."

"Mark never said a word to me about this," Rebecca said, a little perturbed. "He had no right to step in and take over."

"Ms. Rebecca, he was a blessing," Lynn said. "He was looking out for you and the company. You should be so grateful to have him, especially when it comes to all that medical stuff. I had no clue what they were talking about. He loves you so much. You have his heart. All you need to do is say 'I need' or 'I would like to have' and it's yours. You also have an extra bonus: he loves Sarah. Don't forget about him and put all your attention and time on her."

"Lynn, Mark is a grown man. Sarah is a child. He understands things, and she is learning. Right now, she needs me more than Mark does."

"They both need you, Rebecca, but in different ways," Lynn said wisely. "Have you prayed about all this?"

"I've prayed about Sarah, but not Mark. He'll understand." Dismissing the subject, she opened the door to the new building, stepped inside, and said, "Oh, my, this is perfect! The colors, the layout—it's all great. Can't wait till opening day!"

Twenty-seven

REBECCA ALWAYS HAD THINGS TO DO IN THE EVENINGS WHEN SHE got home. Even if it was office work, Sarah stayed close by. Rebecca didn't want anyone to take Sarah unless she could go too. Mark wanted to talk about the wedding, but Rebecca never seemed to have time. One afternoon, Mark picked Sarah up after school so they could spend some time together. They went home, saddled up the horses, and went for a ride.

Once they were a good distance from the house, Mark asked, "Sarah, how would you like to help plan a party? But you must keep it a secret."

"I love parties, but who is it for?" she asked.

"You know I have asked Rebecca to marry me, and she said yes. But she is so busy with the grand opening where she works that she doesn't have time to plan a wedding. So I thought we could surprise her and plan it for her. Mary and my mom will be helping."

"What do I get to do?"

"They will need help in picking out a dress for Rebecca and one for you," Mark explained. "Also, you will need to help them decorate the church, but we can't let Rebecca know."

"When you marry Mama Rebecca, will you be my daddy?"

"I would love to be your daddy," Mark answered. "What do you think about having a daddy?"

"I don't know. I never had a daddy before."

"You know what? I've never had a daughter before, but I think I am going to like it, especially since it's going to be you."

"Will we do things together?" she asked. "At school, you can bring your dad and show him off. He tells the others what he does."

"I would love to go to school with you, and we can do things at home as a family also."

"Will this make Mama Rebecca happy?"

"I think it will," Mark replied. "Will it make *you* happy?"

"I think so," she said.

"Then we need to plan a big surprise party. You can decide on what color the flowers need to be and the color for your dress."

"This is going to be fun," Sarah said. "So, I can only talk to you, Ms. Irene, and Ms. Mary about this?"

"That's right."

Every day after school, Sarah, Mary, and Irene looked at dresses, invitations, and flowers and wrote down lists of people to invite. They were having so much fun. Irene contacted Phillip, and he said he knew just the dress for Rebecca. And when they gave him Sarah's measurements, he said he would make her a dress that would go perfectly with Rebecca's.

One afternoon, Sarah asked Irene, "What am I supposed to call you, Ms. Irene?"

"Child, you can call me whatever feels right for you," she answered. "I am Mark's mother, so you could call me Grandmother, Granny, Mimi, Nana, Grammy, Nona, Mam-maw—there are so many names. And if they don't sound good to you, you can still call me Ms. Irene. You decide, okay?"

"Okay," she said. "What do I call Ms. Mary?"

Mary had just walked in and said, "I'll answer that. You can call me Aunt Mary. What do you think?"

"I like that," Sarah said. "I've never had a grandparent before, or an aunt. This is so much fun. I'm going to see what Sammy wants me to call him. I have such a big family now."

After dinner, the doorbell rang. Mary went to see who it was, and when she opened the door, there stood Lacey.

"Is Mark here?" she asked.

"Yes, he is," Mary replied. "Won't you come in?"

Mary led Lacey to the den where Mark, Irene, and Sarah were. Before Mary could say a word, Lacey spoke up. "Mark, I need to have a word with you in private."

He got up and led her into another room to see what she had to say.

"So I understand you gave Rebecca a wedding ring and asked her to marry you," she barked. "What is wrong with you?"

"Lacey, it's good to see you, as always," Mark replied, staying calm. "First, I'm a grown man who can make his own decisions. I happen to love Rebecca, and she loves me."

"But that child in there, her mother died, and Rebecca plans to raise her as her own," Lacey said sharply. "What kind of marriage will it be to start off with a ready-made family? It's bad enough that you're thinking marriage, but one with a child? What's wrong with you?"

"I realize this is hard for you to understand," Mark answered, "but I love Rebecca with all my heart, and I love Sarah just as much. That little girl is so precious, so wonderful, and Rebecca and I are so blessed to have her. Don't you ever let me hear you say anything negative about either one of them. They are my world and my life, and if you can't except that, then you need to stay away and keep your mouth shut. Thanks for stopping by." He walked out of the room and headed for the front door.

As Mark opened the door for Lacey, she turned to him and spat out, "You will regret this one day when you see that I'm right, and you'll wish you had listened to me." Mark just held the door open.

When he closed the door behind Lacey, he saw Sarah standing there. "Does she not like Mama Rebecca and me?"

"That lady doesn't like much of anything," Mark replied.

- *A Journey for Rebecca* -

"Did you really mean it when you said Mama Rebecca and I mean the world to you?"

"Yes, honey, I did. You two ladies are everything to me. We are soon going to be one big, happy family." Reaching down, he picked up Sarah to hold her. "I love you very much, Sarah, and I always will."

A minute or two later, Rebecca came in looking exhausted. She asked Mark, "Was that Lacey I saw leaving here?"

"Yes, and you didn't miss a thing," he said. "How are things at the office? Have you set a date on when the new part will be open?"

"Yes, next Wednesday is the big day. Hopefully things will settle down and get back to normal then." She turned her attention to Sarah. "What have you been doing tonight? Did you enjoy the visit with Lacey?"

"We were having a good time till she came by," she replied. "She doesn't like me."

Surprised, Rebecca looked at Mark. "Sarah, how could you say such a thing? Everybody likes you."

"She doesn't," Sarah said frankly. "She told Mr. Mark he was making a big mistake. I don't think she likes kids."

"Honey, I hate to say this," Rebecca said, "but Lacey only likes herself. She is very unhappy and has a hard time understanding people who are happy."

"Then we need to pray for her," Sarah said. "Didn't you say we needed to pray for people who are sad and didn't know God?"

"Yes, I did," Rebecca said, pleased. "When we say our prayers tonight, we will have to add Lacey's name to them. Are you about ready for bed?"

"Can I stay with Ms. Irene and Ms. Mary while you take your shower?" she asked.

"Sure. Come on to bed in about twenty minutes. You have school tomorrow."

Rebecca was so tired and felt awful about not spending more

time in the evenings with Sarah. Hopefully after the next week, Sarah would be able to come to the after-school program she had worked so hard to develop. After taking her shower, Rebecca stretched out on the bed to wait for Sarah and went sound to sleep. Mark tucked Sarah into bed beside Rebecca, and they said their prayers. He went around to Rebecca and kissed her on the forehead. In two weeks, she would be his wife, and then he would be able to lay beside her and hold her close.

On Wednesday morning, both Lynn and Rebecca were at work early. Rebecca had invited Irene to come around nine for she wanted her to be the one to cut the ribbon.

"Rebecca, this is wonderful!" Irene exclaimed. "Looking at the blueprints in the beginning, I thought it was a wonderful idea, and now, here it is! It's no longer on paper but right before our eyes.

She added, "I am so proud of what you have done for this company. You are a blessing and an inspiration to all of us."

"I wouldn't go that far, Irene," Rebecca said, "but it will certainly help the people here at McKay's, myself included."

"Oh, Mark said this morning that he was going to come by for the ribbon-cutting ceremony. He is very proud of you also."

"What about his patients?" Rebecca asked.

"He had his secretary move them around so he could be here. I think it's wonderful that he wants to come and support you."

"Your right. He is so good to Sarah and me. We are lucky to have him. Oh, here he is now."

Mark parked and quickly approached the group. "I was afraid you had already started. I left work on time, but traffic was terrible." Turning his attention to the building, he said, "This place looks terrific! You did a wonderful job, and everyone is going to be so pleased."

"I think they will," Rebecca agreed. "Some have already wandered around, and they have nothing but good things to say. Oh, here comes Lynn. They must be ready for us."

"Rebecca, the news media is here, and they have all the cameras ready," she announced. "Nearly all the employees are here, eager to come in and look around. They are all so happy and excited."

"That's wonderful. Okay, Irene, are you ready to cut the ribbon?" Rebecca asked.

"My dear, I still think you should be the one to cut the ribbon," Irene said. "This was all your dream. I can't take credit for any of it."

"But this company belongs to your family," Rebecca countered. "You were the one backing this project. I wouldn't dream of having it any other way. You should do the honors. Besides, I'm not a McKay—yet." She looked at Mark and smiled.

Little did Rebecca know that her wedding was pretty much all planned and, in two weeks, she would become Mrs. Mark McKay.

As they gathered in front of the building, Irene stepped up to the microphone. "I want everyone to know that I feel so unworthy to do the ribbon cutting. Rebecca Clark came to me with a desire to make McKay's a better place for the employees. Before you now is the realization of the dream she had. She is like a daughter to me and has been from the first time we met. I prayed for God to send us someone who would love the company as much as I do, and little did I know that when I first met her, she would be the person to take over and have such a great love for each employee of this company. She mingles with you during work so she can know you personally and have a better understanding of who you are and the lives you have. She has brought you all closer together; we are truly like a family. You all love one another and are so willing to help one another out, and it's all because of Rebecca Clark. Before she was hired, I thought McKay's was the best company around. But she made McKay's the number-one company as judged by many other people as well. She listened to what they had to say, what would be of great benefit to them, and what hardships they were under. She took everything to heart, prayed about it, and waited for God to guide her. Every morning, this company starts the day with prayer. The employees come to her for advice regarding work, family, and how to know God better. She is their friend. I have seen her come home burdened down with concern for one of the employees. It is a great honor to stand here beside her to look at what all she has done. In fact, I have already fixed up the papers, and McKay's will be owned by Rebecca Clark. And soon, she will be Rebecca McKay. Now for those scissors." She reached out her hand.

Rebecca gasped. She had no idea this was coming. She just stood in shock, unable to move or say anything.

Irene turned around to see tears forming in Rebecca's eyes.

"Now, child, no need for tears. You earned this, and I couldn't be happier." She turned and cut the ribbon to much applause. She turned back to Rebecca and said, "The ribbon is cut, and McKay's is all yours."

Wrapping her arms around Irene, Rebecca was still at a loss for words. Finally, she made her way to the microphone and looked out over the crowd. "I am so speechless right now. So I'll just say that we have refreshments inside, and we are all eager to show you around and answer any questions you may have." Stepping back, she reached out to Irene and hugged her again, tears streaming down her face. This was not how she had planned the day to go.

Mark came up to Rebecca to give her a hug. "I had no idea my mother was going to do this," he said. "She never said a word, but I think she made a very wise decision."

Hugging Mark, Rebecca could not stop the flow of tears. As people passed by, they patted her on the back or offered words of congratulations, and some reached out to hug her and Mark.

Finally able to compose herself, Rebecca found Lynn, who was already giving tours.

"Ms. Rebecca, I am so happy for you!" she gushed. "You are truly the best boss ever, and we are so lucky to have you."

"Lynn, please, if I'm not careful, I'm going to start crying again."

The day was a total success, and the employees were thrilled with the upgrades to the company. By the time the day was over, Rebecca was exhausted and overwhelmed by the day's events. She hoped that the next day everything would be back to normal. It was six o'clock, and she needed to get home to Sarah.

Walking in the door, she noticed the house was quiet. Rebecca wondered if they had all gone out to eat and she had forgotten to meet them. Then the lights came on, and banners of "Congratulations" hung all around. Sarah ran over to Rebecca. "I'm so proud of you, Mama Rebecca!"

Giving Sarah a big hug, Rebecca soon forgot how tired she was. God had blessed her with not only an awesome job but an awesome family. Giving thanks to him didn't seem like enough.

Twenty-eight

AFTER A WEEK, THINGS AT THE PLANT SEEMED TO BE GOING VERY smoothly. The new section was operating practically on its own. Employees had already signed for child care, as well as those who wanted to use the gym. Parking was sectioned off, those with children at the day care parked in one area, and those with no children parked in another. Rebecca and Lynn were so pleased at how everything had fallen into place.

"Lynn, you have been such a big help to me," Rebecca told her. "Again, I must say, I don't know how I could have done it without you. Why don't you take some time off? You and your husband can take a trip, relax, and enjoy life."

"What about you?"

"Oh, I have too much to do to take any time off," she answered. "Now that everything here is working so well, I really do need to start thinking about a wedding. Mark has been so good about not pressuring me to set a date, and really, he hasn't said much about the wedding to me at all. I think he knew I had a full plate here at work and trying to find time for Sarah. In fact, Mark and Sarah seem very close."

She brought her thoughts back to Lynn. "So you take some time off, and then I'll take some time for a honeymoon. Sarah will soon be out for summer break, so we can all three go somewhere together."

"Rebecca, for a honeymoon, it needs to be only you and Mark. You two deserve some time together, just you two. You will have plenty of time for all three of you to go places together and make memories, but for your honeymoon, it's to be just you and Mark."

"I'll think about it," Rebecca said hesitantly, "but for now, you and Tony need to find somewhere to spend a nice, relaxing week. Boss's orders."

As Rebecca was walking out the door, Lynn could hardly contain herself. She knew that, on Saturday, Rebecca would be getting married. She could only hope that Rebecca didn't become upset over not planning her own wedding, but from what Mark had told her, she would love it. He had spared no expense on making this wedding perfect, and of course, she had been able to help him with a few details, which she was delighted to do.

On Friday afternoon, Lynn knocked on Rebecca's office door.

"Come in."

"Ms. Rebecca, would you mind if I left a little early today? Tony and I have some plans, and I could use the extra time off."

"Absolutely! Where are you two taking off to, if you don't mind my asking?"

"Right now, we have some things we need to do before tomorrow," Lynn said vaguely. "I can explain more to you later."

"Sounds good. You two have a great time wherever you go." As Lynn left, Rebecca knew she would miss her greatly, even if it was for just a week or two. They had become so close that Lynn was more like a sister to her than a coworker. But she needed the time off as much as Rebecca did, and with a wedding to plan, Rebecca would be taking time off later, so it was only right that Lynn take some time now.

As Rebecca was leaving work, she couldn't help but notice that everyone seemed so happy and upbeat. Could the new addition make this much of a difference? She didn't think so, but whatever it was, it was a good thing. When she pulled into the garage at home, she still felt as if something was amiss, but what? Mark's car was not there, so she thought maybe he had to work late. Even inside the house, it seemed as if things were different. She couldn't put her finger on it. Had she been so tied up with the grand opening at work that she had missed out on something? She would talk to Mark when he got home and see what his thoughts were.

Then Rebecca saw Irene. "I was beginning to think no one was home," she said. "The house is so quiet. Where's Sarah?"

"Hello, my dear," Irene replied. "Sarah is with Sammy and will be home later. Mary had to go check on a friend and will be back shortly."

"Is Mark having to work late?" Rebecca asked. "He usually sends me a text if he does, and I haven't heard from him."

"I believe he had some things to check on. I wouldn't worry."

"Are you all right, Irene? You seem a little jumpy."

"My dear, I am fine," Irene asserted. "I have a project I'm working on and want to get it completed. Now if you'll excuse me." She headed for the door.

"Is there anything I can do to help you?"

"Oh, no, no. You just take it easy and enjoy the quiet. Relax— that's something you haven't done in some time. Now I must be going. Bye."

With that, Irene was out the door.

Rebecca wasn't sure how she should be feeling at the moment, but the feeling that something wasn't right made her very uneasy. She decided she would fix something to eat and take a shower, and maybe everyone would be home by then.

About nine o'clock, Sammy and Sarah came in.

"Sarah, I have missed you so!" Rebecca said. "Where have you and Sammy been?"

"We had things to do," she replied. "I know it's late, so I'll go get ready for bed. Mama Rebecca, could we just do our Bible reading tonight and say our prayers? I'm tired and don't really want to read our bedtime book."

"Sure, Sarah. Are you all right? You're not feeling sick, are you?"

"No, I'm fine. I just want to get ready for bed." Turning, she went to her room.

"Sammy, what have you and Sarah been doing today?" Rebecca asked, obviously concerned. "Why is she so tired?"

"Now, Ms. Rebecca, you know how Ms. Sarah and I are when we are together," Sammy replied. "We go and enjoy ourselves as if today is our last. That little girl just blesses my heart. I'm so glad we have her. Can I do anything for you before I turn in?"

"No, thanks, Sammy. I appreciate your spending time with Sarah. You know that little girl has a heart full of love for people."

"Well, we all love her," he said. "Good night. See you tomorrow."

"Good night, Sammy, and thanks again."

When Rebecca went to her room, Sarah had just finished her bath and was heading to the bed. "I laid your Bible on the pillow and am ready to snuggle," she announced.

"You must really be tired," Rebecca said. "What did you and Sammy do all day?"

"We did a lot of things. Can we talk about it tomorrow? I just want to stretch out and go to sleep."

"Sure, honey. I hope you're not coming down with anything." Feeling Sarah's head, Rebecca determined she wasn't running a fever. So Rebecca opened her Bible. They had recently started reading from Proverbs, and this night she started in the third chapter and read verses 1–6.

> My son, do not forget my teaching, but keep my commandments in your heart, for they will prolong your life many years and will bring you peace and prosperity. Let love and faithfulness never leave you; bind them around your neck, write them on the tablet of your heart. Then you will win favor and a good name in the sight of God and man. Trust in the Lord with all your heart and lean not on your

own understanding: in all your ways acknowledge
him, and he will make your path straight.

Sarah was almost asleep, not hearing what Rebecca was reading.
But for some reason, Rebecca reread the scripture. She knew God
was talking to her through his word. Taking Sarah in her arms,
Rebecca was so thankful for all God had blessed her with. Life had
not always been easy, but then Jesus didn't have an easy life either.
With tears running down her cheeks, Rebecca prayed for guidance,
wisdom, and love as she raised Sarah. She prayed that Sarah would
always allow God to be a part of her life.

She covered Sarah up and then decided to take her shower,
reasoning that Mark may be home by the time she finished. But she
went to Mark's room after her shower, and he still had not made it
home. So she sent him another text. This was not like Mark to not
respond to her text. She hoped nothing serious had happened at the
hospital.

Rebecca noticed that the porch light was on, so she went to turn
it off and then decided to go out on the porch. As she looked down
the driveway, she remembered the first time she had driven down
it. How she had marveled at this house, the well-groomed lawn,
and all that seemed so perfect. The thought of her living here was
more like a dream, but here she was, living in this beautiful home,
the owner and CEO of McKay's, engaged to Mark, and the mother
of a beautiful little girl. Looking up at the sky, she smiled and felt
tears in her eyes. "Lord, I am so unworthy of all that you have given
me," she said aloud. "You have blessed me so much. This is really
all yours. Help me that I will always do what's best, what you would
have me do. Thank you, Lord. Thank you."

The next morning, Rebecca woke to Sarah tapping her on
the arm.

"Mama Rebecca, wake up. You have to get up."

"Sarah, why are you up so early?" she asked. "Why are you already dressed? What are you up to?"

"Come on! Get dressed and I'll show you. Come on, you have to hurry."

Rebecca got up and change clothes. She had no idea what Sarah was up to, but she knew she was excited. As they made their way to the living room, Rebecca saw that it was full of people, some from the church. Mary and Irene were standing there smiling, with clothes laying around them, as was a lady with makeup and hair products.

"Come on, Mama Rebecca! This is your special day!" Sarah urged her.

"What are you talking about?" Rebecca asked.

The doorbell rang, and Lynn walked in with breakfast.

Shocked, Rebecca said, "Lynn, what are you doing here? You are supposed to be on vacation."

"Oh, I wouldn't miss this day for anything," Lynn said with a broad smile.

"Okay, I must have missed the memo for today. What's going on?"

Irene walked over to Rebecca and said calmly, "My dear, it's your wedding day. You have been so busy that we all decided to take some stress and worry off you. We have asked you at different times about what you would like regarding your wedding, so we took note and put it all together for you. Mark is at a friend's house because he is not to see you till you walk down the aisle. The sun is out, it's a beautiful day for a wedding, and my dear, you deserve only the best."

Not knowing what to say, Rebecca could feel tears in her eyes again. She looked around at the people who had given up their time to make this day so special for her. Again, she thought, *Lord, I am so unworthy of all this. Thank you.*

"Sarah, have you known about this all along?" Rebecca asked in disbelief. "You have not said one word. Is this part of what you and Sammy were doing yesterday?"

"Yes!" Sarah answered excitedly. "Wait till you see your dress and mine. Daddy Mark said only the best dresses for his two women. They are just beautiful."

Soon, Mary brought out the wedding dress. It had a very fitted bodice with a full, floor-length skirt made from taffeta. The fitted bodice was covered with lace, as were the sleeves that went down to her wrists and were filled with pearls and crystal rhinestones. The V-shaped neckline made the dress even more elegant. The back of the dress came down to a point and was also covered with lace, pearls, and crystal rhinestones. Sarah's dress was made to be very similar to Rebecca's, except her neckline was round and the back was not as open.

Irene handed Rebecca a headpiece that matched the dress perfectly. "My dear, this is what I wore on the day of my wedding. I sent it to Phillip to make the proper adjustments to go with your dress. This is your something old. I pray that you and Mark are blessed with the love and happiness that Charles and I had. I wish he could be here today. He would be so happy."

The women gathered around Rebecca, all preparing for the day. Before long, they left for the church.

At one o'clock, everything was in perfect order. Rebecca could not believe how beautiful it all was.

"Irene, I haven't practiced walking down the aisle," she said nervously. "What am I supposed to do?"

"Don't worry," Irene said. "Sammy will be walking you down the aisle. Just follow his lead. Sammy and Sarah practiced several times yesterday. Lynn is your maid of honor, and Sarah is your attendant."

Again, tears started forming in Rebecca's eyes.

"Now, now, my dear, no time for tears. Before I go out to be seated, I want you to know how happy I am to have you as my daughter-in-law. You're more like a daughter, and I love you very much. You have brought so much joy and happiness to our home. You are a blessing from God and an answer to so many prayers."

Trying hard not to cry, Rebecca hugged Irene. "God blessed me when I was born with a precious, godly mother, and then she was taken away. You have filled that void, and if it's all right, I would like to call you Mama."

"Oh, my dear, I can't think of anything better," Irene said sweetly. "Now I'm going to cry."

Lynn came over to give Rebecca her bouquet. "I know how much you love flowers, so I did some research. In your bouquet you have lily of the valley, which represents happiness; hyacinths, for steady love; ivy, for fidelity and friendship; myrtle, the emblem of matrimony; and sweet William, which signifies gallantry."

"Oh, Lynn, this is just perfect," Rebecca said. "Knowing what each flower represents makes this bouquet even more special. How could I ever repay you for what you have done? You are such a blessing."

Finally, when she was alone in the dressing room, Rebecca looked in the mirror one last time before going to the chapel. She could not believe this was her wedding day. Her dress was so beautiful. Phillip had outdone himself again. She bowed her head to give thanks for all God had blessed her with. Her journey in life had been hard, but God had always been there, and in the end, she had been blessed. "Lord, I feel so unworthy of all that you have blessed me with. As I now go into a new chapter of my life, I ask that you be with us all. Every day, guide us that we will always seek to do your will. Thank you for my new family and all the wonderful friends you have brought into my life and for those who made this day possible. Thank you, Lord. Amen."

With everyone in their places, Rebecca, Lynn, Sarah, and Sammy were ready for the signal to start the walk down the aisle toward Mark. Just before they got to the door, Sarah walked up beside Rebecca and took her hand.

"God took my mama Rachel, but he gave me you to take her place, just like he gave you Renny"

"Renny? Is that what you are going to call Ms. Irene?" Rebecca asked.

"Yes, she said I could pick out a name for her, and I think Renny is good. It sort of goes with Irene. But I'm not going to call you Mama Rebecca anymore, just Mama. And Daddy Mark will be Daddy. I have a big family now."

Holding back tears once more, Rebecca leaned down to give Sarah a hug and a kiss.

"I love you so much, Sarah. Thank you."

The wedding music start, and Rebecca could feel her heart beating so hard. As she walked up to the doorway, there stood Mark, smiling and looking straight at her. She took Sammy's arm for she needed some support. He patted her hand. "Ms. Rebecca, you are going to be all right. I'm right here, and when we get to the end of the aisle, Mr. Mark is there to take over and care for you from now on."

It was five o'clock before Mark and Rebecca were able to leave the church. Sarah came running up to them to give them hugs and kisses. They were only going to be gone for a few days, and later the three of them would take a vacation together.

"I love you, Mama and Daddy. Hurry home because I'm going to miss you."

Rebecca replied, "We love you too, Sarah. I'll call tonight before you go to bed, and we will have our prayer time over the phone."

Sarah made her way back to Renny, took her hand, and said, "I have the best family ever. As Mama says, 'God is good all the time.'"

Epilogue

As soon as spring break came, Mark and Rebecca took Sarah to Disney Land for a few days and then went to the beach. It was as if they were meant to be a family. The next year, Rebecca became pregnant, and they all were so excited—especially Sarah, knowing she was going to become a big sister. Then Rebecca found out she was going to have twin boys. To make Sarah feel part of the new addition, they decided to let her pick out the names. The big day finally arrived, and the boys were born. When the time came that Sarah could go to the hospital to visit her new baby brothers, she was very excited.

Mark said to Sarah, "Well, the big day is here. What names did you decide on for your baby brothers?"

With a big smile on her face, Sarah stated she had come up with two names from the Bible. Her Sunday school teacher, Ms. Kristy, had talked about a certain family in the Bible, and she thought how great it would be to have those names for her baby brothers. Since her name was Sarah, the boys would be called Abraham and Isaac.

Mark and Rebecca agreed that Sarah could not have come up with any better names.

Looking at her precious family, Rebecca told Mark, "On the day I graduated from college, I felt like I was all alone after I received the news my parents were both gone. I followed the advice they had given me years earlier, that no matter where you are or what is happening in your life, God is always with you. As I look back, I can see that God has been with me every step of the way. At the time, I just did not see it, but the journey he has taken me on is a journey I will always cherish."

They agreed that God is good and faithful all the time.

> Give thanks to the Lord, for he is good; his love endures forever. (Psalm 107:1)

> The Lord bless you and keep you;
> the Lord make his face shine upon you
> And be gracious to you;
> The Lord turn his face toward you
> And give you peace. (Numbers 6:24–26)